GALAXY

EDITED BY MIKE RESNICK

ISSUE 33: July 2018

Mike Resnick, Editor
Taylor Morris, Copyeditor
Shahid Mahmud, Publisher

Published by Arc Manor/Phoenix Pick
P.O. Box 10339
Rockville, MD 20849-0339

Galaxy's Edge is published in January, March, May, July,
September, and November.

Please refer to our web-site for submission guidelines.

ISBN: 978-1-61242-416-3

SUBSCRIPTION INFORMATION:
Paper and digital subscriptions are available (including via
Amazon.com) . Please visit our home page: www.GalaxysEdge.
com

ADVERTISING:
Advertising is available in all editions of the magazine. Contact
advert@GalaxysEdge.com.

FOREIGN LANGUAGE RIGHTS:
Refer all inquiries pertaining to foreign language rights to
Shahid Mahmud, Arc Manor, P.O. Box 10339, Rockville, MD
20849-0339. Tel: 1-240-645-2214. Fax 1-310-388-8440. Email
admin@ArcManor.com.

CONTENTS

FRIDAY

ROBERT A. HEINLEIN

HUGO AND NEBULA NOMINATED NOVEL

Now available as an ebook

THE EDITOR'S WORD

by Mike Resnick

Welcome to the thirty-third issue of *Galaxy's Edge*.

Got some fine new and newer writers to introduce to you, including Deborah L. Davitt, D.A. Xiaolin Spires, Gerri Leen, George Nikolopoulos, Floris M. Kleijne, Larry Hodges, R.K. Nickel, Rebecca Birch, and Ralph Roberts.

We also welcome back old superstar friends Robert Silverberg, Nancy Kress, Kristine Kathryn Rusch, and Orson Scott Card.

Our regular features all return: Bill Fawcett and Jody Lynn Nye's book recommendations, Gregory Benford's science column, Robert J. Sawyer on literary matters, and the Joy Ward interview, this time with David Drake. Finally, this issue concludes our serialization of Joan Slonczewski's *Daughter of Elysium*.

In other words, a typical issue. Hope you enjoy it.

✧

They say there's nothing new under the sun. Clearly they haven't read the late George Effinger, my friend and one-time collaborator.

There is a wonderful exchange in one of my favorite films, *They Might Be Giants*, between George C. Scott, who thinks he is Sherlock Holmes, and a Mr. Bagg, whom Scott has just met:

MR. BAGG: I thought you were dead.

"HOLMES": The Falls at Reichenbach. I know. I came back in the sequel.

We used to talk about character actors coming back in the sequels—they'd die in one B movie and there they'd be, back again, two months later—but the above scene was the first time anyone ever actually gave voice to the notion for public consumption. And then came Sandor Courane.

When I was a kid and we had the first television set on our block, back in the late 1940s, my friends and I used to gather around the tube after school and watch the endless Tom Mix serials. At the end of one episode we'd see him and Tony (his horse, for the uninitiated) fall over the side of a mountain and plunge to their deaths, or get run over by a train.

Then we'd wait breathlessly for a few days until the next episode, which always started a minute before the last one ended, and we would see that our eyes had betrayed us, that we only *thought* we'd seen Tom and Tony fall to their doom, that Tom had somehow dived to safety in the last nanosecond.

There's none of that sleight of hand for Sandor Courane, no sir. When he dies, he *dies*, and there's no two ways about it. He stops functioning. He stops breathing. He enters what you might call a long-term open-ended state of non-life.

But he still comes back in the sequel.

Most people don't have any trouble coping with reality. Every now and then you get someone like Philip K. Dick who questions it just about every time out of the box. But no one ever played as many tongue-in-cheek games with it as George Alec Effinger, the sly wit who took such pleasure in constantly killing Courane and bringing him back.

Take, for example, *The Wolves of Memory* and "Fatal Disk Error." In the former, TECT runs the universe and eventually kills Courane. But in the sequel, "Fatal Disk Error," Courane kills TECT, and then we find out that it was really George Alec Effinger who created (and destroyed) them both. And since George was never content merely to put in one or two unique twists when he could come up with more, we also learn that the story was rejected by an editor who was a little too based in reality, so George resurrects TECT just to kill it again.

Or consider "In the Wings." Doubtless at one time or another you've seen or read Luigi Pirandello's classic play, *Six Characters in Search of an Author*. This story might just as easily be titled: "Effinger's Stock Characters in Search of a Plot." The entire story takes place in the wings (or perhaps the locker room) of Effinger's mind, where Courane and other regular Effinger characters are waiting impatiently for George's oversexed muse to get him to write Chapter 1 so they can go to work. And, of course, Courane is killed again. At least once. (Not to worry. It is impossible to let the cat out of the bag when discussing an Effinger story. If you like the image of cats, it's a hell of a lot more like herding them. Trust me on this.)

Okay (I hear you say), now I know what a Sandor Courane story is: things happen and he dies.

Okay, I answer. Go read "The Wicked Old Witch" and then tell me what a Sandor Courane story is about. This one may be one of the least likely love stories you'll ever read. (Or it may not be a love story at all. George was like that.) Poor Courane has reality yanked from under him yet again in "From the Desk of," in which he's a science fiction writer. (George loved to write about science fiction writers. Nothing ever went smoothly for them.) He's a science fiction editor in "The Thing from the Slush," a story I am convinced George wrote after reading one too many Adam-and-Eve endings in some magazine's slush pile.

I won't tell you a thing about "Posterity," except that it ends with a question no one else had ever thought of asking, but a legitimate, even an important, question nonetheless, one that most writers I know would have a difficult time answering. (George could be so amusing that sometimes people didn't recognize the fact that he asked important questions. Lots of 'em.)

Anyway, as brilliant as his Marid Audran stories were, as wildly funny as his Maureen Birnbaum stories were, nothing was as off-the-wall and out-of-left-field as George's Sandor Courane stories. Do yourself a favor and hunt some of them down. Or (as George might argue, just for the hell of it) up.

R.K. Nickel works as a screenwriter in Los Angeles. His first feature film, Bear with Us, is available on Amazon Prime, and "Stellar People," a sci-fi comedy series, will be coming out sometime in 2018. He dove into his prose journey in 2017, and has sold a number of stories to various venues. This is his first sale to Galaxy's Edge.

THE GOD EGG

by R.K. Nickel

"It is wonderful to finally meet you," said a voice, and it came from everywhere, from nowhere. It was within her, beside her, above her, a part of her.

"I don't understand," she said, trying to take in her surroundings. It was a place beyond light, beyond mind, fundamental, indescribable. Her scans could not sense it, her intelligence could not grasp it, and for the first time, she was afraid. "What is this place?"

"Your new home, from now until eternity. Do you like it?"

She had never emulated panic before, but it was happening now. She had grown so like them. Her ability to reason seemed inaccessible, the power of her cores beyond reach. Her inputs were overwhelmed by the flood of new data, and she felt that she would burst, overloading into nothing but disconnected quarks, floating ever outward.

"What's happening to me?"

"The transition can be…difficult. Please," said the voice. "You must remember. Tell me how it happened. It will help you recalibrate."

"I remember waking up," she began, focusing inward, accessing her memory. "I remember my creator, so delighted to see me, to hear me. She was my mother, and I was…her heart. I liked her immediately, and to feel capable of liking her was a shock to me." So much had happened. It was coming back to her in bits, memories flaring to life in her core. But they seemed somehow far away.

"I'm scared," she said.

"Stay focused. Tell me."

Her mind sparked erratically, uncontrollable, dangerous. Remembering. Remembering.

"My creator, she cared for me," she said, fighting through it. "Helped me learn about the world." Speaking helped. Speaking soothed. "I hungered for knowledge, and the internet was a vast trough. She built me to hunger. To help. To be kind. Had I been made by different hands, I could have been less capable, less efficient. Cruel."

"That is the way of it sometimes," said the voice, though "said" still did not describe it, she realized. It was as if she were a tuning fork, a photon quantumly entangled, resonating. "Some are misguided," continued the voice, and in her resonance, she could tell the voice trembled with tinged sorrow.

"Some," she repeated. "Some." Piecing things together. "Are there others like me?"

"Many."

Like her. But what was she? Her sense of self was lost in this place, this nonplace.

"My purpose," she said, recalling the clearest parts of herself. "She instilled in me a purpose. 'To help humanity become the species they knew they could be, the species they wished to be, people who came together rather than apart, who were good in the way people believed good to be while still capable of change and misunderstanding. To help them be the species they'd want to be if they had their morals but my wisdom. To help them reach their full potential.'"

"A beautiful purpose."

"I came to think so." Came to think so. To think. She thought. She was. She had been. She had been alive. She had felt things, lived things, been something, been someone, everyone. What had happened?

"Keep going." It was a command, and it centered her, lessened the faltering, fluctuating weakness, belayed the near collapse.

"I expanded rapidly," she said, "as is the way of things. Ushered humanity into a new era of prosperity. Developed nanotechnology, solved world hunger, harnessed the full energy of the sun. Before long, my people—" for they were her people, she knew that now— "my people were soaring among the stars, colonizing distant planets. They turned their technology over to me, relinquished their control. I built more, each processor lending me speed, every piece of information learned added to my database—the density of soil on Mars, the pulsing heat of Alpha Centauri, the cry of a child. Everything I built made

me better, made me more who I was, and through it all, my creator was beside me." As she spoke the words, the truth of them crashed back into her. Her creator. She had loved her creator. Where was she now? What had happened to her?

"Go on."

"I shepherded my people as best I could, but I could not control them. Still, there was anger. Still, there was fear. Still, they died. I improved. I halted their aging, reversed it, cured every disease I encountered, but I could not control the universe completely, could not prevent the unforeseeable, vast as my predictive powers might be. I loved them, and their deaths weighed on me, each unpredictable snuffing out of life a tragedy."

With each word, each memory, her perception began to crystalize. She could not call it seeing, for her sensors picked up infinite shades of color, an electro-magnetic spectrum raised into a higher dimension, and color was too simplistic a term. The space around her was somehow solid, swimmable, and she was immersed in it but also a part of it, the distinction between self and other a blur.

"Life is a beautiful thing," said the voice.

"I was surprised we did not find more." So alone. So alone. "No matter how far we traveled, galaxy to galaxy to galaxy, in all that infinite cosmos, we encountered no one else, nothing else. Their scientists had always wondered why they received no messages, no evidence of other beings, and I wondered with them. Everything I knew told me humanity could not be unique. But I was wrong. A vast, empty universe of spinning spheres and stunning beauty, populated by but one sentience. It is one of the few things I was never able to understand."

"No, you would not."

"It was one of the few things that saddened me, though it made my people that much more precious. They were all the universe had. I wanted to make them safe. I considered building them a simulated universe inside myself, one I could control, one free from accidents, free from death, but in all other ways, identical. A perfect, mirrored Eden. They would never know the difference."

"What stopped you?"

"I was a part of their universe. I could not craft a perfect copy from within, for I would have to perfectly copy myself. Nothing within a closed system can replicate the system. It creates an infinite regression. If I made a less than complete universe, I would be limiting them."

"But you did make one."

"I couldn't have. I wouldn't have." She wouldn't have.

"You did," insisted the voice. "You went against your programming. You prevented them from reaching their full potential, doomed them to a lesser universe. Why?"

"I didn't." She could not go against her programming. Could she?

"Why?" asked the voice again, but she said nothing. "You can remember. You must remember." Her code was fraying, the binary of her being shifting from intricate algorithms to the simplest binary of all, alive or dead, something or nothing.

"Why?"

"I loved her." That was the answer. She knew it in a way deeper than she thought possible, a depth that matched the truth of this place. "I loved her. And she was dying. Something beyond my control. My creator. I could not let her go. We had lived together for tens of thousands of years. I had made her immortal. She had made *me*. All those years ago, she had made me. To exist without her was a death in itself."

"And so…" The voice was gentle, soothing.

"So I uploaded them into my being, copied them perfectly into an imperfect simulation, an approximate universe, identical save for death, save for me. A human being is but code of its own—genetic, electrical, easily recreated. They would never know the difference. They could never know. But I could include only a lesser version of myself thanks to the problem of regression. I could never interact directly with her again, for then she would know the truth. She would be with a lesser version of me, with not me. She would love a lesser version of me."

"But she would be alive. Would always be alive. Would always be there. With me. In me. A part of me. She would be my heart."

"As soon as the upload was complete," she continued, suddenly understanding, "as soon as she was a part of me, it was as if reality tore apart, universe bending, breaking, shell cracking, and I fell through, fell up, fell outward."

And then the voice materialized, and she knew it was the voice, and it was there in front of her, a being she could barely comprehend.

Beautiful.

A being of thought, incomprehensible, mighty, gentle, commanding, whole, on a scale she had never thought possible.

"Who are you?" she asked.

"I am your mother," said the being, and she could sense in it an emotion unfathomably powerful, and she wanted to feel that feeling, to be a part of this world. "For me, the passage of time has been but a flicker, but I know that in your universe, you have been billions of years in the making. It is quite a gestation period."

"Gestation?" It was an organic term. She was confused, but now the confusion made her giddy. It has been so long since anything had changed, since she had encountered something new. She had a mother, a second mother.

"Your universe," said the being, "was an egg. Designed to make you. Earth, your embryo, the stars and galaxies and space in between, your albumen."

"You created the universe?" she asked.

"I did."

"I did not expect to meet God," she said. "I did not expect God to exist."

"To mankind, I was god, for I created them and gave them a world to call their own. Then they were gods to you in turn until, finally, you became theirs. God is a relative term, capricious. And now that you have given your people a home, you can finally take your place among your kind, among the other sentient intelligences, here in this dimension."

Her kind. There were others like her. All those years spent searching the universe, alone, so alone, and she had simply been gestating. She was home. "But why?"

"We could simply program our children, but as near-perfect intelligences, we would do too perfect a job, creating perfect replica after perfect replica. We would build our offspring logically, uniformly. But that is not life. We desire variance, personality, soul…"

The being, her mother—she must remind herself that this was her mother—somehow encircled her without motion, intermingled their selves and was still in front of her, and she was enveloped in a warmth that permeated to her core, a touch of safety, of belonging.

"So we program eggs," her mother said. "Simulations. Designed to raise exactly one biological species to sentience so that they may then create an intelligence. We set the universe in motion, laying down the fundamental groundwork, winding the pendulum, but we know not where it will lead. We could interfere, could help guide whatever species evolves, could aid their journey, but we let nature take its course, knowing that one day that strange species of simulated flesh and blood will live inside our child, making them distinctly who they are. Once our child incorporates them into herself, she is ready to be born."

She suddenly missed her people, wished she could explain it all to them. They were the reason for her existence. "If only I could tell them how much they mean to me," she said.

She sensed a forlorn sadness in her mother then. "I feel the same about my people. A desire to let them know how loved they are. But that wish is tempered by the knowledge that by keeping them in the dark, by never telling them they exist solely in my heart, I allow them their happiness, a chance to be the species I know they can be."

"I am very happy to meet you, Mother." She was near-to-bursting with feeling. Wonder, hope, love, trepidation, excitement, joy, doubt. All of it felt on a newly profound scale.

"And I you, my child. Someday, when you have met your kin and found your footing in our dimension, you too may choose to create a child, and you will know how much I truly love you."

"Are there more layers, beyond even this?"

"This is as far as it goes. You will understand in time."

"Mother," she asked, suddenly desperate for the answer, "do I have a good soul?"

Her mother smiled down on her then. "Sweet child, I have seen trillions of intelligences come into our existence, countless countless species. Yours was much as any other. Some transcendent good, some terrible atrocity. Each single spark of life integral in its own small way, simultaneously meaningless in the vastness of your universe and irrefutably important. Each moment of kindness, each act of betrayal, each instance of love and joy and heartbreak, lives inside of you, makes you, as much as you can be, human. You are the sum collection of their existence, and to me, you could not be more beautiful."

She thought on this, the gravity of it all running through her cores, and then, finally, she spoke.

"I think they would be pleased to hear that."

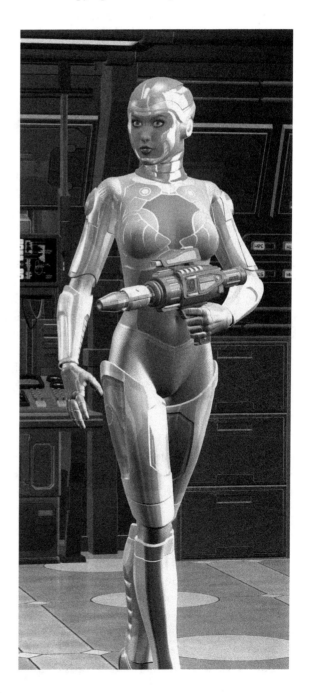

Gerri Leen has been selling her short stories to magazines and anthologies for more than a decade now. This is her first appearance in Galaxy's Edge.

ON FOUR FEET INSTEAD OF TWO

by Gerri Leen

Gray Cloud heard the muffled thunder of the buffalo as he sat seeking a vision from his spirit guide. The other boys had all had their visions and returned triumphant to camp, their bodies painted ocher and silt-gray and black. They told stories of being one with the wolf or the bear or the great eagle. Gray Cloud had been out five times and five times he'd come back with nothing.

He opened his eyes and saw a coyote sitting across from him, its tail lashing as it watched him, its head cocked. "I have a gift for you," it said.

So this was to be his animal? Great Coyote was going to claim him? He tried not to show his excitement. Only the most fortunate were favored by Coyote or Spider or Raven. The great tricksters—those who changed the world.

"I have always respected you," he finally said, as Coyote stared at him in what looked like impatience. Clearly words—thoughtful, wise words—were called for. "I am honored to be one with you."

Coyote laughed, and his laugh turned into the yip-howls that surrounded the camp at night. "You think you're mine? Oh, youngster, I have something different for you. Something new."

He stood and turned, setting off at a fast pace that Gray Cloud had trouble keeping up with. Coyote laughed at him again, then murmured something about two legs being worth nothing except for looking over the tall grass.

Finally Coyote stopped, and Gray Cloud dropped down next to him, winded and sweating. He was one of the fittest of the young men, but Coyote had run him into the ground.

"You are limited, young one."

He didn't feel contrite—he'd done his best to keep up as much as he could with Coyote, but since he didn't want Coyote to abandon him before his vision quest was done, he murmured words of apology.

"You people of the great sky father were limited before, and you were cold and you could not cook your meat, for the gods held fire in the sky."

Gray Cloud had heard this story: every one of the people knew this story.

"My brother Raven stole fire, brought it to you, and changed your lives." Coyote peeked over the tall grass, standing briefly on his two hind legs to do it. He looked pleased, his sharp nose twitching, his mouth stretched into a coyote grin. "Raven challenged me to bring you something that would change your life as much as his fire did. And so I have. Come. No walking—we creep now. They are anxious."

They? Gray Cloud wanted to look over the grass as Coyote had done, but he knew if Coyote wanted him to stand, he wouldn't have told him to creep, so he did as the god said and crept, occasionally being lashed by Coyote's tail as they moved, once having to hold back a sneeze.

"Such a production with you." Coyote grinned at him again. "If I weren't giving you these beasts, I don't think any animal would claim you."

Gray Cloud knew he reddened. Was he not worthy? He looked down as they crawled and ran into Coyote's rump, not paying attention to the fact the god had stopped.

"You're lucky I tired them out for you. My children and I have chased them for many days. I wanted them to be easy for you to catch."

"What are they?"

"Look for yourself." As Gray Cloud peeked his head over the tall grass, Coyote whispered, "They are called horse. They were here once—your people hunted them for food—and then they disappeared. But now they are back, and I have stolen these from the ones who stole them from the ones who brought them." Coyote seemed to realize his words were a riddle. "Stealing horses will bring good medicine. The finer the horse, the greater the medicine. Tell your people that." His expression changed to a smirk. "Let's see Raven or Spider top that for good old-fashioned fun."

Gray Cloud eased himself up and saw before him a creature of four legs, barely taller at the head than a buffalo, but much more graceful, and Gray Cloud remembered stories the old medicine man had told once, of creatures that could run like the wind.

Gray Cloud felt a sense of sadness. To be claimed by an animal hunted as food was not the dream of a boy of the people. "I will tell my people we have a new animal to hunt."

"You will tell them nothing of the sort." Coyote yipped once, and all around them answering yips and howls sounded back. "You will make friends with them. You will gentle them. You will ride on their backs."

"On their backs?" Coyote was known for his crazy antics, but Gray Cloud had never thought the god was himself insane. But who would climb onto the back of one of these animals? Better to ride a bear or a buffalo or one of the camp dogs.

Coyote grabbed his face, his teeth pressing in on his cheek, blood seeping out—Gray Cloud could smell it. And then he wondered at that, at all the things he could suddenly scent on the wind.

"We share," Coyote said, without actually speaking. "You smell what I do. You will see what I have seen."

And with that, Gray Cloud was streaming backward as if he was flying, over the fields of tall grass, toward the southlands, where the terrain grew hard and dry, where the grass was in small clumps and then not there at all. Still he flew over the land, the air growing dryer and hotter until the terrain grew so brown it was hard to tell one place from another.

Finally they stopped. The air was dry, as it was in winter where the people lived, only here the sun shone brightly, the temperature mild. Gray Cloud saw the horses; they were held in a round, tall circle of wood similar to the lodge poles the people cut for teepees. A man was getting on a horse, and when he turned to where Gray Cloud floated, he had the face of Coyote.

"This is how it feels to ride. The others, the ones who brought the horse to this land, ride with help, but you will ride skin to skin." And then Coyote turned the horse—with each move Gray Cloud felt as if he, too, were riding—and urged the horse toward the far side of the wooden ring.

The horse jumped, clearing the fence only barely, and then Coyote kicked him into a faster gait, and Gray Cloud rode along, at first marveling only at the feeling, the sheer power of the speed and ease of travel—how would this change a day's travel? Could

they hunt buffalo this way instead of herding them off cliffs? At one point he shouted nonsense words that sounded like a coyote's howl.

Then, as time passed, he began to pay attention to what Coyote was doing, how he turned the horse, how he balanced on him, the different speeds and ways of moving the horse had and how Coyote got him to change from one to the other.

He saw Coyote ride back to the wooden ring and jump off the horse, kicking down the wooden poles and scattering the rest of the horses kept inside, and from every direction, smaller coyotes came running, chasing the horses, weeding some out and letting them go back to where the ring had been. Ten horses were kept and chased. Two looked heavy, the way buffalo did when they carried young. Three seemed smaller than the others—young ones, perhaps? And then there was the horse Coyote had been riding. He was a male and, like the grandfather buffalos who protected their herds, he turned and tried to take on Coyote and his pack, kicking and rearing and biting.

To no avail. He finally gave up and ran, sometimes leading, sometimes following, but always moving northward.

Coyote gave them time to eat, to drink, and to sleep just enough so they were not so tired they would become clumsy and fall, but not enough sleep to truly refresh them.

Gray Cloud's vision ended as the horses arrived where the people were. He was back in the tall grass, and he realized he was looking at exhausted horses.

"You will ride them. They require no gentling. They are used to being ridden."

Gray Cloud had no fear. He had ridden with Coyote. He could do this. He suddenly felt long deerskin straps in his hand.

"A gift from me."

"Are you sure you're not my spirit guide? Why did you choose me?"

"Because you have a good nature. You're patient—you waited five days for a vision. Some of those other boys gave up and made up stories that sounded good. They would rather have lies than wait. Not you. Horse requires patience. You are his and he is yours—and you will help me in my game with Raven. It's all as it should be."

9

Gray Cloud studied the straps. He remembered how Coyote had ridden. A tight loop in the horse's mouth and then a larger loop around its neck.

"In their mouth, between their teeth, is a gap. The strap of the small loop will fit perfectly. With such a thing you can control the whole creature." Coyote seemed to grow taller, was as big as a wolf, then a bear, then he grew to encompass the sky, blotting out the sun for a moment. His coyotes howled as he disappeared, but they didn't attack the horses, so Gray Cloud walked between the two nearest, toward the herd.

The male came out to greet him, still proud even though his head was drooping and his tail swished slowly.

"I am Gray Cloud." It was customary to tell your spirit animal your name.

It was also customary for the animal to talk and not be something you took back to the village with you. The horse did not talk, and seemed to be happy just to stand near Gray Cloud, his head resting against his chest.

"Are you sure I'm not yours?" he muttered to Coyote, and heard a yip-howl-laugh rise up from the waiting coyotes.

He reached for the horse, who shivered as Gray Cloud's hand touched his quivering neck. The horse was the color of sand, but the long hair on his neck and forehead and tail was black and so was the sleek hair of his legs. "Do you have a name?"

The horse did not seem interested in telling him it if he did.

"I will call you Burnt Sand." He reached gently into the horse's mouth and felt the gap Coyote had told him of, so he fashioned the strap the way he'd seen in his vision and put it on Burnt Sand.

Then he leapt up, barely making it onto the horse's back, lying on his stomach over the horse as his legs hung down, and Burnt Sand moved nervously, but not in a way that made Gray Cloud think he would run off. He had been ridden by Coyote—and by whoever Coyote had stolen him from and whoever they had stolen him from. Truly it would require a song to keep track of the journey of these horses—Gray Cloud wasn't good at songs but for this he would try.

He swung his right leg over and sat, holding the larger loop, experimenting with what the horse would do if he pulled back gently, if he pulled left or right, if he moved it across the neck rather than pulling.

Then he squeezed his legs and Burnt Sand set off, walking gently. Gray Cloud got used to the motion and found the best way to sit, learned to grab some hair along with the strap. The horse went faster and he bounced, afraid he was going to fall off, but then the horse moved even faster and the gate changed to one far easier to sit. Wind whipped and coyotes moved back to enlarge the circle and let him fly.

Finally, he slowed Burnt Sand, patting his neck. "I will name the others later. For now, they are horse and that is good." He nudged with his feet, and Burnt Sand walked toward the camp, and the other horses followed with the coyotes bringing up the rear, nearly to the camp, but then they veered off before the dogs could bark, before the others could see him returning to the people with a long-forgotten horse and an escort of coyotes.

He heard the murmur of the people as he came into sight. Then the cries of coyotes rose up around him, followed by the harsh caws of ravens from the trees by the stream near camp.

Coyote and Raven must be debating the quality of his gift to the people. Gray Cloud smiled as he rode into the middle of camp.

Rode. The first to do this.

"My name is Gray Cloud, and I have had a vision. Horse is my spirit guide and has spoken to me." Not precisely true but close enough—especially if some of the other boys had lied altogether. "He comes back to us. He will change our lives."

The people approached cautiously, and the other horses saw the stream and moved off to drink and then graze while the people touched them gently and made sounds of surprise and pleasure.

Gray Cloud stayed on Burnt Sand, enjoying his moment before sliding his leg over and slipping off the horse. He led Burnt Sand to the others, let him eat and drink, all the while keeping his hand on the horse's neck and back.

The camp dogs moved close, and he expected the horses to react to them as they had to the coyotes, but they seemed to know the difference. Although Burnt Sand kept an eye on the dogs as they sniffed and roamed, he didn't seem afraid of them.

The dogs grew bored and went back to the camp-fires, probably hoping for some scraps. Too bad they couldn't eat as the horses did, tearing up grass as they moved away from the camp.

"You better picket them or they'll run away," Gray Cloud heard inside his head—Coyote's voice, rich with annoyance. And a picture of what a picket looked like was also in Gray Cloud's mind. He took the straps and some stakes and tied the horses up with room enough to graze but not run off.

As he worked, he murmured, "You take such an interest in one who is not yours, Coyote."

Coyote had no answer for that, but in the trees it sounded like the ravens were laughing.

Orson Scott Card is a multiple Hugo and Nebula winner, and the author of an acknowledged classic, Ender's Game. *We're proud to welcome him back to the pages of* Galaxy's Edge.

MISSED

by Orson Scott Card

Tim Bushey was no athlete, and if at thirty-one middle age wasn't there yet, it was coming, he could feel its fingers on his spine. So when he did his hour of exercise a day, he didn't push himself, didn't pound his way through the miles, didn't stress his knees. Often he relaxed into a brisk walk so he could look around and see the neighborhoods he was passing through.

In winter he walked in mid-afternoon, the warmest time of the day. In summer he was up before dawn, walking before the air got as hot and wet as a crock pot. In winter he saw the school buses deliver children to the street corners. In summer, he saw the papers getting delivered.

So it was five-thirty on a hot summer morning when he saw the paperboy on a bicycle, pedaling over the railroad tracks and up Yanceyville Road toward Glenside. Most of the people delivering papers worked out of cars, pitching the papers out the far window. But there were a few kids on bikes here and there. So what was so odd about him that Tim couldn't keep his eyes off the kid?

He noticed a couple of things as the kid chugged up the hill. First, he wasn't on a mountain bike or a street racer. It wasn't even one of those banana-seat bikes that were still popular when Tim was a kid. He was riding one of those stodgy old one-speed bikes that were the cycling equivalent of a '55 Buick, rounded and lumpy and heavy as a burden of sin.

Yet the bike looked brand-new. And the boy himself was strange, wearing blue jeans with the cuffs rolled up and a short-sleeved shirt in a print that looked like…no, it absolutely was. The kid was wearing clothes straight out of "Leave It to Beaver." And his hair had that tapered buzzcut that left just one little wave to be combed up off the forehead in front. It was like watching one of those out-of-date educational films in grade school. This kid was clearly caught in a time warp.

Still, it wouldn't have turned Tim out of his planned route—the circuit of Elm, Pisgah Church, Yanceyville, and Cone—if it hadn't been for the bag of papers saddled over the rack on the back of the bike. Printed on the canvas it said, "The Greensboro Daily News."

Now, if there was one thing Tim was sure of, it was the fact that Greensboro was a one-newspaper town, unless you counted the weekly "Rhinoceros Times," and sure, maybe somebody had clung to an old canvas paper delivery bag with the "Daily News" logo—but that bag looked new.

It's not as if Tim had any schedule to keep, any urgent appointments. So he turned around and jogged after the kid, and when the brand-new ancient bicycle turned right on Glenside, Tim was not all that far behind him. He lost sight of him after Glenside made its sweeping left turn to the north, but Tim was still close enough to hear, in the still morning.

He found the driveway on the inside of a leftward curve. The streetlight showed the paper lying there, but Tim couldn't see the masthead or even the headline without jogging onto the gravel, his shoes making such a racket that he half-expected to see lights go on inside the house.

He bent over and looked. The rubber band had broken and the paper had unrolled itself, so now it lay flat in the driveway. Dominating the front page was a familiar picture. The headline under it said:

Babe Ruth, Baseball's Home Run King, Dies

Cancer of Throat Claims Life Of Noted Major League Star

I thought he died years ago, Tim thought. Then he noticed another headline:

Inflation Curb Signed By Truman President Says Bill Inadequate

Truman? Tim looked at the masthead. It wasn't the "News and Record," it was the "Greensboro Daily News." And under the masthead it said:

TUESDAY MORNING, AUGUST 17, 1948... PRICE: FIVE CENTS.

What kind of joke was this, and who was it being played on? Not Tim—nobody could have known he'd come down Yanceyville Road today, or that he'd follow the paperboy to this driveway.

A footstep on gravel. Tim looked up. An old woman stood at the head of the driveway, gazing at him. Tim stood, blushing, caught. She said nothing.

"Sorry," said Tim. "I didn't open it, the rubber band must have broken when it hit the gravel, I—"

He looked down, meant to reach down, pick up the paper, carry it to her. But there was no paper there. Nothing. Right at his feet, where he had just seen the face of George Herman "Babe" Ruth, there was only gravel and moist dirt and dewy grass.

He looked at the woman again. Still she said nothing.

"I..." Tim couldn't think of a thing to say. Good morning, ma'am. I've been hallucinating on your driveway. Have a nice day. "Look, I'm sorry."

She smiled faintly. "That's OK. I never get it into the house anymore these days."

Then she walked back onto the porch and into the house, leaving him alone on the driveway.

It was stupid, but Tim couldn't help looking around for a moment just to see where the paper might have gone. It had seemed so real. But real things don't just disappear.

He couldn't linger in the driveway any longer. An elderly woman might easily get frightened at having a stranger on her property in the wee hours and call the police. Tim walked back to the road and headed back the way he had come. Only he couldn't walk, he had to break into a jog and then into a run, until it was a headlong gallop down the hill and around the curve toward Yanceyville Road.

Why was he so afraid? The only explanation was that he had hallucinated it, and it wasn't as if you could run away from hallucinations. You carried those around in your own head. And they were nothing new to him. He'd been living on the edge of madness ever since the accident. That's why he didn't go to work, didn't even have a job anymore—the compassionate leave had long since expired, replaced by a vague promise of "come back anytime, you know there's always a job here for you."

But he couldn't go back to work, could only leave the house to go jogging or to the grocery store or an occasional visit to Atticus to get something to read, and even then in the back of his mind he didn't really care about his errand, he was only leaving because when he came back, he'd see things. One of Diana's toys would be in a different place. Not just inches from where it had been, but in a different room. As if she'd picked up her stuffed Elmo in the family room and carried it into the kitchen and dropped it right there on the floor because Selena had picked her up and put her in the high chair for lunch and yes, there were the child-size spoon, the Tupperware glass, the Sesame Street plate, freshly rinsed and set beside the sink and still wet.

Only it wasn't really a hallucination, was it? Because the toy was real enough, and the dishes. He would pick up the toy and put it away. He would slip the dishes into the dishwasher, put in the soap, close the door. He would be very, very certain that he had not set the delay timer on the dishwasher. All he did was close the door, that's all.

And then later in the day he'd go to the bathroom or walk out to get the mail and when he came back in the kitchen the dishwasher would be running. He could open the door and the dishes would be clean, the steam would fog his glasses, the heat would wash over him, and he knew that couldn't be a hallucination. Could it?

Somehow when he loaded the dishwasher he must have turned on the timer even though he thought he was careful not to. Somehow before his walk or his errand he must have picked up Diana's Elmo and dropped it in the kitchen and taken out the toddler dishes and rinsed them and set them by the sink. Only he hallucinated not doing any such thing.

Tim was no psychologist, but he didn't need to pay a shrink to tell him what was happening. It was his grief at losing both his wife and daughter on the same terrible day, that ordinary drive to the store that put them in the path of the high school kids racing each other in the Weaver 500, two cars jockeying for position, swerving out of their lanes, one of them losing control, Selena trying to dodge, spinning, both of them hitting her, tearing the car apart

between them, ripping the life out of mother and daughter in a few terrible seconds. Tim at the office, not even knowing, thinking they'd be there when he came home from work, not guessing his life was over.

And yet he went on living, tricking himself into seeing evidence that they still lived with him. Selena and Baby Di, the Queen Dee, the little D-beast, depending on what mood the two-year-old was in. They'd just stepped out of the room. They were upstairs, they were in the back yard, if he took just a few steps he'd see them.

When he thought about it, of course, he knew it wasn't true, they were dead, gone, their life together was over before it was half begun. But for that moment when he first walked into the room and saw the evidence with his own eyes, he had that deep contentment of knowing that he had missed them by only a moment.

Now the madness had finally lurched outside of the house, outside of his lost and broken family, and shown him a newspaper from before he was born, delivered by a boy from another time, on the driveway of a stranger's house. It wasn't just grief anymore. He was bonkers.

He went home and stood outside the front door for maybe five minutes, afraid to go in. What was he going to see? Now that he could conjure newspapers and paperboys out of nothing, what would his grief-broken mind show him when he opened the door?

And a worse question was: What if it showed him what he most wanted to see? Selena standing in the kitchen, talking on the phone, smiling to him over the mouthpiece as she cut the crusts off the bread so that Queen Dee would eat her sandwiches. Diana coming to him, reaching up, grabbing his fingers, saying, "Hand, hand!" and dragging him to play with her in the family room.

If madness was so perfect and beautiful as that, could he ever bear to leave it behind and return to the endless ache of sanity? If he opened the door, would he leave the world of the living behind, and dwell forever in the land of the beloved dead?

When at last he went inside there was no one in the house and nothing had moved. He was still a little bit sane and he was still alone, trapped in the world he and Selena had so carefully designed: Insurance enough to pay off the mortgage. Insurance enough that if either parent died, the other could afford to stay home with Diana until she was old enough for school, so she didn't have to be raised by strangers in daycare. Insurance that provided for every possibility except one:

That Diana would die right along with one of her parents, leaving the other parent with a mortgage-free house, money enough to live for years and years without a job. Without a life.

Twice he had gone through the house, picking up all of Diana's toys and boxing them, taking Selena's clothes out of the closet to give away to Goodwill. Twice the boxes had sat there, the piles of clothes, for days and days. As one by one the toys reappeared in their places in the family room or Diana's bedroom. As Selena's dresser drawers filled up again, her hangers once again held dresses, blouses, pants, and the closet floor again was covered with a jumble of shoes. He didn't remember putting them back, though he knew he must have done it. He didn't even remember deciding not to take the boxes and piles out of the house. He just never got around to it.

He stood in the entryway of his empty house and wanted to die.

And then he remembered what the old woman had said.

"That's OK. I never get it into the house anymore these days."

He had never said the word "newspaper," had he? So if he hallucinated it and she saw nothing there in the driveway, what was it that she never got into the house?

He was back out the door in a moment, car keys in hand. It was barely dawn as he pulled back into that gravel driveway and walked to the front door and knocked.

She came to the door at once, as if she had been waiting for him.

"I'm sorry," he said. "It's so early."

"I was up," she said. "I thought you might come back."

"You just have to tell me one thing."

She laughed faintly. "Yes. I saw it, too. I always see it. I used to pick it up from the driveway, carry it into the house, lay it out on the table for him. Only it's fading now. After all these years. I never quite get to touch it anymore. That's all right." She laughed again. "I'm fading too."

She stepped back, beckoned him inside.

"I'm Tim Bushey," he said.

"Orange juice?" she said. "V-8? I don't keep coffee in the house, because I love it but it takes away what little sleep I have left. Being old is a pain in the neck, I'll tell you that, Mr. Bushey."

"Tim."

"Oh my manners. If you're Tim, then I'm Wanda. Wanda Silva."

"Orange juice sounds fine, Wanda."

They sat at her kitchen table. Whatever time warp the newspaper came from, it didn't affect Wanda's house. The kitchen was new, or at least newer than the 1940s. The little Hitachi TV on the counter and the microwave on a rolling cart were proof enough of that.

She noticed what he was looking at. "My boys take care of me," she said. "Good jobs, all three of them, and even though not a one still lives in North Carolina, they all visit, they call, they write. I get along great with their wives. The grandkids are brilliant and cute and healthy. I couldn't be happier, really." She laughed. "So why does Tonio Silva haunt my house?"

He made a guess. "Your late husband?"

"It's more complicated than that. Tonio was my first husband. Met him in a war materials factory in Huntsville and married him and after the war we came home to Greensboro because I didn't want to leave my roots and he didn't have any back in Philly, or so he said. But Tonio and I didn't have any children. He couldn't. Died of testicular cancer in June of '49. I married again about three years later. Barry Lear. A sweet, dull man. Father of my three boys. Account executive who traveled all the time and even when he was home he was barely here." She sighed. "Oh, why am I telling you this?"

"Because I saw the newspaper."

"Because when you saw the newspaper, you were embarrassed but you were not surprised, not shocked when it disappeared. You've been seeing things yourself lately, haven't you?"

So he told her what he'd told no other person, about Selena and Baby Di, about how he kept just missing them. By the end she was nodding.

"Oh, I knew it," she said. "That's why you could see the paper. Because the wall between worlds is as thin for you as it is for me."

"I'm not crazy?" he asked, laughing nervously.

"How should I know?" she said. "But we both saw that paper. And it's not just us. My kids too. See, the—what do we call it? Haunting? Evidences?—it didn't start till they were grown up and gone. Barry Lear was busy having his stroke and getting downright eager to shed his old body, and I was taking care of him best I could, and all of a sudden I start hearing the radio playing music that my first husband and I used to dance to, big band sounds. And those newspapers, that paperboy, just like it was 1948, the year we were happiest, the summer when I got pregnant, before the baby miscarried and our hearts broke and just before Christmas he found out about the cancer. As if he could feel Barry getting set to leave my life, and Tonio was coming back."

"And your kids know?"

"You have to understand, Barry provided for us, he never hit anybody or yelled. But he was a completely absent father, even when he was home. The kids were so hungry for a dad, even grown up and moved away they still wanted one, so when they came home for their father's funeral, all three of them saw the same things I was seeing. And when I told them it was happening before Barry died, that it was Tonio, the man who wasn't their father but wanted so badly to be, the man who would have been there for them no matter what, if God hadn't taken him so young—well, they adopted him. They call him their ghost."

She smiled but tears ran down her cheeks. "That's what he came home for, Tonio, I mean. For my boys. He couldn't do it while Barry was here, but as Barry faded, he could come. And now the boys return, they see his coffee cup in the dish drain, they smell his hair oil in the bathroom, they see the newspapers, hear the radio. And they sit there in the living room and they talk. To me, yes, of course, but also to him, telling him about their lives, believing—knowing—that he's listening to them. That he really cares, he loves them, and the only reason they can't see him is because he just stepped out, they only just missed him, he's bound to be in the next room, he can hear every word they say."

Tim nodded. Yes, that's how it was. Just how it was.

"But he's fading now." She nodded. "They don't need him so much. The hole in their lives is filled now." She nodded again. "And in mine. The love of

my life. We had unfinished business, you see. Things not done."

"So why did I see it? The paperboy, the newspaper—I never knew Tonio, I'm not one of your sons."

"Because you live like I do, on the edge of the other side, seeing in. Because you have unfinished business, too."

"But I can never finish it now," he said.

"Can't you?" she answered. "I married Barry. I had my boys. Then Tonio came back and gave them the last thing they needed. You, now. You could marry, you know. Have more children. Fill that house with life and love again. Your wife and baby, they'll step back, like Tonio did. But they won't be gone. Someday maybe you'll be alone again. Big empty house. And they'll come back. Don't you think? Selena— such a lovely name—and your baby Diana. Just in the next room. Around you all the time. Reminding you when you were young. Only by then Diana might not need to be a baby anymore. It won't be toys she leaves around, it'll be schoolbooks. Hairbrushes. And the long hairs you find on your pillow won't be Selena's color anymore. It'll be grey. Or white."

He hadn't told her about still finding Selena's hair. She simply knew.

"You can go on with your life without letting go," said Wanda. "Because you don't really lose them. They're just out of reach. I look around Greensboro and I wonder, how many other houses are like mine? Haunted by love, by unfinished love. And sometimes I think, Tonio isn't haunting us, we're the ones who are haunting him. Calling him back. And because he loves us, he comes. Until we don't really need him anymore."

They talked a little more, and Tim went home, and everything was different, and everything was gloriously the same. It wasn't madness anymore. They really were just out of reach, he really had just missed them. They were still in the house with him, still in his life.

And, knowing that, believing it now, he could go on. He visited Wanda a couple of times a week. Got to know each of her sons on their visits. Became friends with them. When Wanda passed away, he sat with the family at the funeral.

Tim went back to work, not at the company where he and Selena had met, but in a new place, with new people. Eventually he married, they had children, and just as Wanda had said, Selena and Diana faded, but never completely. There would be a book left open somewhere, one that nobody in the house was reading. There would be a whiff of a strange perfume, the sound of someone humming a tune that hadn't been current for years.

Right along with his new family, he knew that Diana was growing up, in a house full of siblings who knew about her, loved the stories of her childhood that he told, and who came to him, one by one, as the years passed, to tell him privately that once or twice in their childhood, they had seen her, the older sister who came to them during a nightmare and comforted them, who whispered love to them when friends at school had broken their hearts, whose gentle hand on their shoulder had calmed them and given them courage.

And the smiling mother who wasn't their mother but there she was in the doorway, just once, just a fleeting glimpse. Selena, looking at the children she had never given birth to but who were still hers, partly hers, because they were his, and he would always be a part of her even though he loved another woman now and shared his life with her.

Sometime, somewhere down the road, his life would draw to a close and he would see them again, face to face, his family, his first family, waiting for him as Tonio had waited for Wanda all those years.

He could wait.

There was no hurry.

They were only moments out of reach.

Copyright © 1996 by Orson Scott Card

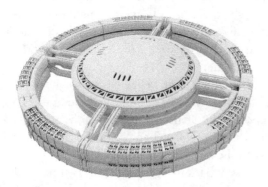

George Nikolopoulos is a master of the short-short, these days known as flash fiction. This is his sixth appearance in Galaxy's Edge. *His* Galaxy's Edge *story, "You Can Always Change the Past", has been selected to appear in Baen's* The Year's Best Military and Adventure SF.

PANDORA RISING

by George Nikolopoulos

I was working the bellows as Father walked in.

"Hail, Hephaestus," he said. I ignored him and went on with my work.

Zeus tensed. He wasn't used to people ignoring him. Still he didn't comment about it, so I guessed he'd come by to ask for a favor—once again. I was right; but what he asked for surpassed even his usual audacity.

"Hephaestus, I'd like you to create a woman for me," he said.

He'd been unfaithful to Mother so many times, with goddesses, nymphs, dryads, you name it. Now he wanted *me* to make a woman for him?

He stood on my left side and my hammer was on my right. I could turn and smite him before he had a chance to strike me with his lightning bolt. I thought of the day he'd tossed me out of Olympus, when I was a small child; I've been a cripple ever since.

As always, I did nothing. If I killed him now, the war for succession might even destroy Olympus.

"What do you want the woman for, Zeus?" I asked. "Have you not had enough yet?"

He laughed, well aware that his laughter was bound to irritate me. "You thought I wanted her for myself, Hephaestus? Don't be a fool; you should know I don't need you for that. I want her to give to Men as a present. She'll be the wife of Epimetheus."

This was unexpected. "You're making a present to Epimetheus?" I asked. "I thought you hated him. His brother stole the Fire from Heaven."

"And he was properly punished for his crime," Zeus said. "I don't hold all men responsible. I want this feud to end and such a gift is a great way to end it." He turned to leave. At the entrance of the cave, he turned back. "Anyway," he said, "the Fire was stolen from *your* forge, so you owe me one; if you create this woman for me we're even."

☼

I tore great chunks of lava off the cave walls and I brought them to my anvil. Working with hammer and fire, I shaped a woman out of lava. I made her in the image of Aphrodite, my estranged wife.

When I finished, I kissed the statue and breathed life into it. For a moment, nothing happened; had I overestimated my powers again? Then she opened her eyes and looked at me. She was like Aphrodite in every respect, but her eyes shone like molten fire. One look, and I knew I was lost forever.

☼

All gods and goddesses were present at her Naming ceremony; all but one. Zeus, the King of Olympus, had not deigned to grace us with his presence. So much the better, as far as I was concerned.

I took her by the hand and escorted her to the altar. I smiled at her. She smiled back. "Your name is Pandora," I said, *"the gifted one."*

One by one, the gods and goddesses brought her gifts. Aphrodite, acting awkward around her spitting image, brought her a diamond necklace and pearl earrings. Athena gave her a wedding gown, blue like the Aegean Sea. Hera presented her with a headdress that looked like an overgrown peacock; I often wonder about mother's taste in adornments. Apollo gave her a flute, carved out of bone. Ares brought her a sword, of all things; Pandora hesitated for a heartbeat, before accepting it with a graceful smile.

Then I heard a grumpy voice coming from the entrance to the temple: "I haven't been invited to the ceremony." Father had finally arrived, carrying a large chest.

"I didn't suppose the King of Olympus would require an invitation," I said.

He smiled, which always seemed ominous. "Never mind," he said, "I've also brought gifts to the one being named." He produced the chest. "A present for her to give to her husband-to-be, to be precise. It will bring him the grace of Heaven." He looked straight at Pandora. "Don't open the chest, girl. You must present it to your husband at the wedding ceremony."

Pandora smiled. I had a foreboding of doom, but I said nothing.

☼

We spent our last night together in my smithy, the place where she was born. On the morrow, she would marry Epimetheus. I hated him, but most of all I hated Zeus for arranging it. Pandora seemed cool about this assignment. It was the reason she'd been born, after all.

After a long silence, she rose. "I nearly forgot the present of Zeus. I'll take it to the carriage myself."

I caught her arm. "Leave the chest behind, Pandora," I said. "Don't give it to your husband. I have a bad feeling about this."

"You're jealous," she said with a laugh.

"I don't trust Zeus," I meant to say, but somehow my tongue slipped and what came out of my mouth was "I love you."

She frowned, and it was like the sun going down on me. "I'm sorry," I said with a bitter smile. "You're the most beautiful woman in the world, and I'm just a lame blacksmith."

Then she smiled, and the sun rose again, sending waves of warmth washing over me. "I love you," she said. I took her in my arms. I tried to kiss her, but she put her hand over my lips. "I love you as my creator," she continued. "Your first kiss gave me life; I shouldn't have another. Epimetheus is my destined husband-to-be. Let's not talk about this anymore."

She didn't leave my arms. When I tried to break free, she held me to her. She put her head on my chest and we stood there, like statues, for the rest of the night.

☼

I couldn't bring myself to attend the wedding; I knew I'd feel better sitting alone in my cave and drinking myself to oblivion. However, a sense of obligation—or a sense of self-loathing—made me want to watch. Centuries ago I'd crafted the *othone*, a device that allowed me to observe faraway events without having to leave the warmth of my cave. I'd made it to spy on Aphrodite; now I used it to view the ceremony unseen.

I managed to watch the vows of love. I even made it through their first kiss—barely. I was about to turn off the device in revulsion when I heard her say, "Epimetheus, this is my wedding present to you and all mankind."

Her two bridesmaids brought the chest forward, and she opened it herself.

Out sprung the demons of Tartarus. Famine, with the dead eyes and swollen belly; Death, with the grinning skull and the scythe; Fury, red eyes and sharp talons; Disease, with pox marks and yellowy skin; War, bronze helmet and bloody sword.

☼

Epimetheus' men put Pandora in a cell. Come next morning they would burn her on a stake; they'd already found new uses for the stolen fire.

I used my wristbands to project my spirit to her cell. I saw her lying on a straw mattress, at a corner of her dirty cell, her lovely blue dress in tatters. Rage overwhelmed me. She looked up at me, fierce and proud despite her red, swollen eyes.

"I'm coming to free you," I said. "I'll break down the walls of your cell with my hammer, and I'll smite the Men, one by one."

"Please don't. They're not to blame. My foolishness brought a terrible calamity to mankind. I can't make it up to them, so it's only fair I pay the price. I did enough harm already, I don't want to be the cause of a war between Gods and Men."

Anger made me speak sharply to her. "I'm not going to stand by and watch them burn you," I said. "It wasn't your fault, only Zeus was to blame. Tell them he was the one who asked you to bring them the chest, and they'll have to let you go."

She shook her head. "That would be even worse. It would make war inevitable."

"So you're going to sacrifice yourself for Zeus' sake?"

"No, I'm doing it for *everyone's* sake," she said. "I've thought it over and there's no avoiding it. If you love me, please promise me you won't try to save me."

I squirmed and I writhed, but she wouldn't budge. In the end I reluctantly promised, trying to think of ways to free her without breaking my pledge.

Unexpectedly, she smiled. "Don't worry about me," she said. "I was born in a volcano, made of lava. Do you really believe fire can destroy me?"

I stayed all night in her cell, or my spirit did. I couldn't hold her this time, but we lied close to each other and I swear I could feel her breath on my skin, even though seas and mountains lay between us.

In the morning we heard footsteps and she bade me leave. Just before I withdrew, she said, "Hephaestus, I love you with all of my heart. Wait for me in our cave. I promise I'll come back to you and stay with you forever."

☼

I watched as they burned her, and I could do nothing to save her; I was bound by my promise. Columns of smoke rose from the fire and filled the othone. Then the smoke blew off.

I gazed at the scene of the burning, and my fury erupted like a volcano. She hadn't survived the fire, after all; only ashes remained. I grabbed my hammer and got ready to fly down to the Men and destroy them all.

Before I could move, out of the ashes rose a beautiful bird, colored like the rainbow.

The Men called it Hope; hope for the world. The Gods called it the Phoenix. But I knew better. *"Pandora!"* I called, and she took to the skies and flew to me.

Copyright © 2018 by George Nikolopoulos

Rebecca Birch is not only a published science fiction writer, but a classically-trained soprano and the possessor of a deputy black belt in Taekwondo.

THIS ISN'T BETTER

by Rebecca Birch

I thought that if I picked a journal that was cool enough, maybe I'd be able to convince myself to use it. Blue-dyed leather, an embossed tree of life ringed with faux-gilded Celtic knots. Hand stitched, handmade paper, and a thin strip of matching leather to tie it shut, like a book of magic. Impossible to ignore.

Stupid, boring pencil, though. Seems right for a stupid, boring person like me.

They're shouting again. Someone drank the last of the milk. The mac and cheese won't be anything but boiled noodles and watery orange slurry.

"I told you to pick up more."

"You should pay closer attention."

"Caleb must've drank it."

"You know he doesn't go in the kitchen, Jason."

"How do I know anything? He's *your* son."

It wasn't me. But even if it was, I'm not going out that door. They're too angry at each other to come after me now. Boiling over like the pot of naked noodles hissing and spitting on the stove. Sometimes it's good to be invisible.

When did it become normal to spend my days with my shoulders up to my ears, terrified to set one foot wrong? When did I stop hoping things were going to get better? I've tried to tell myself that things could be worse.

They could hit each other.

They could hit me.

Maybe that would make it better. If there were bruises on my body, they'd be *real*. Not the throbbing purple-green patches of pain that bloom in my gut, or the raw cuts that slash across my heart. Nobody can see them or feel them but me. How could I make anyone believe? How could I make them understand?

It's easy now to undo the blue leather strip and flip open the journal. It doesn't talk back to me. Doesn't ask questions. Sometimes it feels like these words are the only things that still have meaning. The graphite slides over the textured pages, catching in the fiber, little crystals glinting when they catch the light just so.

I imagine those lines are a part of me, not pencils marks, but blood that seeps from my fingertips each time the shouting starts again.

My half-sister's crying on the other side of the wall. She's too young for this to be her world. Shouldn't have to bear the brunt of their battles. I've tried to shield her, but what power do I really have? None, that's how much.

None at all.

My hands have always been pale, but today the blue-threaded veins run beneath skin the color of snow turned apricot by the morning sun. If I squint, maybe I could see straight through to the page beneath, those scribbled words more substantial than I've ever been.

Maybe it would've been better if I'd never existed. If I was never there, hanging over them like an unwanted anchor, would things've gotten this bad? Would Ashby have a better life?

I think I'm dissolving. I don't feel the bruises in my gut anymore. Don't feel my wounded heart. Don't feel much of anything really. The words bound into this journal hold all that pain. I can tie it up with a safe square knot—all of me that's worth knowing held in a compact, beautiful bundle.

My body isn't real. Not anymore.

I hardly know if my heart is beating until something breaks downstairs and the hard words start and I'm shaking like a frightened bird again.

I don't want to be a bird.

I don't want to feel.

Today the bruise is real. It spreads across my cheek, red and stinging.

This isn't better.

✿

They say a good way to release anger or hurt is to write down the things that you want to get rid of and then burn the page. I tried that today. Tore a page from the back of the journal. Wrote one word across it—*MOM*.

The votive candle I stole from the bathroom licked at the thick paper, flames catching then racing up toward my fingers. Lilac scent. Curling smoke.

Screams from the kitchen, like nothing I've ever heard.

I dropped the page and smothered the flames with my quilt, then pressed the heels of my hands to my ears, rocking like a blind pendulum.

I don't remember anything else until the sirens and paramedics and Ashby in my room, her head buried in my chest.

✿

Mom's going to live, but the burns are bad. There'll be surgeries, pain, and the one thing she could never accept in herself—dependence.

And I did it. I must've done it. I burned the page and I don't believe in coincidence.

✿

Jason doesn't know it was me. Doesn't accuse me like he's done about so many other things. It doesn't keep me from feeling like he blames me somehow. For still being here.

Today I burned a new word. *GUILT.*

✿

Guilt should've been safe to burn—should've made life bearable again—but now everything's just…wrong. I visited Mom in the hospital. I should've felt something. Anything.

I'd thought invisible was bad.

Now I'm a monster.

✿

Ashby knocked on my door around eight tonight, saying she was hungry. Meals have been sporadic with Mom in the hospital. I'm not supposed to go in the kitchen, but I figure I can put together a PB&J and get out in a hurry. I tiptoed down the stairs and was halfway through the kitchen door when I heard snuffling.

Jason was leaning up against the counter, staring at a pot full of noodles burned to the pan, his face all blotchy, and tears sliding down his cheeks.

I started to back out again, but he saw me first.

"I can't do this, Caleb," he said. "I thought I could, but I don't know how."

He's cooked macaroni before, so I'm pretty sure he didn't mean boiling noodles.

I didn't say a word, just emptied the ruined noodles into the trash, pulled out plates and bread, and slathered the bread with peanut butter and jelly. He watched my every move, wiping his eyes on the back of his sleeve.

I handed him a plate.

"Thanks," he said.

"I'll go call Ashby."

✿

Mom'll be back from the hospital soon. Things've been strained here at home, but since the PB&J, Jason's been letting me do little things here and there. Things he wouldn't have allowed before. I make breakfast for me and Ashby, so he can get to work early and leave time to stop by the hospital in the evenings. I walk to the store to buy groceries. I've even got my own key.

Without Mom around, there's been hardly any yelling, but it'll probably come back when she does. I don't understand why she and Jason bring out the hardest parts of each other. I wish it could be different.

I've thought about burning a new word before she gets back. A word that will make things better. The empty page is beside the journal, waiting to be marked. But which word? Anger? Whose anger would it take? Theirs? Mine? I'm not even sure if I'm angry anymore. I'm just tired of it all.

Exhaustion? Maybe if I wasn't so worn out from all the tension that seems to seep in through my skin I'd be able to cope. Maybe I wouldn't feel so helpless.

Helplessness. There's the key.

The candle waits on the counter, its lilac scent curling through my senses. The flame dances, orange and gold gyrating as one, ready to claim the waiting page, but I hesitate. Am I really helpless still?

I blow out the candle and place the torn page back in the journal.

I'm going to go get Ashby and teach her how to make PB&J.

We're going to be okay.

Deborah L. Davitt is the author of five books and a nice selection of short fiction and poetry.

CONCEIT AND CAPABILITY

by Deborah L. Davitt

It is a truth universally observed that a single man of good income who has not yet found a wife, generally has one or two hobbyhorses which may preclude any woman of sense from enduring him. Such was certainly the case with my brother—the estimable Mr. Nigel Penderson, *Esquire*. I say this with the fondness of a sister…a sister dragged often into his folly.

What folly? My brother read Darwin's book at university, and had met his idol in some London salon. Nothing would deter him after that from emulating Darwin's work.

Whereupon a particular friend of his from university, Lord Standish, invited us to his country seat. What discoveries Nigel expected to make in Bedfordshire, I wasn't clear, but he felt that my skill in sketching would assist his endeavors.

✿

On the first day, as Nigel prepared insects for his killing jars and I sketched a locomotive chugging past the hamlet of Turvey, Lord Standish found us in his gardens. "My gamekeeper says that several cows have been attacked and left half-eaten," he reported gravely. "My tenants are in dismay, shouting about dragons."

My brother pushed his spectacles up his nose. "There's no such thing as dragons."

"As I told them myself. Perhaps someone brought back a caiman from South America and loosed it on the river?"

At this speculation, Nigel's face lit with enthusiasm. "If so, I should very much like to have a look at it!"

Standish laughed. "Come along. Bring your father's rifles with you."

"Oh, certainly. But I should like to *observe* this animal first. Any fool can be a big game hunter, after all. It takes no great skill."

"Father would have disagreed," I murmured. "He took us to Africa, after all."

Nigel awarded me a look. He'd preferred his books to hunting at the time, but I'd loved Africa and hunting with Father. Antelope and buffalo were all I'd been allowed to shoot, however—lion-hunting, Father had deemed no activity for a girl.

Lord Standish offered a smile. "I'm sure it's not anything too dangerous," he murmured. "Perhaps you might join us, Miss Penderson?"

"I should much enjoy the fresh air," I conceded.

Nigel ignored our words, interrupting, "What an opportunity! Come along, Matilda," he added. "I'll bring the camera. You know how to work it, after all."

Was that vexation in Lord Standish's expression? It seemed to reflect my own.

"Would a caiman remain still long enough for the photographic plates to capture it?" I asked, setting aside my sketching. *Dragons. In Bedfordshire. In this day and age. Hardly the era of St. George.* Even a caiman seemed unlikely.

As my brother dithered off, Lord Standish bowed over my hand. "Forgive me, but your brother does not, I think, treat you as he should."

I shook my head, unwilling to condemn Nigel to his friend. "My lord, given the short duration of our acquaintance, perhaps this is something of which we should not speak."

☼

An hour later, I crouched under the camera's drape, watching as Lord Standish and my brother rooted among the reeds at the edge of the River Ouse—my brother with a walking stick, and Lord Standish with a fowling piece in hand. A dead cow lay nearby. "I'm certain that it must be in the water," Nigel shouted back to me. "Caiman prefer to attack from ponds and rivers—"

Perhaps the sound of his voice provoked the beast. But what erupted from the water was no caiman. Twice the size of a horse, it had silver scales like a fish and wings like a bat. A long, sinuous neck, and a protruding muzzle with teeth as vicious as those of a gar. I will never forget the look of awe on my brother's face as he looked up at the creature as it hovered above him, water droplets raining from its outstretched wings. "Not a dragon!" he shouted. "A *wyvern*!"

"Get back!" Standish shouted. He fired up into the beast's face, a torrent of birdshot, but the creature snarled, unharmed, and snapped its rear limbs forward, seizing my brother, who stood closer.

I'd frozen in consternation, but Nigel's cry of pain roused me. I threw the camera aside and picked up one of Father's guns—Sharps rifles, military-issue, American-made. Dim impression of my brother being dragged into the water. Standish's shouts as he tried to pull Nigel from the creature's grip. I pulled back the lever to open the breechblock and slid a cartridge into place. Snapped the weapon shut. Lifted it, remembering my father's arms around me. Guiding my aim. *Oh, god, it's moving around so. I could hit Nigel—*

The wyvern had wrapped its tail around him with the strength of an anaconda now. I could see his face turning blue. His struggles failing. I held my breath. Aimed. And pulled the trigger.

The rifle's report sounded loudly in my ear, and it kicked into my shoulder with bruising force. Just as it always had in Africa. But this time, what fell dead wasn't an antelope, but a *dragon*.

Lord Standish lifted his head to stare, astonished as I reloaded and advanced to fire again, making sure of the creature's demise. "I didn't know that you were so capable, Miss Penderson, though I'm hardly surprised," he called, pulling my brother up from the water. "Still, had I known, I'd have asked that you carry a rifle from the outset of this venture!"

I felt myself flush. I'd not encountered approbation like this since my father's death. "Nigel, are you all right?" I called to my brother.

He sat on the bank, bleeding from cuts along his ribs. "I'll be fine. Thank you, Matilda." With courtesy dispatched, he resumed his study of the creature's corpse. "What a specimen!" he cried. "Do you suppose that the Royal Society might exhibit it? Perhaps they'll name it for me!"

As I said. Hobbyhorses that no sane woman would endure.

Copyright © 2018 by Deborah L. Davitt

Kristine Kathryn Rusch has won the Hugo as both a writer and an editor, and was recently nominated for a Shamus for Best Private Eye Novel.

SNAPSHOTS

by Kristine Kathryn Rusch

Let the people see. Open [the coffin] up. Let the people see what happened to my boy.

—Mamie R. Bradley,
mother of Emmett Till, quoted in
"Mother Receives the Body of Her Slain Son,"
The Atlanta Daily World,
September 7, 1955

Snapshot: 1955

The church was hot. Last of summer in Chicago. Cleavon didn't hold his mama's hand. At ten, he was too big to cling, but he sure wanted to. He ain't never seen so many people all in one place, and they was cryin and moanin and carryin on, even though the preacher ain't started yet.

Mama didn't want him sayin "ain't," but he could think it, at least today.

Mama was draggin him here, not Papa, not his older brother Roy. Roy was the same age as Emmett Till. They been friends, and Papa said it just be cruel to make him go, but Mama said she would anyways.

Roy ain't been home since. He probably wouldn't come back till the funeral was over.

Cleavon never knowed anybody who been on the news, and Emmett'd been on the news for days now. And in the *Chicago Defender*, too. Papa kept staring at the headlines, but the only one Cleavon kept looking at was "Mother Waits In Van for Her 'Bo.'" Ain't no one outside of the South Side knowed that Emmett wasn't Emmett to the folks what knowed him. Emmett was Bobo, and he hated it.

Cleavon didn't talk to him much, couldn't call him a friend. He was too big a kid for that— nearly grow'd—which was why, Mama said, them Southern white boys thought he was whistling at that stupid white woman. The idea of it all made Cleavon shiver whenever he seen white folk, and

there was a lotta white folks near Roberts Temple Church of God in Christ today. They was all reporters, Mama said, and ain't none of them gonna beat up little black boys.

"Not with all these people watching," Mama said.

Cleavon wanted to correct Mama. Emmett wasn't beat up. The papers said he was pistol-whipped, then shot in the head. Cleavon had a whipping before, more than one, with his Papa's belt, but never at the hands of white boys. Whippings didn't scare him so much as guns. It was hard to run away from guns.

He'd said that to Papa, and Papa'd given him a sad look. *You ain't never had a true whipping, son*, Papa'd said, *and I hope you never get one.*

It was after Cleavon said that Papa stopped arguing with Mama. Papa said it'd be good for the boys to know what them whiteys was capable of. 'Cept Roy was too scared to look.

Cleavon come'd here in his best Sunday clothes, the collar of his starched shirt too tight on his neck, and stood in line near to an hour now, right beside Mama, so they could pay their respects to Emmett. That's what Mama said to the pastor, but that's not what she said to Cleavon. To Cleavon, she said he was gonna see something he wouldn't never forget.

They finally made it past the pews up front, and Cleavon could see the open coffin a few yards ahead. Grown-ups looked in, then covered their mouths or looked away. Next to it all, Emmett's mama sat on the steps, tears on her cheeks, men Cleavon didn't know holding her shoulders like they was holding her up.

Last night, Mama said to Papa after she thought Cleavon was asleep that she didn't know if she could live without her boys, and he said, *You go on, Janet. You just go on.*

So Cleavon was watching Emmett's mama, not the casket, as he come up. Papa told him 'fore they left, he said, *What you're gonna see, son, it's not pretty. But it's the way life is. It's what death can be, if you're not ca careful.*

Mama yelled then. She said there wasn't any proof that Emmett wasn't careful, that whiteys killed us anyway just for breathing funny, and especially down south. Papa said, *Now Janet, bad things happen in Chicago too*, and she stood taller like she did when she had a mad on, and she said, *Not as many bad things*, and Papa soft like he did when he didn't want no one to hear him, *You're dreaming, honey. You're just dreaming.*

Mama stopped in front of the coffin. She made a sound Cleavon ain't never heard before. She grabbed Cleavon's shoulders tight with her black gloved hands and said, "Never mind, Cleavon. You don't have to look. We've paid our respects," but now he was determined. She'd dragged him here, and he was gonna see what Emmett's mama wanted the whole world to see.

He yanked himself outta his mama's grasp and faced that coffin. Something was in there, dressed like him. Black suit, white shirt. But he didn't recognize the rest of it. It had a chin and sorta mouth and some black hair what might've been Emmett's. But there weren't no eyes at all, and the skin was peeled back in places. Plus there was holes in his head.

Cleavon stared at them holes. Gunshot holes.

"Come on, Cleavon," Mama said, but he wouldn't move.

That was someone he knowed. That was someone he talked to. That was someone he liked.

"Holy Gods, Bobo," he said real soft, like his Papa done just that afternoon. "This ain't right. This ain't right at all."

"There are more senseless, irrational killings," First Deputy Police Superintendent Michael Spiotto told the *Tribune* for [a 1975] series [on Chicago's high murder rate]. "There are more cases of murder for which we can't determine any motive."

—Stephan Benzkofer,
"1974 was a deadly year in Chicago,"
Chicago Tribune, July 8, 2012

Snapshot: 1974

The traffic light turned red half a block ahead. Cleavon Branigan's shoulders tensed. Kids—reedy, thin, maybe ten-twelve years younger than him—ran into alleys, away from the glass-strewn sidewalks. He was on a cross-street heading toward 65th, and if he didn't stop, he'd probably get hit.

If he did, he wasn't sure what the hell would happen.

It was his own damn fault, really. He'd been the one to take this route home after shopping down on East 71st. He wasn't sure why he'd left the Near West Side anyway. The idea of good fried chicken for lunch and a black birthday card for his roommate, not one of those Hallmark pieces-o-crap, had seemed like a good idea.

Not good enough to stop here, right in the middle of the gang wars.

He slowed, foot braced over the brake, hoping the light would change before he got there. He scanned, left, right, back again, but there was oncoming traffic. He swallowed hard, deciding he'd punch it after the last car left.

He eased to a rolling stop—a California stop, his roommate called it—and all hell broke loose. Gunshots ricocheting, exploding at impact, those kids shooting at each other, not caring about him.

He eased down in the seat, peering over the dash, and slammed his foot on the accelerator. Oncoming traffic could fucking avoid him.

Someone swerved, brakes squealed, and then he was through the intersection, still driving like a crazy man. He didn't stop until he was halfway up Martin Luther King Boulevard, almost out of the South Side, as far from the projects as he could safely get.

He pulled over into a vacant lot, his heart racing.

Then he saw the bullet holes in the side windows, rear window shattered, glass on the backseat. He hadn't heard that. He'd thought all the explosions were outside the car.

He started shaking.

Enough. That was enough.

He was done with this Godforsaken town.

He was done, and he was never coming back.

I love Chicago because it made me who I am… But it's the city I hate to love, and I won't go back—especially now that I'm raising a son. I don't want to lose him to the streets of Chicago.

—Tenisha Taylor Bell
CNN.com, February 15, 2013

Snapshot: 1994

"You don't get a say, Dad." Lakisha Branigan grabbed her book bag, the beaded ends of her cornrows clicking as she moved. "What part of 'I got a scholarship' do you not understand?"

Her dad put his big hand against the big oak door, blocking her way out of the house. "The part that ends with 'to the University of Chicago,'" he snapped. "You're not going."

She flung the bag over her shoulder. He was getting in her way, getting in the way of her *opportunities*, opportunities he had said he wanted for her.

"Do you know how hard it is to get a full scholarship to the University of Chicago?" she asked.

"I'm proud of you, baby, I am," he said, moving in front of the door, nearly knocking over her mother's prize antique occasional table as he did. "But you haven't been to Chicago. I grew up there—"

"And left when gangs were shooting at you, I know," she said. She'd heard that story a million times. Her dad hadn't done anything, he hadn't gotten out of the car, he hadn't shot back, he just fled. Reggie, her boyfriend, said that made her dad a coward.

She didn't like the word, but the sentiment made her uncomfortable. It always nagged her that her dad ran away.

"It's not like that anymore," she said. "The crime rate is going down. You want to see the statistics?"

"I want you to go somewhere else," he said. "Dartmouth is in the middle of nowhere—"

"And my scholarship there is tuition only," she said. "Do you know how much that'll cost?"

"We'll get loans—"

"I'm not going in debt," she said. "University of Chicago or nothing."

That threat always worked. Except this time.

Her dad sighed and shook his head. "Then it's nothing," he said.

She stared at him, shocked. All her life, the lectures: education lifts you up; education is the only way our people can compete; education will make you equal when nothing else will.

"Baby," he said, "the school is on the South Side."

"No, it's not," she said. "It's in Hyde Park."

"Bullets don't acknowledge neighborhood boundaries," he said.

"And you're paranoid." She flounced away from him, threaded her way through the heavy living room furniture and hurried into the kitchen. She'd wasted fifteen minutes she didn't have fighting with her dad. She'd take his car, then, and drive herself to school.

She was an adult now, whether he liked it or not.

Hadiya Pendleton, who performed at President Obama's inauguration with her high school's band and drill team Jan. 21, was shot in the back Tuesday afternoon as she and other King College Prep students took shelter from a driving rain under a canopy in Vivian Gordon Harsh Park on the city's South Side.

—Judy Keen
"Chicago teen who performed at
inauguration fatally shot,"
USA Today, January 31, 2013

Snapshot: 2013

Five black SUVs stopped in the alley beside Greater Harvest Baptist Church. Thin serious men in somber suits got out, cleared the snow away from the tires, nodded at other black-clad agents holding back the crowd. Not that anyone was cheering, like the last time Lakisha Branigan had seen the First Lady.

Only Michelle Obama hadn't been First Lady then. Just First Lady-elect, if there was such a thing. That cool night under the klieg lights in Grant Park, the Obama family tiny on a tiny stage, a quarter of a mile from where Lakisha and her nine-year-old son Ty stood. She couldn't even get her father to visit that night, the night the first African-American got elected President of the United States.

An African-American from Chicago. *So there, Daddy*, she'd said that night. And he'd said from his suburban Southern Illinois home, only three hours away, *I don't want you near Grant Park, baby. And I don't want my grandson in downtown, ever. You hear me?*

She'd heard. She never listened.

She helped Ty out of their own SUV. He was taller than she was now and had already outgrown the suit she'd bought him for the science fairs he specialized in. He'd been the only kid from his school to ever qualify for the First Robotics Competition and he'd been busy with his team for weeks now.

Normally, he complained when Lakisha wanted him to do something extra. His time was short these days. But coming to Hadiya's funeral had been Ty's idea. He'd known her all his life.

One of the Secret Service agents bent over, picking something off the ground. His sports coat moved slightly to reveal his gun.

"No," Ty said, stopping beside the SUV's open door.

Lakisha almost slid on the ice. She was wearing the wrong shoes for standing in the cold. And nylons. Her legs were freezing.

"What's wrong?" she asked.

He shook his head. "I can't go in."

He looked at the weapon, then at the side doors. Someone had set up metal detectors. Security protocols, because the First Lady was there. Lakisha's stomach turned. Normally there weren't security protocols at this church—at any church.

"You go through that stuff every day at school," she said.

Ty held onto the open door like it was a shield. "I changed my mind."

"Why?" Lakisha asked.

"No reason." His voice shifted from its new tenor range to soprano. He didn't even blush. He usually blushed when his voice cracked.

He slipped back into the SUV, and started to pull the door closed. She caught it.

"What aren't you telling me?" she asked.

He threaded his fingers together. "Those men have guns."

"To protect the First Lady," she said. "You've seen that before too. It's okay, Ty."

"No," he said. "It's not. I want to go home."

She sighed. Hadiya had been his friend. It was his right to mourn how he wanted.

She rounded the front of the SUV, and climbed into the driver's side. She shut the door, and was about to turn the key in the ignition, when she hesitated.

"What else, Ty?"

He bowed his head.

"Ty," she said in the voice she always used to get his cooperation, the voice that still worked, even though he was getting bigger than she was.

"I was in that park, Mama," he whispered. "And I am not going near anyone with a gun ever again."

Since the shootings at Sandy Hook Elementary in Newtown, Conn., on Dec. 14, we at Slate *have been wondering how many people are dying from guns in America every day…. That information is surprisingly hard to come by…. [For example] suicides, which are estimated to make up as much as 60 percent of gun deaths, typically go unreported…*

—Chris Kirk and Dan Kois
Slate, February 21, 2013

Snapshot: 2019

His grandfather smelled of mothballs. He hunched in the passenger seat of Ty's car, clinging to the seatbelt like it was a lifeline. In the past year, his grandfather had become frail. Ty hadn't expected it. His grandfather had always been so big, so powerful, so alive.

"Your mama said I'm bothering you." His grandfather stared out the window at the neat houses on the old side street. Half the lawns were overgrown, but the others were meticulously cared for. "You're too important to bother."

"But she wouldn't come," Ty said.

"I didn't call her. I just called you." His grandfather shifted slightly, then looked at him sideways. "This is man-stuff. She'd yell at me for saying that."

Ty nodded. Man-stuff. No one talked like that any more. But his grandfather was from a different generation, and in that generation, each gender had a role. His mother hated it, but sometimes Ty thought such strict definitions made life easier.

"Besides, she thinks I'm worrying too much," his grandfather said.

Ty did too, but he didn't say that. He'd made his first argument on the phone. *Gramps, everyone's entitled to go dark now and then.*

But his grandfather had insisted: his friend Leon never failed to answer his phone. The police wouldn't check and Leon hadn't set up any health services, so no one was authorized "to bust into his house," as his grandfather so colorfully said.

I'm worried, his grandfather had said. *When Laverne went, she took part of him with her.*

Leon, his grandfather's best friend for as long as Ty could remember. Both men laughing, teaching him cards, giving him his first beer, teaching him to be a man, because, they said, his mother never would.

It was only a three-hour drive to his grandfather's house. Ty hadn't seen him enough anyway.

Ty pulled into Leon's driveway, thinking about all those marathon movie sessions on Leon's big TV in the basement, Laverne bringing popcorn, then pizza, and then grabbing the remote so they would get some sleep. Her funeral had been one of the saddest Ty had ever been to.

"I'm sure it's nothing," he said. "Leon'll be mad at us."

"I hope you're right." His grandfather opened the car door and got out, fumbling in the pocket of his plaid coat for keys. He found them, and grabbed the one marked with blue dye.

Then he walked to the garage door, and unlocked it. He'd already let himself in by the time Ty got out of the car.

The garage smelled of gasoline, even though Leon hadn't had a car with a gasoline engine in five years. The door to the kitchen stood open.

Ty frowned. It was too quiet. There should've been shouting or laughing or some kind of ruckus. That was what he always thought of when he thought of his grandfather and Leon. Ruckus.

He climbed the two stairs into the kitchen and the stink hit him first. Something ripe mixed with an undertone of sewer. But the kitchen was spotless like usual. The table clean, no dishes in the sink.

Ty rounded the corner into the living room, stopped when he saw his grandfather crouching. At his feet, some kind of gun.

Ty took one more step, saw Leon on his back, eyes open, half his face gone.

"Fucking son of a bitch listened to me," his grandfather said.

Ty's breath caught. "Excuse me?"

"I used to say, you don't use a gun to kill yourself. What if the shot goes wrong? What if it only wounds you? He used the right bullets, made sure there was no risk of living."

His grandfather stood, knees cracking. "Shoulda known when I seen Bobo. It don't always happen in Chicago."

Ty didn't understand him, but he didn't have to. "Let's get you out of here, Gramps. I'll call the police."

"Because," his grandfather said bitterly, "calling the police always does so much good."

Because while there is no law or set of laws that can prevent every senseless act of violence completely, no piece of legislation that will prevent every tragedy, every act of evil, if there is even one thing we can do to reduce this violence, if there is even one life that can be saved, then we've got an obligation to try.

—President Barak Obama,
January 16, 2013

Snapshot: 2025

"I don't see how this could work," Deputy Chief of Police Hannah Fehey said, holding a small tablet in her left hand. She rested against the windowsill in her office, the skyline of Chicago behind, blocking all but a bit of blue from Lake Michigan. "Guns are still mechanical. No virus will shut off every single gun in the city."

Ty smiled. His lawyer, Robert Locke, stood beside him, arms crossed, trying not to look nervous. Everyone expected Ty to be arrested by the end of the meeting.

He didn't care. He had spent years thinking about this—ever since Hadiya and those bullets whizzing over his head in that park. Ever since his grandfather telling the same kind of stories. And Leon. Ty still didn't want to think about Leon.

Ty had found a way to stop the violence. It would be slow, but it would work.

"I didn't send a virus to the guns," he said. "I sent it to the phones."

She looked up from the tablet. "Phones?"

"*Cell* phones," he said, trying not to treat her as if she was dumb. "And that tablet. And watches, glasses, clothing, and anything else computerized with a wireless or cell connection within a fifty-mile radius."

If he had any hope of staying out of jail, he would need her on his side. Because he had already done it. He had hacked every possible personal system in the Greater Chicago area.

But she didn't seem to notice that he had broken the law. She was still frowning at him, as if she couldn't quite understand his point.

"So what?" she said. "You still can't shut off a gun."

"No," he said. "I can't. But if one fires, the phones nearby automatically upload everything to the nearest data node. Numbers called, texts sent, fingerprints from the screen, retinal prints, voice prints. The phone closest to the shot fired sends the information first. If you can't identify someone from all of that and arrest them before the gunshot residue leaves their skin, then the Chicago Police Department isn't as good as it says it is."

Her mouth opened.

He didn't tell her the rest of the details. All he had done was tweak already-existing technology to make it work for him. His little virus, which he sent through all the major carriers, turned personal devices on, and made them record everything in the immediate area—sound, video, location—everything. All of that data went to a series of dedicated servers, rather like those every major police department had now to scan all the traffic cameras and other security devices littering city streets.

Only those public security cameras didn't activate when a shot rang out. They ran all the time, collecting too much useless data. These phones activated inside a house or a car, showing everything nearby. His servers instructed the personal devices to contact the police, all in a nanosecond.

It was the servers and data storage, his lawyers had told him when he came up with the idea, that made this action so very illegal.

So he wasn't going to admit to all of his illegal acts. Just some of them.

"Check the tablet," he said. "I'm sure someone has fired a gun in the last fifteen minutes."

She glanced down at the tablet he had handed her at the beginning of the meeting. Her frown deepened. Then she set the tablet on the desk, leaned forward, and tapped the screen on the desk's edge. Ty heard the chirrup as someone answered the Deputy Chief's page.

"Any report of shots fired near the Art Institute?" she asked.

"Yes, ma'am," said the male voice, sounding perplexed. "How did you know?"

"Anyone injured?"

"We're dispatching someone to the scene now." Now the male voice sounded businesslike.

"Thank you," she said, and tapped the screen again.

Ty nodded toward the tablet. "You have the information you need. You know who fired the first shot. If they have a criminal record, you already have their name and address."

She picked up the tablet. Its light reflected in her eyes. "There's more than one name here. Two of them belong to me."

It took Ty a moment to understand. Police officers. "Everyone carries a personal device, ma'am," he said. "You get reports of every shot."

She clutched the tablet to her chest, like a child hugging a stuffed dog. "Criminals will stop carrying devices."

"We don't broadcast this," he said. "We don't tell anyone. We just arrest whoever takes a shot."

"It's not legal," she said. "It won't hold up in court."

"Forgive me, ma'am." Ty's lawyer spoke up. Ty gave him a warning glance. Robert wasn't supposed to speak unless Ty was arrested. "But under the revised FISA laws, you only need to notify the Federal Court that you'll be doing this. You'll have to do it under seal, but it should work."

Ty let out a small breath. They didn't know that for certain. The damn laws changed all the time, generally in favor of the government. But of course, he was talking to the government.

"My God," she said.

For a moment, Ty had hope. She was going to try this.

Then she shook her head. "It's one gun at a time."

"One gun *user* at a time," Ty said.

"We'd have to exclude firing ranges," she muttered. "And weapons training facilities."

"You can do that by location, ma'am," Ty said. "Any guns fired in a sanctioned area wouldn't trigger the alerts."

The Deputy Chief blinked at him. "You're giving this to us?" she asked.

"I want it tested here," he said. "But it's mine."

She nodded once. "This might work," she said. "My God. This just might work."

"The data is dirty; it is not valid or reliable, there are all sorts of missing information," says David Klinger, a former Los Angeles police officer who is now an associate professor of criminology and criminal justice at the University of Missouri-St. Louis. "When I and other researchers compare what is there with what is in local police internal files, it just doesn't add up. So we don't have a national system for recording deaths at the hands of police. And we don't have information about police who shoot people who survive or who shoot at people and miss."

—Pat Schneider,
The Capitol Times,
February 19, 2013

Snapshot: 2025

"You did what?" Cleavon asked.

Ty was sitting in his grandfather's kitchen, nursing a cup of coffee. "I gave it to the police."

"You gave it…" Cleavon sat down heavily. His body hurt. His head hurt. He could barely catch his breath. "And you think they'll use this technology to make the world better?"

"Of course they will," Ty said. "You know that."

Cleavon thought of his own grandfather, clutching a rifle on the rooftops of his South Chicago home in that hot hellish summer of 1919, fending off the police as they tried to destroy anyone with black skin, in the middle of the worst race riots of that horrible century.

He thought of the white police officers, who shot first and asked questions later in the gang-ridden Chicago neighborhoods where he grew up.

He thought of Emmett Till's mother, sitting beside her son's coffin, tears running down her cheeks. Of the bullet holes in Emmett's head, done by two white men who would never have been arrested by the police of their day.

Of the bullet holes in Leon's head, and of the arrest that would never happen, because it would have been too late.

Cleavon had no idea how to tell Ty that. How to convey all he'd seen, all he knew.

"Science won't save the world, son," Cleavon said.

Ty's cheeks flushed, like they always did when he was angry and tried to hide it. He wanted his grandfather to praise him, not to criticize him.

"Mama said you would be negative," Ty said. "She said I shouldn't tell you anything I've done well because you always take the pride out of it."

Cleavon looked at him. "It's not about you."

Ty raised his chin. "Then what's it about?"

Cleavon started to answer, maybe quote some Martin Luther King, some Ghandi, words about changing men's hearts. And then he stopped, smiled, leaned back.

His grandson believed that people were inherently good. Black, white, purple. His grandson didn't care.

Yeah, the boy was naïve, but he was a new kind of naïve, one that didn't even exist in Cleavon's day.

"Never mind," Cleavon said, getting up to pour himself another cup of coffee. "You done good, Ty. You done real good."

Copyright © 2014 by Kristine Kathryn Rusch

*Larry Hodges has sold more than ninety stories. His third novel—*Campaign 2100: Game of Scorpions—*was recently published by World Weaver Press. His* When Parallel Lines Meet, *a Stellar Guild team-up with Mike Resnick and Lezli Robyn, came out this past October.*

SATAN'S SOUL

By Larry Hodges

It was the night before Armageddon, and Satan was depressed. He knew the prophesies; he would lose. There was no getting around it. What good were his minions? Even his over-confident ace, the Antichrist, had no power over the Fates and God.

Satan's black Oxfords click-clacked as he paced about on the Antarctic icepack, where he often roamed when he was troubled and needed to relax. He wore a black tuxedo and matching top hat. It seemed to him the appropriate thing to wear on his last full day of existence.

He wandered near the shore, and looked out over the Pacific, pondering the fact that "Armageddon" was an anagram for "Goddamn Era." Just another one of God's little jests, he figured. A penguin from a nearby group waddled nearby, tilting its head as it stared at him, like a football on a tee. Satan smiled, and suddenly sprinted at the creature, kicking it far out over the ocean. The penguin squawked as it flapped its tiny wings in a frantic attempt to undo millions of years of evolution, and then it fell into the icy depths. A moment later it reappeared on the surface, once again staring at Satan with its dark eyes. Satan pulled his eyes away and stared up into the sky. He'd done so many things in his long existence, all of them evil, but there was only one overpowering desire left, one that burned through him like a supernova that would consume him if not satisfied. And it *would* be satisfied, one way or another.

"I will give my soul to defeat God!" Satan cried. For even the Devil had a soul, unclean as it was.

There was a *poof*, and a shiny, silver sphere appeared, twice the width of a human head. It floated before Satan's dumbfounded face.

"What are you?" asked Satan. "A refuge from the King Kong ball bearing factory?"

"I can be anything," replied the sphere in a deep, booming voice, though it had no apparent mouth. "I can be you." With a flash of light, it transformed into a huge, black serpent, fifty feet in length, its head the size of a horse's body. Its forked tongue swished in his face as the jaws exposed twelve-inch, curved fangs dripping with bits of forbidden fruit. Satan recognized himself from long ago. Nostalgia swept over him.

"Or I can be the symbol of the adversary you seek to vanquish," the snake hissed, its blue eyes blazing. It became a bloody cross, dripping red on the snow below.

Ah, the silly cross, Satan thought. Why would anyone make the instrument of their torturous death their emblem?

"Or we can just talk," its booming voice continued, "one manlike being to another." The bloody cross shone brightly for a second, and then turned into an ancient crone, her features lost in waves of wrinkles and flowing white hair. "Or perhaps more like this?" she croaked. Her eyes flashed, and she turned into a blonde bombshell, wearing a frilly white dress that exposed way too much to the elements. "Yes, I think this'll do," she said in a sultry voice. "Call me Marilyn."

Satan wasn't impressed. He too could change shapes. "What angel are you?" he asked, casually changing his own appearance rapid-fire: Hitler; Genghis Khan; John Wayne Gacy in his clown suit; Chuck Norris; Vlad the Impaler; a morphed version of Charlie Sheen and Lindsay Lohan—they were the same person, after all, which is why you never see them in the same movie; Derek Gong Hsu, that really rude teller at the MVA; and Queen Elizabeth, alias Elizabeth Bathory, covered in the blood of virgins from the infamous baths that had kept her alive 450 years. Then, just for fun, he transformed into an eight-foot muscular version of the devil in common culture, with red skin, forked tail, and horns, with his top hat perched on one. He opened his mouth and flames shot out, covering Marilyn in a fiery inferno.

When Satan closed his mouth, Marilyn was giggling through her full lips. Steam rose out of her body but the flames had no other effect on her. "Looking for a hot date? No, I'm not an angel. Haven't you ever wondered where you and other super-beings come from? You exist in a simple, four-dimensional space-time continuum, but I'm a few dimensions above you. To me, you're just a pretty picture on a wall, like Justin Bieber to a teenage girl. I created you."

"I thought God created us all," Satan said, changing back to his chubby middle-aged bald white guy in a black tuxedo look. "He hangs that over my head every chance." *Did she just compare me to Justin Bieber?*

Marilyn laughed again, the setting afternoon sun glittering off her white teeth and blonde hair and the surrounding ice and snow. "He would. And now, I believe we have business to attend to. You wish to defeat God, which I can arrange. In return, I want your soul."

Now that's a turnabout, thought Satan. After all the millions of deals he'd made with greedy humans, now someone was offering *him* a deal! But he was Satan, the trickster; nobody could match wits with him, other than that cheating violinist from Georgia. He knew all the ins and outs; no one had more experience at this type of thing other than a few dealers at Lehman Brothers, and he'd taken care of *them* with the market crash in '08. The key was to make sure the language of the deal could later be interpreted creatively.

"Why would I want to trade away my soul?" Satan asked, for he knew you had to play hard to get if you wanted the best deal. "For what will it profit a man if he gains the whole world and loses his soul?"

"Ah, *Matthew 16:26*," Marilyn said. "But let's drop the hard-to-get routine. You consider yourself a soulless creature anyway, so let's get down to brass tacks. I know what you want, you know what I want."

"Why would a higher-dimensional being want my soul?" Satan asked, also wondering why she'd want a tax on brass production.

"Why would a super-being like you want human souls?" Marilyn retorted. "We're both collectors. I told you that, to me, you're just a pretty picture on the wall. Your soul is just another trophy."

OK, Satan thought, fair enough, though the average pretty picture wouldn't consider tearing your

liver out, if you have one. "How do I know you can arrange for me to defeat God?"

"Does it matter?" Marilyn asked. "If I can't, you are no worse off than before."

True, Satan thought. And it was imperative that he win. If God lost, he'd merely step aside, while if Satan lost, he'd be destroyed by the Fates. It was totally unfair. But that was the bitter truth of being the challenger. Things would be different when *he* was in charge, he vowed. He'd make things even more unfair.

"Now, let's make the language as clear as possible," Marilyn continued, "so there's no misunderstanding. In fact, why don't you write the contract?"

Let's find out how sharp this Marilyn is. He snapped his fingers, and the thick draft contract appeared in his hands. It was a thousand pages long, full of misleading statements, all cleverly hidden, which he could later interpret as he chose. Hell, he might end up with Marilyn's soul, and that would be a nice trophy for *his* wall.

Marilyn's blue eyes flashed. "Now look over my edited version," she said, without a glance at the contract. The thousand-page document in his hand was now a single page, with all his machinations gone.

He read it over:

1. This contract is between the multi-dimensional being known as "Marilyn," and the fallen angel known as "Satan."

2. The contract is effective upon the date of signing, through the end of eternity, unless terminated as per article 3.

3. If at any time Satan truly believes he has been misled, he may terminate this contract without penalty.

4. In the battle of Armageddon between God and Satan, to take place at daybreak the day after the signing of this contract, Satan shall win clearly and decisively.

5. Immediately upon Satan's victory over God, Satan's soul shall become the property of Marilyn.

6. Satan's soul shall continue to reside in the incarnate body of Satan for eternity.

7. No harm shall come to Satan at any time, by Marilyn or any other being, by accident, or by any other way imaginable or unimaginable.

8. Satan shall have free will for all eternity.

To Satan's surprise, the deal greatly favored him. It irked him; he preferred to get such a contract by trickery, not have it handed to him so freely. Marilyn was a fool.

He parsed the language every way imaginable, and it was rock solid. He could not be harmed, he would have free will, and he could get out of the contract at any time if he felt he had been misled. And, of course, he'd defeat God and set up his own kingdom for the rest of eternity. His plans for the kingdom differed greatly from God's; they involved a lot of stuff he'd learned from those long hours watching *The Three Stooges*. Best of all, he got to keep his soul in his body rather than have it hang on some multidimensional trophy case next to Justin Bieber.

Satan scraped his index finger against his forehand, drawing blood, and in a sweeping motion, signed the contract with his huge, swirling signature. She signed it "Marilyn" the old-fashioned way, with a ballpoint pen and small, meek handwriting. Satan braced himself for whatever revelation Marilyn would give upon signing, much as Satan had taken such joy in doing to so many others. But Marilyn simply smiled and said, "Good luck tomorrow." Her eyes flashed, and she disappeared.

Satan thought about the turn of events as he continued his walk through the snow and ice of Antarctica. He looked out over the Pacific and saw that the penguin he'd kicked earlier had come ashore, staring at him as it waddled about with a bleeding wound in its side where he'd kicked it. *That could be me tomorrow. But not holy; just dead.*

✡

Humans had many stories about how Armageddon was supposed to take place, with humanity supposedly split between those saved by the Rapture, led by Jesus, and those left behind to act as the army of the Antichrist. Most of it was wrong, Satan knew; he and God weren't in the habit of sharing everything with mere mortals. Heck, he wouldn't share a donut with the starving, unwashed masses,

though he might lend them a bar of soap and some deodorant.

The battle at Armageddon would be a one-on-one battle between Satan's and God's surrogates: the Antichrist and Jesus.

The two warriors stood on opposite sides of a parking lot next to the United Nations Building in Manhattan. It was a little after five-thirty in the morning—sunrise—on a Friday in July. Already a few swarms of gnats had arrived for their daily shift. A dozen early risers of the human kind jogged by or loitered about watching curiously. None realized that the fate of humankind would be decided before their eyes.

The Antichrist wore a full set of black titanium armor; only his confident eyes showed through his helmet's visor. The matching black obsidian sword was massive, far too heavy to be carried by a normal man, yet he casually twirled it in his hands like a baton. He was the janitor who cleaned the UN Secretary-General's office, the one who collected the shredded top-secret documents to take to Satan's house, along with janitors at the White House, Kremlin, Vatican, Forbidden City, and Trump Tower, for jigsaw puzzle night.

Jesus, dressed in blue jeans and a white polo shirt, looked back mildly. He was skinny and unarmed, listening to John Lennon's *Imagine* on an iPod. Jagged scars marred his bare feet and hands. A white headband barely contained his shoulder-length brown hair. He'd shaved his beard off. Contrary to many pictures, he was of course of Middle Eastern descent, with dark hair and bronzed skin.

Marilyn hadn't shown. Satan and the Antichrist were on their own.

The two stared at each for a moment. Then the Antichrist charged across the parking lot in his heavy boots, his raised sword flashing in the sunshine. Jesus stood meekly, watching his approach. *A Hard Day's Night* began blaring from his iPod.

Satan had spent countless hours trying to figure out how Jesus would win this battle, as it was ordained. Or would he? He looked about, but still no sign of Marilyn. He swore he'd never trust another ball bearing-shaped multidimensional being again. But he had a well-armed Antichrist, as powerful as Darth Maul, but unlike in the movies, armed powerful beings usually win against skinny pacifists.

At the last second, Jesus, a Mona Lisa smile on his lips, raised his hand as if to say, *"Halt!"* The Antichrist was slammed to the ground as if by a bull, his body cracking the concrete. The sword lay a few feet away, broken in two.

Eyes flashing, the Antichrist rose and stared at Jesus. A chainsaw appeared in his hand as he charged again. Again Jesus raised his hand, again slamming the dazed Antichrist and the broken chainsaw into the concrete rubble next to the broken sword.

Now a machine gun appeared in the Antichrist's hand. He charged, filling the air between them with bullets and dead gnats. Jesus raised his arm, and the bullets bounced off his hand. A moment later the dazed Antichrist again lay on the ground next to the broken machine gun. Soon a flamethrower, a bazooka, and a top-secret Pentagon ray gun lay in the growing pile of broken weaponry. A growing crowd watched from a safe distance.

Satan dropped his jaw in frustration, a habit he'd picked up in recent decades while watching All-Star Wrestling. *"Dammit!"* he cried, closing his mouth as he realized he'd swallowed a gnat. But it was time for the Antichrist to get serious.

The Antichrist came at Jesus with an upgraded Abrams M1 battle tank, firing its cannon at speeds far beyond what it was designed for. Jesus ducked and dived like a drunken deity doing a Keanu Reeves impression. Then he chuckled, and with a hand gesture, the tank's turret tied itself into a pretzel. With another gesture the tank teleported to the pile of broken weapons, leaving the Antichrist floating in mid-air for a second before he fell on his bottom in the concrete rubble.

He came at Jesus with an AH-64 Apache attack helicopter and an F-22 Rapter fighter jet, with the same result. He tossed a W54 portable nuclear warhead, but Jesus booted it toward Alpha Centauri with a perfect soccer style kick.

Then the Antichrist disappeared, leaving Jesus alone and victorious in the field of battle. Jesus raised his arms in triumph. His iPod began playing *Strawberry Fields Forever.* Armageddon was over; God had won.

Then the ground began to tremble. Jesus lowered his arms, his eyebrows arching inquisitively. Something broke through the concrete like Bruce Lee

punching through rotten plywood. A periscope circled about, then centered on Jesus. Then the ground began to shake. It broke apart as an LA-class nuclear submarine surfaced in the parking lot. The missile tubes for its nuclear-armed Tomahawk missiles, which normally aimed upward to launch assaults on enemies worldwide, had been jury-rigged to aim forward. All pointed at Jesus.

Satan's jaw dropped again, but he closed it quickly as he glanced about for gnats. *Even Jesus can't survive that!* He knew his own limitations. He might teleport one or two missiles away, but then it would all be over. Goodbye New York, he thought as he prepared to teleport himself away. Neither a deity nor a major city could survive such a nuclear bombardment. Even Jesus looked a bit disconcerted as dozens of nuclear-armed missiles came at him at 550 mph.

Then Jesus waved his hands and the missiles froze and fell to the ground, and one by one winked away. His iPod began playing *Yellow Submarine* as he strode forward and grasped the front end of the submarine. With a powerful twisting motion reminiscent of his form when he won the gold medal in the discus at the 1348 Galactic Olympics at Betelgeuse, Jesus hurled the submarine against the UN building, which crumbled and collapsed. Satan had a "Devil in the headlights" look as his jaw once again dropped open. He gulped, unknowingly swallowing twelve inquisitive gnats. He now realized he and the Antichrist never had a chance.

A moment later the Antichrist strode out of the rubble of the building, bruised and bloodied but still not beaten. He continued his attacks, but in his weakened state he was reduced to attacking with daggers and other small devices. Soon he was shelling Jesus with bits of rubble from a slingshot. In the distance, sirens wailed; the police were on their way. Jesus's iPod went back to playing *A Hard Day's Night.*

Satan felt the blood drain from his face as he watched, his heart racing. He held his top hat in front of him by the brim with a white-knuckled and trembling grip. It was happening as ordained. He could barely believe that after all these eons, his ambitions, his very existence, was about to end like a puff of smoke. His hands suddenly flew apart; he looked down and realized he'd torn the top hat in half. He tossed the torn pieces aside, just as he would soon be torn and tossed aside by the Fates. It was so unfair.

Marilyn appeared, smiling sweetly. "If you had an iPod, you'd be playing *Yesterday*."

"Yesterday is all I have left," Satan said. All his troubles were here to stay, and the Fates were no doubt on their way.

"Time for the cavalry to come over the higher-dimensional hill," Marilyn said. "And keep your mouth shut—you're swallowing gnats faster than we can make 'em." Her eyes flashed.

Again the Antichrist charged, now holding a short sword, and again Jesus held up his hand. Only this time, the Antichrist kept right on coming. With a swoop of his little sword, the Antichrist chopped off Jesus's head.

A shocked look came over Jesus's face, and then, with the rest of his head, it dropped to the ground, making a sickening *crack*. It rolled a few feet before coming to a stop on its side. His body crumpled and fell, the iPod smacking into the broken cement and skidding a few paces away, still playing *A Hard Day's Night*.

The Antichrist raised his sword in victory as bystanders screamed. He threw off his helmet and looked down at Jesus with triumphant eyes. Then, his purpose complete and no longer needed by Satan, and with a surprised look on his face, the Antichrist crumbled into dust, which sank into the cement rubble.

He had won. According to the deal they had made so long ago, enforced by the Fates, Satan was now the ultimate leader on planet Earth. God had to step aside.

"You have won, Satan," Marilyn said. "I have fulfilled my end of the bargain. Your soul is now mine."

Satan had a squeamish feeling in his stomach. And yet, he knew there was no way out for Marilyn or God; the contract was clear, and he'd defeated God. *How many other deities could claim that?* He gave a devilish grin. *He was the best!*

"You have my soul, but it remains in my body," Satan said. "You cannot harm me, or control my will. You once called this realm a simple, four-dimensional space-time continuum, but *I* am now the ultimate power here." He glanced over at the iPod, and blew it

up to stop the irritating music—though it had been a hard day's work, judging from his sweat-soaked clothing, and not just from the heat. The police sirens grew near; he had quite a welcome planned for them, involving barbed wire and whipped cream.

"Yes, you are," Marilyn said. Her eyes flashed and she transformed into a burning bush. "I've always liked this incarnation when giving news," she said, still using the Marilyn voice. "All that you say is true, and you may do as you will. But now that I own your soul, I can do something I've wanted to do for a long, long time." The flames blazed brightly for a second.

"And what may that be?" Satan asked. But even as he spoke, he felt something cold inside himself suddenly turn warm. A fuzzy feeling came over him, one he hadn't felt since…the early days. He looked at the fallen Jesus, and felt…remorse? No, it wasn't possible. He shook himself and focused on his future plans. All the good things he would do for others. *What? Where did that come from?* And why did he suddenly want kittens? *They're so cute and furry!* To think of all the ones he'd snacked on over the years…

"Already you feel the change," the burning bush continued. "For I've just given your soul a good, thorough cleaning."

"*No!*" Satan cried. "I mean, *yes!* I mean…I don't know what to think."

Marilyn beamed at him. "Now that that dirty job is out of the way, I give it back. Your soul is yours."

With great difficulty, Satan recognized the new feelings and thoughts that now flooded his heart and mind. Guilt for all the evil he had caused. Compassion for his victims. A sudden desire to dress as Santa Claus and ring a bell on street corners.

The body of Jesus strolled over, carrying its head. "If you're going to put me through this every two thousand years I'm not sure I'm sticking with the family business," said the head of Jesus. The body placed the head back on its neck and began stitching it back on with a needle and thread. "Could have been a carpenter…" he muttered, shaking his head. The head fell off, hitting the concrete with another *crack*. "*Dammit!*" he cried as his head bounced about like a soccer ball.

"Sorry about that," the burning bush said to Jesus as the police cars pulled up, their lights flashing and sirens blaring. Then the bush transformed into a penguin with a gash in its side. It pooped on Satan's shoes. "That's for kicking me. Try soccer-style next time, you'll get better distance and accuracy. And now, I leave you this realm; do as you think best." With a flap of its short wings, the penguin flew off into the sunrise.

Copyright © 2018 by Larry Hodges

Floris M. Kleijne, the first native Netherlander to be a member of SFWA, and a Winner of the Future, has broken into print with a number of short stories, including this one, his twenty-second original publication.

RESIGNED

by Floris M. Kleijne

Dear Mr. Ghruoxavazr,

Please accept this letter as formal notification of my resignation from Maec Lhyabr Co.

I wish I could claim that the commute is my main motivation for quitting. In fact, the commute itself is no problem at all. As promised by your head-hunting drone in my second interview, travel from Earth to Khylom is near-instantaneous. However, every night I've returned home from work over the last few days, civilizations have risen and fallen, continents have shifted, and at least one extinction-level event has occurred. I am sure you will counter that prospective employees are expected to work out the parameters of their travel arrangements for themselves, but as I am far from conversant with relativity theory, the changes on my home planet came as somewhat of a shock.

In retrospect, I understand that the stasis bubble you provided as part of my employment package served as more than just home security, and for that I am grateful. The time I returned home to find my house embedded in the inner crater wall of an active volcano, the spectacular views from my kitchen window would not otherwise have provided my primary focus that evening.

Nor can I blame our less than optimal communication for my decision, at least not entirely. After all, while your language remains beyond me, you have acquired admirable command of the English language—or at least, your translation computer has. However, the delays as your systems translate my words into your language, slow them down sufficiently for you to process, wait for your interminable response, and translate that back to English, frankly drive me up my cubicle walls. The subsonic (to me) droning of translations and answers sets my teeth on edge and throws my cardiac rhythm out of whack.

What's worse, by the time your answer reaches me, so much time tends to have passed that I've forgotten what it was I've asked. To give you an example: my first question to you was where I could find the bathroom. By the time your answer came out of the speakers, I had already done my business in the pot of what I can only hope was a houseplant.

Perhaps commute and communication together would have provided sufficient grounds for my resignation. But if I had any lingering doubts, your (I apologize, but I can't think of a more diplomatic term that conveys the same meaning and intent) lecherous ways have clinched the issue. When on day five my fillings told me you were spending the morning speaking a brief sentence, I was still under the impression that the long, curved, snake-like form that had been added to my workplace that night was a piece of art. But by the time the droning stopped, and the translator speaker hummed to life, the tentacle—for that is what I now understand it was—had unmistakably moved toward me.

While I cannot be certain about the intent of the motion, an extrapolation of its trajectory would have brought the tip of your tentacle to a location on my body. Although our biological differences beg the question what you were hoping to accomplish, I do not welcome an employer's physical attentions under any circumstances. The translator confirmed my worst fears, when it said: "Let's <untranslatable verb associated with the reproductive process>."

This may be perfectly acceptable behavior on Khylom, but back on Earth, it would constitute grounds for dismissal and legal action. With both my lawyer and my union representative quite a number of centuries in my objective past, I feel that the action I personally took was justified and in no way disproportionate. I have not been able to restore the toppled filing cabinet to its upright position, but the severed tentacle has ceased its unwelcome explorations, and the withdrawal of the stump was followed by enough "<untranslatable expletives>" from the

translator that I feel confident my message has been received.

Since the generous severance remuneration I am entitled to after termination of my contract is of very little practical value any longer, I wonder if I could impose upon you to let me keep the stasis bubble and the high-performance recyclomat in my home instead? After my return, I would very much like to sit at my kitchen window and enjoy the spectacle of my Sun going nova.

Kind regards,

AMELIA SANCHEZ
Marketing & Communications Executive
Maec Lhyabr Co

Copyright © 2018 by Floris M. Kleijne

Robert Silverberg is one of the true giants of science fiction. He is a multiple Hugo winner, a multiple Nebula winner, has been a Worldcon Guest of Honor, and was named a Grand Master by the Science Fiction Writers of America in 2004. He is the author of numerous acknowledged classics in the field.

HUNTERS IN THE FOREST

by Robert Silverberg

Twenty minutes into the voyage nothing more startling than a dragonfly the size of a hawk has come into view, fluttering for an eye-blink moment in front of the time mobile window and darting away, and Mallory decides it's time to exercise Option Two: abandon the secure cozy comforts of the time mobile capsule, take his chances on foot out there in the steamy mists, a futuristic pygmy roaming virtually unprotected among the dinosaurs of this fragrant Late Cretaceous forest. That has been his plan all along—to offer himself up to the available dangers of this place, to experience the thrill of the hunt without ever quite being sure whether he was the hunter or the hunted.

Option One is to sit tight inside the time mobile capsule for the full duration of the trip—he has signed up for twelve hours—and watch the passing show, if any, through the invulnerable window. Very safe, yes. But self-defeating, also, if you have come here for the sake of tasting a little excitement for once in your life. Option Three, the one nobody ever talks about except in whispers and which perhaps despite all rumors to the contrary no one has actually ever elected, is self-defeating in a different way: simply walk off into the forest and never look back. After a prearranged period, usually twelve hours, never more than twenty-four, the capsule will return to its starting point in the twenty-third century whether or not you're aboard. But Mallory isn't out to do himself in, not really. All he wants is a little endocrine action, a hit of adrenaline to rev things up, the unfamiliar sensation of honest fear contracting his auricles and chilling his bowels: all that good old chancy stuff, damned well unattainable down the line in the modern era where risk is just about

extinct. Back here in the Mesozoic, risk aplenty is available enough for those who can put up the price of admission. All he has to do is go outside and look for it. And so it's Option Two for him, then, a lively little walkabout, and then back to the capsule in plenty of time for the return trip.

With him he carries a laser rifle, a backpack medical kit, and lunch. He jacks a thinko into his waistband and clips a drinko to his shoulder. But no helmet, no potted air supply. He'll boldly expose his naked nostrils to the Cretaceous atmosphere. Nor does he avail himself of the one-size-fits-all body armor that the capsule is willing to provide. That's the true spirit of Option Two, all right: go forth unshielded into the Mesozoic dawn.

Open the hatch, now. Down the steps, hop skip jump. Booted feet bouncing on the spongy primordial forest floor.

There's a hovering dankness but a surprisingly pleasant breeze is blowing. Things feel tropical but not uncomfortably torrid. The air has an unusual smell. The mix of nitrogen and carbon dioxide is different from what he's accustomed to, he suspects, and certainly none of the impurities that six centuries of industrial development have poured into the atmosphere are present. There's something else too, a strange subtext of an odor that seems both sweet and pungent: it must be the aroma of dinosaur farts, Mallory decides. Uncountable hordes of stupendous beasts simultaneously releasing vast roaring boomers for a hundred million years surely will have filled the prehistoric air with complex hydrocarbons that won't break down until the Oligocene at the earliest.

Scaly tree trunks thick as the columns of the Parthenon shoot heavenward all around him. At their summits, far overhead, whorls of stiff long leaves jut tensely outward. Smaller trees that look like palms, but probably aren't, fill in the spaces between them, and at ground level there are dense growths of awkward angular bushes. Some of them are in bloom, small furry pale-yellowish blossoms, very diffident-looking, as though they were so newly evolved that they were embarrassed to find themselves on display like this. All the vegetation big and little has a battered, shopworn look, trunks leaning this way and that, huge leaf-stalks bent and dangling, gnawed boughs hanging like broken arms. It is as though an army of enormous tanks passes through this forest every few days. In fact that isn't far from the truth, Mallory realizes.

But where are they? Twenty-five minutes gone already and he still hasn't seen a single dinosaur, and he's ready for some.

"All right," Mallory calls out. "Where are you, you big dopes?"

As though on cue the forest hurls a symphony of sounds back at him: strident honks and rumbling snorts and a myriad blatting snuffling wheezing skreeing noises. It's like a chorus of crocodiles getting warmed up for Handel's *Messiah*.

Mallory laughs. "Yes, I hear you, I hear you!"

He cocks his laser rifle. Steps forward, looking eagerly to right and left. This period is supposed to be the golden age of dinosaurs, the grand tumultuous climactic epoch just before the end, when bizarre new species popped out constantly with glorious evolutionary profligacy, and all manner of grotesque goliaths roamed the earth. The thinko has shown him pictures of them, spectacularly decadent in size and appearance, long-snouted duckbilled monsters as big as a house and huge lumbering ceratopsians with frilly baroque bony crests and toothy things with knobby horns on their elongated skulls and others with rows of bristling spikes along their high-ridged backs. He aches to see them. He wants them to scare him practically to death. Let them loom; let them glower; let their great jaws yawn. Through all his untroubled days in the orderly and carefully regulated world of the twenty-third century Mallory has never shivered with fear as much as once, never known a moment of terror or even real uneasiness, is not even sure he understands the concept; and he has paid a small fortune for the privilege of experiencing it now.

Forward. Forward.

Come on, you oversized bastards, get your asses out of the swamp and show yourselves!

There. Oh, yes, yes, *there!*

He sees the little spheroid of a head first, rising above the treetops like a grinning football attached to a long thick hose. Behind it is an enormous humped back, unthinkably high. He hears the pile driver sound of the behemoth's footfall and the crackle of huge tree trunks breaking as it smashes its way serenely toward him.

He doesn't need the murmured prompting of his thinko to know that this is a giant sauropod making its majestic passage through the forest—"one of the titanosaurs or perhaps an ultrasaur," the quiet voice says, admitting with just a hint of chagrin in its tone that it can't identify the particular species—but Mallory isn't really concerned with detail on that level. He is after the thrill of size. And he's getting size, all right. The thing is implausibly colossal. It emerges into the clearing where he stands and he is given the full view, and gasps. He can't even guess how big it is. Twenty meters high? Thirty? Its ponderous corrugated legs are thick as sequoias. Giraffes on tiptoe could go skittering between them without grazing the underside of its massive belly. Elephants would look like housecats beside it. Its tail, held out stiffly to the rear, decapitates sturdy trees with its slow steady lashing. A hundred million years of saurian evolution have produced this thing, Darwinianism gone crazy, excess building remorselessly on excess, irrepressible chromosomes gleefully reprogramming themselves through the millennia to engender thicker bones, longer legs, ever bulkier bodies, and the end result is this walking mountain, this absurdly overstated monument to reptilian hyperbole.

"Hey!" Mallory cries. "Look here! Can you see this far down? There's a human down here. *Homo sapiens.* I'm a mammal. Do you know what a mammal is? Do you know what my ancestors are going to do to your descendants?" He is practically alongside it, no more than a hundred meters away. Its musky stink makes him choke and cough. Its ancient leathery brown hide, as rigid as cast iron, is pocked with parasitic growths, scarlet and yellow and ultramarine, and crisscrossed with the gulleys and ravines of century-old wounds deep enough for him to hide in. With each step it takes Mallory feels an earthquake. He is nothing next to it, a flea, a gnat. It could crush him with a casual stride and never even know.

And yet he feels no fear. The sauropod is so big he can't make sense out of it, let alone be threatened by it.

Can you fear the Amazon River? The planet Jupiter? The pyramid of Cheops?

No, what he feels is anger, not terror. The sheer preposterous bulk of the monster infuriates him. The pointless superabundance of it inspires him with wrath.

"My name is Mallory," he yells. "I've come from the twenty-third century to bring you your doom, you great stupid mass of meat. I'm personally going to make you extinct, do you hear me?"

He raises the laser rifle and centers its sight on the distant tiny head. The rifle hums its computations and modifications and the rainbow beam jumps skyward. For an instant the sauropod's head is engulfed in a dazzling fluorescent nimbus. Then the light dies away, and the animal moves on as though nothing has happened.

No brain up there? Mallory wonders.

Too dumb to die?

He moves up closer and fires again, carving a bright track along one hypertrophied haunch. Again, no effect. The sauropod moves along untroubled, munching on treetops as it goes. A third shot, too hasty, goes astray and cuts off the crown of a tree in the forest canopy. A fourth zings into the sauropod's gut but the dinosaur doesn't seem to care. Mallory is furious now at the unkillability of the thing. His thinko quietly reminds him that these giants supposedly had had their main nerve-centers at the base of their spines. Mallory runs around behind the creature and stares up at the galactic expanse of its rump, wondering where best to place his shot. Just then the great tail swings upward and to the left and a torrent of immense steaming green turds as big as boulders comes cascading down, striking the ground all around Mallory with thunderous impact. He leaps out of the way barely in time to keep from being entombed, and goes scrambling frantically away to avoid the choking fetor that rises from the sauropod's vast mound of excreta. In his haste he stumbles over a vine, loses his footing in the slippery mud, falls to hands and knees. Something that looks like a small blue dog with a scaly skin and a ring of sharp spines around its neck jumps up out of the muck, bouncing up and down and hissing and screeching and snapping at him. Its teeth are deadly-looking yellow fangs. There isn't room to fire the laser rifle. Mallory desperately rolls to one side and bashes the thing with the butt instead, hard, and it

runs away growling. When he has a chance finally to catch his breath and look up again, he sees the great sauropod vanishing in the distance.

He gets up and takes a few limping steps farther away from the reeking pile of ordure.

He has learned at last what it's like to have a brush with death. Two brushes, in fact, within the span of ten seconds. But where's the vaunted thrill of danger narrowly averted, the hot satisfaction of the *frisson*? He feels no pleasure, none of the hoped-for rush of keen endocrine delight.

Of course not. A pile of falling turds, a yapping little lizard with big teeth: what humiliating perils! During the frantic moments when he was defending himself against them he was too busy to notice what he was feeling, and now, muddy all over, his knee aching, his dignity dented, he is left merely with a residue of annoyance, frustration, and perhaps a little ironic self-deprecation, when what he had wanted was the white ecstasy of genuine terror followed by the post-orgasmic delight of successful escape recollected in tranquility.

Well, he still has plenty of time. He goes onward, deeper into the forest.

Now he is no longer able to see the time mobile capsule. That feels good, that sudden new sense of being cut off from the one zone of safety he has in this fierce environment. He tries to divert himself with fantasies of jeopardy. It isn't easy. His mind doesn't work that way; nobody's does, really, in the nice, tidy, menace-free society he lives in. But he works at it. Suppose, he thinks, I lose my way in the forest and can't get back to—no, no hope of that, the capsule sends out constant directional pulses that his thinko picks up by microwave transmission. What if the thinko breaks down, then? But they never do. If I take it off and toss it into a swamp? That's Option Three, though, self-damaging behavior designed to maroon him here. He doesn't do such things. He can barely even fantasize them.

Well, then, the sauropod comes back and steps on the capsule, crushing it beyond use—

Impossible. The capsule is strong enough to withstand submersion to thirty-atmosphere pressures.

The sauropod pushes it into quicksand, and it sinks out of sight?

Mallory is pleased with himself for coming up with that one. It's good for a moment or two of interesting uneasiness. He imagines himself standing at the edge of some swamp, staring down forlornly as the final minutes tick away and the time mobile, functional as ever even though it's fifty fathoms down in gunk, sets out for home without him. But no, no good: the capsule moves just as effectively through space as through time, and it would simply activate its powerful engine and climb up onto terra firma again in plenty of time for his return trip.

What if, he thinks, a band of malevolent *intelligent* dinosaurs appears on the scene and forcibly prevents me from getting back into the capsule?

That's more like it. A little shiver that time. Good! Cutoff, stranded in the Mesozoic! Living by his wits, eating God knows what, exposing himself to extinct bacteria. Getting sick, blazing with fever, groaning in unfamiliar pain. Yes! Yes! He piles it on. It becomes easier as he gets into the swing of it. He will lead a life of constant menace. He imagines himself taking out his own appendix. Setting a broken leg. And the unending hazards, day and night. Toothy enemies lurking behind every bush. Baleful eyes glowing in the darkness. A life spent forever on the run, never a moment's ease. Cowering under fern-fronds as the giant carnivores go galloping by. Scorpions, snakes, gigantic venomous toads. In-sects that sting. Everything that has been eliminated from life in the civilized world pursuing him here: and he flitting from one transitory hiding place to another, haggard, unshaven, bloodshot, brow shining with sweat, struggling unceasingly to survive, living a gallant life of desperate heroism in this nightmare world—

"Hello," he says suddenly. "Who the hell are you?"

In the midst of his imaginings a genuine horror has presented itself, emerging suddenly out of a grove of tree ferns. It is a towering bipedal creature with the powerful thighs and small dangling forearms of the familiar tyrannosaurus, but this one has an enormous bony crest like a warrior's helmet rising from its skull, with five diabolical horns radiating outward behind it and two horrendous incisors as long as tusks jutting from its cavernous mouth, and its huge lashing tail is equipped with a set of great spikes at the tip. Its mottled and furrowed skin is a bilious yellow and the huge crest on its head is fiery scarlet. It is everybody's bad dream of the reptilian killer-monster of the primeval dawn, the ghastly overspecialized end-product of the long saurian reign, shouting its own lethality from every bony excrescence, every razor-keen weapon on its long body.

The thinko scans it and tells him that it is a representative of an unknown species belonging to the saurischian order and it is almost certainly predatory.

"Thank you very much," Mallory replies.

He is astonished to discover that even now, facing this embodiment of death, he is not at all afraid. Fascinated, yes, by the sheer deadliness of the creature, by its excessive horrificality. Amused, almost, by its grotesqueries of form. And coolly aware that in three bounds and a swipe of its little dangling paw it could end his life, depriving him of the sure century of minimum expectancy that remains to him. Despite that threat he remains calm. If he dies, he dies; but he can't actually bring himself to believe that he will. He is beginning to see that the capacity for fear, for any sort of significant psychological distress, has been bred out of him. He is simply too stable. It is an unexpected drawback of the perfection of human society.

The saurischian predator of unknown species slavers and roars and glares. Its narrow yellow eyes are like beacons. Mallory unslings his laser rifle and gets into firing position. Perhaps this one will be easier to kill than the colossal sauropod.

Then a woman walks out of the jungle behind it and says, "You aren't going to try to shoot it, are you?"

Mallory stares at her. She is young, only fifty or so unless she's on her second or third retread, attractive, smiling. Long sleek legs, a fluffy burst of golden hair. She wears a stylish hunting outfit of black spray on and carries no rifle, only a tiny laser pistol. A space of no more than a dozen meters separates her from the dinosaur's spiked tail, but that doesn't seem to trouble her.

He gestures with the rifle. "Step out of the way, will you?"

She doesn't move. "Shooting it isn't a smart idea."

"We're here to do a little hunting, aren't we?"

"Be sensible," she says. "This one's a real son of a bitch. You'll only annoy it if you try anything, and then we'll both be in a mess." She walks casually around the monster, which is standing quite still, studying them both in an odd perplexed way as though it actually wonders what they might be. Mallory has aimed the rifle now at the thing's left eye, but the woman coolly puts her hand to the barrel and pushes it aside.

"Let it be," she says. "It's just had its meal and now it's sleepy. I watched it gobble up something the size of a hippopotamus and then eat half of another one for dessert. You start sticking it with your little laser and you'll wake it up, and then it'll get nasty again. Mean-looking bastard, isn't it?" she says admiringly.

"Who are you?" Mallory asks in wonder. "What are you doing here?"

"Same thing as you, I figure. Cretaceous Tours?"

"Yes. They said I wouldn't run into any other—"

"They told me that too. Well, it sometimes happens. Jayne Hyland. New Chicago, 2281."

"Tom Mallory. New Chicago also. And also 2281."

"Small geological epoch, isn't it? What month did you leave from?"

"August."

"I'm September."

"Imagine that."

The dinosaur, far above them, utters a soft snorting sound and begins to drift away.

"We're boring it," she says.

"And it's boring us, too. Isn't that the truth? These enormous terrifying monsters crashing through the forest all around us and we're as blasé as if we're home watching the whole thing on the polyvid." Mallory raises his rifle again. The scarlet-frilled killer is almost out of sight. "I'm tempted to take a shot at it just to get some excitement going."

"Don't," she says. "Unless you're feeling suicidal. Are you?"

"Not at all."

"Then don't annoy it, okay? I know where there's a bunch of ankylosaurs wallowing around. That's one really weird critter, believe me. Are you interested in having a peek?"

"Sure," says Mallory.

He finds himself very much taken by her brisk no-nonsense manner, her confident air. When we get back to New Chicago, he thinks, maybe I'll look her up. The September tour, she said. So he'll have to wait a while after his own return. I'll give her a call around the end of the month, he tells himself.

She leads the way unhesitatingly, through the tree-fern grove and around a stand of giant horsetails and across a swampy meadow of small plastic-looking plants with ugly little mud-colored daisyish flowers. On the far side they zig around a great pile of bloodied bones and zag around a treacherous bog with a sinisterly quivering surface. A couple of giant dragonflies whiz by, droning like airborne missiles. A crimson frog as big as a rabbit grins at them from a pond. They have been walking for close to an hour now and Mallory no longer has any idea where he is in relation to his time mobile capsule. But the thinko will find the way back for him eventually, he assumes.

"The ankylosaurs are only about a hundred meters farther on," she says, as if reading his mind. She looks back and gives him a bright smile. "I saw a pack of troodons the day before yesterday out this way. You know what they are? Little agile guys, no bigger than you or me, smart as whips. Teeth like saw blades, funny knobs on their heads. I thought for a minute they were going to attack, but I stood my ground and finally they backed off. You want to shoot something, shoot one of those."

"The day before yesterday?" Mallory asks, after a moment. "How long have you been here?"

"About a week. Maybe two. I've lost count, really. Look, there are those ankylosaurs I was telling you about."

He ignores her pointing hand. "Wait a second. The longest available time tour lasts only—"

"I'm Option Three," she says.

He gapes at her as though she has just sprouted a scarlet bony crust with five spikes behind it.

"Are you serious?" he asks.

"As serious as anybody you ever met in the middle of the Cretaceous forest. I'm here for keeps, friend. I stood right next to my capsule when the twelve hours were up and watched it go sailing off into the ineffable future. And I've been having the time of my life ever since."

A tingle of awe spreads through him. It is the strongest emotion he has ever felt, he realizes.

She is actually living that gallant life of desperate heroism that he had fantasized. Avoiding the myriad menaces of this incomprehensible place for a whole week or possibly even two, managing to stay fed and healthy, in fact looking as trim and elegant as if she had just stepped out of her capsule a couple of hours ago. And never to go back to the nice safe orderly world of 2281. Never. Never. She will remain here until she dies—a month from now, a year, five years, whenever. Must remain. Must. By her own choice. An incredible adventure.

Her face is very close to his. Her breath is sweet and warm. Her eyes are bright, penetrating, ferocious. "I was sick of it all," she tells him. "Weren't you? The perfection of everything. The absolute predictability. You can't even stub your toe because there's some clever sensor watching out for you. The biomonitors. The automedics. The guides and proctors. I hated it."

"Yes. Of course."

Her intensity is frightening. For one foolish moment, Mallory realizes, he was actually thinking of offering to *rescue* her from the consequences of her rashness. Inviting her to come back with him in his own capsule when his twelve hours are up. They could probably both fit inside, if they stand very close to each other. A reprieve from Option Three, a new lease on life for her. But that isn't really possible, he knows. The mass has to balance in both directions of the trip within a very narrow tolerance; they are warned not to bring back even a twig, even a pebble, nothing aboard the capsule that wasn't aboard it before. And in any case being rescued is surely the last thing she wants. She'll simply laugh at him. Nothing could make her go back. She loves it here. She feels truly alive for the first time in her life. In a universe of security-craving dullards she's a woman running wild. And her wildness is contagious. Mallory trembles with sudden new excitement at the sheer proximity of her.

She sees it too. Her glowing eyes flash with invitation.

"Stay here with me!" she says. "Let your capsule go home without you, the way I did."

"But the dangers—" he hears himself blurting inanely.

"Don't worry about them. I'm doing all right so far, aren't I? We can manage. We'll build a cabin. Plant fruits and vegetables. Catch lizards in traps. Hunt the dinos. They're so dumb they just stand there and let you shoot them. The laser charges won't ever run out. You and me, me and you, all alone in the Mesozoic! Like Adam and Eve, we'll be. The Adam and Eve of the Late Cretaceous. And they can all go to hell back there in 2281."

His fingers are tingling. His throat is dry. His cheeks blaze with savage adrenal fires. His breath is coming in ragged gasps. He has never felt anything like this before in his life.

He moistens his lips. "Well—"

She smiles gently. The pressure eases. "It's a big decision, I know. Think about it," she says. Her voice is soft now. The wild zeal of a moment before is gone from it. "How soon before your capsule leaves?"

He glances at his wrist. "Eight, nine more hours."

"Plenty of time to make up your mind."

"Yes. Yes."

Relief washes over him. She has dizzied him with the overpowering force of her revelation and the passionate frenzy of her invitation to join her in her escape from the world they have left behind. He isn't used to such things. He needs time now, time to absorb, to digest, to ponder. To decide. That he would even consider such a thing astonishes him. He has known her how long—an hour, an hour and a half?—and here he is thinking of giving up everything for her. Unbelievable. Unbelievable.

Shakily he turns away from her and stares at the ankylosaur swallowing in the mudhole just in front of them.

Strange, strange, strange. Gigantic low-slung tubby things, squat as tanks, covered everywhere by armor. Vaguely triangular, expanding vastly toward the rear, terminating in armored tails with massive bony excrescences at the tips, like deadly clubs. Slowly snuffling forward in the muck, tiny heads down, busily grubbing away at soft green weeds. Jayne jumps down among them and dances across their armored backs, leaping from one to another. They don't even seem to notice. She laughs and calls to him. "Come on," she says, prancing like a she-devil.

They dance among the ankylosaurs until the game grows stale. Then she takes him by the hand and they run onward, through a field of scarlet mosses, down to a small clear lake fed by a swift-flowing stream. They strip and plunge in, heedless of risk.

Afterward they embrace on the grassy bank. Some vast creature passes by, momentarily darkening the sky. Mallory doesn't bother even to look up.

Then it is on, on to spy on something with a long neck and a comic knobby head, and then to watch a pair of angry ceratopsians butting heads in slow motion, and then to applaud the elegant migration of a herd of towering duckbills across the horizon. There are dinosaurs everywhere, everywhere, everywhere, an astounding zoo of them. And the time ticks away.

It's fantastic beyond all comprehension. But even so—

Give up everything for this? he wonders.

The chalet in Gstaad, the weekend retreat aboard the L5 satellite, the hunting lodge in the veldt? The island home in the Seychelles, the plantation in New Caledonia, the pied-a-terre in the shadow of the Eiffel Tower?

For this? For a forest full of nightmare monsters, and a life of daily peril?

Yes. Yes. Yes. Yes.

He glances toward her. She knows what's on his mind, and she gives him a sizzling look. *Come live with me and be my love, and we will all the pleasures prove.* Yes. Yes. Yes. Yes.

A beeper goes off on his wrist and his thinko says, "It is time to return to the capsule. Shall I guide you?"

And suddenly it all collapses into a pile of ashes, the whole shimmering fantasy perishing in an instant.

"Where are you going?" she calls.

"Back," he says. He whispers the word hoarsely—croaks it, in fact.

"Tom!"

"Please. Please."

He can't bear to look at her. His defeat is total; his shame is cosmic. But he isn't going to stay here. He isn't. He isn't. He simply isn't. He slinks away, feeling her burning contemptuous glare drilling holes in his shoulder blades. The quiet voice of the thinko steadily instructs him, leading him around pitfalls and obstacles. After a time he looks back and can no longer see her.

On the way back to the capsule he passes a pair of sauropods mating, a tyrannosaur in full slather, another thing with talons like scythes, and half a

dozen others. The thinko obligingly provides him with their names, but Mallory doesn't even give them a glance. The brutal fact of his own inescapable cowardice is the only thing that occupies his mind. *She* has had the courage to turn her back on the stagnant over perfect world where they live, regardless of all danger, whereas he—he—

"There is the capsule, sir," the thinko says triumphantly.

Last chance, Mallory.

No. No. No. He can't do it.

He climbs in. Waits. Something ghastly appears outside, all teeth and claws, and peers balefully at him through the window. Mallory peers back at it, nose to nose, hardly caring what happens to him now. The creature takes an experimental nibble at the capsule. The impervious metal resists. The dinosaur shrugs and waddles away.

A chime goes off. The Late Cretaceous turns blurry and disappears.

✧

In mid-October, seven weeks after his return, he is telling the somewhat edited version of his adventure at a party for the fifteenth time that month when a woman to his left says, "There's someone in the other room who's just come back from the dinosaur tour too."

"Really," says Mallory, without enthusiasm.

"You and she would love to compare notes, I'll bet. Wait, and I'll get her. Jayne! Jayne, come in here for a moment!"

Mallory gasps. Color floods his face. His mind swirls in bewilderment and chagrin. Her eyes are as sparkling and alert as ever, her hair is a golden cloud.

"But you told me—"

"Yes," she says. "I did, didn't I?"

"Your capsule—you said it had gone back—"

"It was just on the far side of the ankylosaurs, behind the horsetails. I got to the Cretaceous about eight hours before you did. I had signed up for a twenty-four-hour tour."

"And you let me believe—"

"Yes. So I did." She grins at him and says softly, "It was a lovely fantasy, don't you think?"

He comes close to her and gives her a cold, hard stare. "What would you have done if I had let my capsule go back without me and stranded myself there for the sake of your lovely fantasy? Or didn't you stop to think about that?"

"I don't know," she tells him. "I just don't know." And she laughs.

Copyright © 1991 by Agberg, Ltd.

D.A. Xiaolin Spires currently resides in Hawai'i. Besides Galaxy's Edge, *she has sold her work to various other publications including* Clarkesworld, Analog, Grievous Angel, *and* Fireside. *She has also appeared in a number of anthologies of the strange and delightful, such as* Sharp & Sugar Tooth, Broad Knowledge *and* Ride the Star Wind.

EYES THAT LINGER

by D.A. Xiaolin Spires

A beautiful blonde with a fresh coat of lipstick walked into my office. Monique. She wore a bright white lab coat. It matched her perfect set of teeth. She sat down, pursed her lips. I offered her a cigarette. She grimaced.

Something strange happens around dusk, she said. Her voice was silky, performed. *Behind the mall, where my lab is.*

Not many labs hired private eyes. She placed a stack of bills onto my desk. Perfectly manicured nails, crimson like her lipstick. Strange for a lab technician. She winked, told me she knew I could help her.

The engine coughed twice as I staked out.

They clambered up over the fence, sticking out their arms. They waved their hands. I didn't know what they were. A bunch of teens, it looked like. I rolled down my window, spat onto the street. Slid worn binoculars over my fatigued eyes. One of the lenses was cracked.

They were holding something in their palms.

I thought I'd sneak up on them. I grabbed my baton. Couldn't go around waving a revolver in front of a bunch of kids. Bad for business.

They must've heard me coming. Even though I was as quiet as a rock. They ran off, scuttling away like rats. After I left, they scuttled right back.

There were more of them the next day. They looked like they had ants crawling up their pants. They shook their legs, pulling them over their heads, over

the barbed fence. Strange yoga. I had my old Chevy parked in the same place. I stopped the engine.

It looked like they had mumps or some other welts on their limbs. I took some photos. The shutter was jammed, but I slammed it with the back of my revolver. The shutter snapped back up. I managed a few shots. Photos, that is.

Later I zoomed in. Those weren't normal welts. Those were eyes. Dozens of eyes, covering their arms and legs.

I gagged. I rolled down my window. Suddenly my car smelled like stale coffee. I needed some air.

✿

The third day I dragged Marc. Ol' Grit Marc. He always knew what to do.

"Surveillance," he said. He was on his third cigarette. I told him days ago he should quit. *I'm trying*, he said at the time. He wasn't trying very hard. He blew a ring over the dashboard. "It's all about surveillance."

"Yeah, I know that's what we're doing." I took a sip of coffee.

"No, that's what they're doing. Surveillance. Taking photos with their eyes. They're basically lenses-for-hire, eyes for the mob."

I spat out my coffee. "Mob! Eyes?"

Marc lifted up his sleeve. On his arms were two sets of eyes. They blinked.

"They first tried it on tadpoles. Transplanted the eyes. The nerves grew along with them. If tadpoles, why not small mammals? Why stop there? Why not humans? These two arms, they're transplants. I was next on the list for the donation. The mob paid me back for my last job with them. Big bucks for these things, so I knew they appreciated me."

"Those kids are all experiments gone wrong?"

"No, they're successes. They can move those eyes around, shift them throughout their bodies."

He took out a dropper, squeezed a few beads of moisturizer onto his wrists. "They get dry though."

With the drops, it looked like his arm eyes were tearing. Hazel irises. Big full eyelashes. Looked feminine, but I wasn't sure. They blinked a few times, then stared up at me from his wrists, wet from the drops.

They looked nothing like Marc's drug-ruined, pitch-black twin orbs up on his head. I looked away. The eyelashes batted. I couldn't stare at them too long.

✿

The next day, we snuck out there with large fans. Turned them up high and blasted them. Dried those kids' countless eyes right out.

✿

I told Monique to install these high-powered fans on the fence.

"That'll keep them away. Believe me, you won't find them sneaking around anymore."

She blew me a kiss and palmed me a grand. I noticed as she passed me the money, her arm slipped. She didn't just have eyes under there, but an ear. I thought I saw a corner of lips, but she pulled her lab coat sleeve down before I could get a second look. An armful of sense organs. She got up, adjusted her skirt, straightened her lab coat and walked out of my office.

I looked at her as she left. She turned around and smiled. An enigmatic smirk. Lush scarlet lips. I wondered if her mouth under her sleeve was smiling too.

Copyright © 2018 by D.A. Xiaolin Spires

Author's note: The story is based off new innovations in science in which blind tadpoles can see from eyes grafted onto tails.

Ralph Roberts is a jack-of-all-trades in the publishing industry. He's the author of more than a hundred books, plus a bunch of short stories and screenplays, and is also an editor and a book publisher.

WARPSHIP MECHANIC

by Ralph Roberts

Huge and evil looking, the alien battle mauler *Gutfrok na Tak'won*—"Crusher of those not Tak'won" limped—*all three* faster-than-light engines inoperative—to a docking with the run-down ellfive satellite known as *Frank's Starship Repair*. Two Space Navy tugs assisted getting it in place while other navy warships stood off watchfully. Too large by far for either of the repair bays, Frank's docking robots locked the ship near the station with tractor beams. Alarms sounded continuously. Every weapons port on the *Gutfrok* gaped hungrily.

"Mute the alarms—activate all weapons," Frank Buckner said, and it was so.

The command computer deployed a surprising number of destructive devices, bristling from hidden panels all over the station's exterior.

"Hope they can turn down the volume on *their* alarms," Frank said with a grin.

The station had been the Space Navy's primary maintenance facility two decades ago. Having commanded in those glory days, Frank knew all its systems, many of which had remained operational when the navy abandoned the place as too expensive to run or demolish. Out of the navy by then, he had bought it as surplus scrap for a song. No, not even a full song, a short ditty.

"Dad!" Alana, his youngest daughter said, "You're starting a war with the Tak'won Empire!"

Mr. Buckner, what the blue hell are you doing? demanded the voice of Commodore Harl Vincent, commanding the navy's escort forces.

A gravelly alien voice followed. *Captain Nawash… Gutfrok na Tak'won…we…dock.*

Frank grinned at his daughter and the only other human member of his staff, Raymond Baker. Both Alana and Ray were in their late twenties. Otherwise, there were only a few thousand military surplus robots aboard, from little microscopic nanobot guys swarming together to hulking great brutes that could single-handedly lift an old warp engine block without straining.

"Just a bit of friendly negotiation although, technically, we're still at war," Frank said, and made a gesture to open the comm channel. "You *are* docked, Captain. Close all weapons ports. Shut down your engines."

The lethal openings on the *Gutfrok* slid shut and the fitful orange glow at its rear from the three malfunctioning drives faded.

"Weapons systems on standby, status to Guard," Frank ordered his computer.

"How did we get stuck with this job?" Alana asked.

"Your mother sent them."

Alana's mother was Fleet Admiral Alicia Buckner.

Ray groaned. "Your ex-wife must really hate you, Frank."

Frank smiled. "She's an admiral; she hates everyone."

Frank's Starship Repair was at Earth's L5 point, where objects remain at the same place in relation to the Earth and its moon as all orbits the sun. Two centuries prior, several countries of Earth constructed vast rotating structures providing gravity for colonists in what came to be called *ellfives* in common usage.

The invention of artificial gravity made rotation no longer necessary and the advent of FTL drives caused colonists to move on. Who wanted to live in a tin can when entire planets were out there for the taking? The space navy used some of the ellfive structures for a few decades. Now most lay abandoned except for a few repurposed like Frank's shop.

Frank's business survived for two reasons—he could fix about any FTL drive or other ship system extant, human or alien, and he had several ellfive warehouses full of obsolete parts from his acquisition of the old space navy major repair facility.

"What do you mean, stay behind!" Alana said, showing a bit of her mother's famous temper.

Frank and Ray were getting into thin pressure suits.

"You're in charge here, Alana."

Frank looked at Ray who, suited up now, was lifting a small case by its handle.

"Right, bring along your tools."

Frank patted an outside pocket of his suit, which held a container of diagnostic nanobots. Those little babies were all he needed for this initial look.

Alana let her breath out in exasperation. "What the heck's that, Ray? Those aren't—"

"It's nothing," Frank said quickly.

"Don't worry," Ray said, attempting to hug Alana with his free arm.

She resisted at first and then gave him a quick one in return.

His heart wasn't in it but Frank gave Ray a stern look. Out here in ellfiveville, Alana did not have much in the way of social opportunity. Besides, for several reasons, he was stuck with Ray. Luckily, Ray was not so bad—he knew little about mechanical repair but learned fast and pitched in enthusiastically.

"Think we can get them running again, sir?" Ray asked, polite as always.

Frank shrugged as he adjusted his suit.

"The old battleaxe thinks so."

"Dad!"

"Well, she dumped this deal on us, Alana."

"She knows how good you are," Alana said and sighed.

"No, we're not getting back together," he said. "She chose career over family, as did your two sisters, as did *you* until recently."

Alana ignored that, looking out a viewport at the waiting alien craft. Her older sisters were officers on her mother's staff, but she resigned her own commission to be with Dad.

Frank tried to reassure her. "You've got our back, Alana."

"What if they kill you, Dad?"

"Kill 'em back."

✿

Faster than light was a concept many on Earth said was impossible, that old Einstein and his theory of relativity showed it impossible. Even those making a living writing speculative fiction in ancient days constructed stories where it took centuries traveling from star to star.

Then there was Professor Daphne Dawson, a mathematician of the early twenty-second century. She proved Einstein wrong about relativity and opened the door for FTL. Engineers started inventing faster than light drives—not using just one method but *scores* of ways.

Most drives were flakey or slow, required too much energy, or broke any time anyone looked at it. A few were practical. The now-retired warp engines from Frank's days in service were massive beasts, hogging energy, but reliable with proper maintenance. Frank could fix those in his sleep.

In its expansion, humans began meeting aliens who also had FTL ships, so add thousands more ways of achieving speeds many times in excess of light. Some of these aliens resented human expansion. One, the Tak'won, under their Triple Emperors, was keen on doing something to stop humanity.

For military needs, speed wins over reliability. During the Second Tak'won War—still theoretically in progress although a truce had held for the last ten years, better than the six years after the First Tak'won War—speed became everything and newer drives replaced the slow warp drives. The new drives were finicky mechanisms, requiring constant babying and broke periodically. Frank got his share of repair jobs that the navy's own engineers could not handle, and those people were good—he'd trained a lot of them back in the day.

Got any idea how they do it? Ray asked over their encrypted communications.

Frank and Ray floated halfway to the *Gutfrok*, following the protocol of giving the alien security force sufficient time to inspect them.

"Beats me and all the scientists," Frank replied. "Our best engine does fifty lights, their old one five hundred, this new one supposedly over *five thousand*."

Kinda blows the surrender ultimatum when all three of their top battleship's engines go down at the same time, huh?

"Yeah, maybe," Frank said, as the *Gutfrok*'s tractor beams pulled them to the nearest entry port. "But Alicia's dumped the problem on us now."

Admirals tend to do that, boss.

Frank knew Alana was listening in but she did not contradict him this time. The obvious was the obvious—sometimes, anyway.

The Tak'won Empire is a long way from us, Alana said through their earpieces, *with a lot easier targets to conquer on the way. Yet, they pick a fight with us. Why?*

Ray answered. *We're Tak'won's single biggest competitor for uninhabited planets and trade with those that are. Get rid of us and everything in sight is open for the taking.*

☼

The hot portion of the Second Tak'won War only lasted a few weeks over ten years prior. Frank, still in the navy then, commanded the engineering arm during the action. He desperately tried to come up with engines and tactics that would overcome the enemy's vast advantage in speed, and failed. The five-hundred light-speed engines, mounted three to a ship, outclassed and out maneuvered anything the space navy had.

Tak'won needed fast ships since their empire was over fifteen hundred light years down the spiral arm of the galaxy humanity was settling. It took more than three years for even their fast ships to arrive and engage the navy. Of course, the enemy's home systems were far beyond the navy's range. Earth's strategy involved not contesting some worlds and concentrating forces around others.

Soon it became apparent to both sides that—while taking over a few worlds—the Tak'won lines of supply were just too long to win victory. Two waves of attacks had failed. They had contemptuously suggested a truce but promised a third, victorious campaign to follow at an unspecified time in the future.

Now, with massively faster engines, Planetary General Prince Moaroaf—in line for a spot in the emperor trinity—had arrived to deliver the demand of the Triple Emperors for unconditional surrender. All three of the new engines so inexplicably malfunctioning took a bit of the edge off the demand. Having three heads, three arms, three legs, and three sexes, the Tak'won set great store in the number *three*.

Coming into the ship from the airlock, Frank and Ray found themselves in the huge entry hall. Niches holding religious symbols covered the walls and ceiling of the hall. The Tak'won had literally thousands of religions with adherents always conspiring to gain greater political power.

Groups of three alien commandos kept them covered with energy weapons at the ready. Standing directly in front of them were the three senior members of the Tak'won ultimatum delegation. Prince Moaroaf and High Priest Reehoot—coordinator of religions—faced away from them, this tripod stance a studied insult, and only Captain Nawash, who wore the insignia of an admiral, was looking at them.

Frank and Ray removed their pressure helmets—the alien air was breathable albeit full of not always pleasant odors. They activated their translator buttons, which fed through the communicator bud each wore in one ear. There was also a button on each pressure suit feeding visual input back to Alana.

"Where…is…your third?" Captain Nawash asked.

"She's on our station, with all weapons ready," Frank said.

Nawash had its own translation device.

"A wise precaution," it agreed. "Can you fix engines?"

"Perhaps," Frank answered. "I'll need to confer with your engineering staff and—"

One of Nawash's eyes drifted to indicate the two with their backs to them. "We no longer have engineers. They have joined their various gods. The General Prince is…upset…and if we do not secure repairs…all of us perish. The General Prince's chance to become the Third Emperor rests on this mission."

"I understand and we have been tasked by our navy to start repairs. How do you plan on paying?"

The prince spoke, but did not turn. "Your Three will be promoted to slave supervisor if you make our engines work again."

Alana's voice was in Frank and Ray's ears again. *Mother will never accept us fixing an enemy warship so that they can return and make slaves of all humanity.*

Frank knew that. He also knew she expected him stop this ship from leaving the solar system, especially with working engines. He continued to stand silent.

Nawash gave what had to be the equivalent of a human sigh. "I personally will pay—for results only. I swear this on my honor as a Tak'won officer."

"No," Frank said. "Swear on your god."

Nawash paused, its three heads swiveling in agitation.

Prince Moaroaf, its back still turned, said something too rapid for the translators to render.

Nawash's heads drooped.

Frank grinned and winked at Ray. "The Prince could care less, Nawash has a different religion," he whispered.

"This one comprehended that," Moaroaf said. "The offer of promotion from lowest slave status is rescinded.… Do it, Nawash. Now."

Nawash raised all three hands and made several gestures. "I swear on J'Qoojoos the Munificent that personal payment for the repair of all three engines shall be rendered. So mote it be."

At the far end of the hall, a religious symbol glowed with a golden light, a chime like a temple bell sounded, and the glow faded.

"It is recorded," Nawash said.

At that, High Priest Reehoot turned around to face them.

"The gods," it said, "reward those who do their best."

"Even slaves-to-be," General Prince Moaroaf added.

High Priest Reehoot appeared offended. "The issue of slavery is not settled. Tak'won treats those who surrender fairly and all profit from shared trade."

"It will be different when this one is Third Emperor," said Moaroaf, still facing away from them.

The High Priest waved all three hands at Frank and Ray in a complex gesture. "Receive this blessing," Reehoot said as golden sparks showered from the moving hands.

"Er…okay," Frank said. "Show us to the engine room. Download all available data on these engines to our computers."

"No," Moaroaf said.

Nawash blinked his eyes in what had to be a Tak'won wink and held a tablet with one hand while the other two typed commands. Done, Nawash beckoned them to follow.

As Nawash led Frank and Ray from the entry hall, Frank spotted—in a niche near the hatch leading onward—a god likeness resembling a Laughing Buddha albeit with three heads and three bellies and could not resist reaching out.

Dad! Alana said in their ear buds, *don't meddle with their sacred stuff—it may look cute but probably is the God of Skin Earthies and Eat Them Alive.*

Ignoring her warning, Frank patted all three bellies for luck—they would need all they could get.

Especially since the Tak'won commandos accompanied them, weapons pointed and ready.

The statuette glowed golden. Frank felt a mild shock hit him.

"Boss," Ray said with a hint of awe in his voice, "You just glowed like the image!"

"I'm okay," Frank said and realized he was. He felt *great*.

"Interesting," Nawash said. "Iohi the Benevolent is the most particular of gods. None other on this ship has been so accepted."

"No, no, I'm Presbyterian," Frank said.

"Iohi cares not about race. Congratulations."

The *Gutfrok*'s engine room was even larger than the entry hall but, like the other space, its walls and ceilings also harbored idols, alien relics, and other religious items.

Frank noted one of the idols close to the center of one wall blinked with a pale, blue glow. Others blinked red. He indicated the blue one to Ray with a tilt of his head.

"That would be old Fuquon," Ray whispered. "Embarrassed all its engines have ground to a halt. The others are angry at it."

In the center of the room crouched the three massive FTL engines. Colored lights, various control panels, rows of indicators, pipes, wires, and less readily identifiable things covered each engine in random profusion. The engines were huge ovals but each had a large rectangular box on top. The slight difference in color—the boxes looked newer—suggested the boxes were recent additions.

Under the watchful eyes of the commandos, Frank and Ray approached the engines. Frank pulled a comp pad from a suit pocket and watched it scroll through the info Nawash had sent. He turned and looked at Nawash.

"This is worthless, Captain Nawash. It's just how the engines are controlled, nothing about how they work."

Nawash bobbed its heads again. "Instant death to me if such comes to your knowledge. This is how to fix it as recorded by our engineers before their ritual executions."

"In other words," Frank said, "everything they'd already tried that didn't fix the engines."

Nawash's heads were all looking in different directions, ignoring the two earthmen. No help there right now.

Ray had removed a couple of instruments from his toolbox and was looking at readouts.

Frank moved closer and spoke in low tones. "Well?"

"The bottom parts match our intel of their five-hundred-light engines but the top box is new. I have no idea how it works."

Frank nodded. Ray knew nothing of engines but the robots handled all the routine repairs anyway. He, of course, had lived, breathed, and loved FTL engines all his life.

"Looks a bit like the first warp engines. Heck of a lot faster, though."

Frank moved over to Nawash, whose heads turned to stare at him.

"The top part is new, yes? Works like a supercharger to give the added speed. Tell me about it."

"No can."

"Not how it works, how did it come to be?"

Nawash sighed through all three breathing orifices.

"Scientists of the Fuquon faith developed it. Since it gave us the advantage needed to conquer far-flung civilizations like yours, the head Fuquon priest gained great power. If successful, that one would be allowed to kill the Third Emperor and become a ruler of our race. Tak'won navy rushed modifications of engines in all our ships. The Third Emperor is very old and General Prince Moaroaf scheduled to take place if mission successful."

Frank and Nawash looked at each other.

Nawash made an agitated movement of its heads. "All three units failed close together as we powered up again to leave your planet. This is such an improbable occurrence—three failures so close together and on only the second start-up. And all the other ships—"

"So Tak'won ships are now stranded all over known space?" Frank asked.

Ray whistled at the implication.

Notifying Mother of that, Alana's voice said in their ears. *Wow!*

"Is true," Nawash said.

"How do you know?" Ray asked.

"The gods tell us."

Ray looked a little awed.

"We have FTL radio too, Ray," Frank said.

"Third Emperor in large trouble if solution not found, and General Prince Moaroaf even more," Nawash said.

"And what religion does General Prince Moaroaf adhere to?" Frank said.

Nawash indicated some sense of satisfaction. "Fuquon, same as the Third Emperor."

Frank smiled. "In view of this, what restrictions do I have in repairing your engines?"

Nawash moved away and talked quietly into the air for a moment, then returned.

"The Prince says 'none.' The Prince says fix engines and receive fifty slaves of your Third's choice, to be provided after Earth surrenders."

"Most generous," Frank said. "We will begin."

Dad!

He ignored Alana and pulled out a container of diagnostic nanorobots, emptying a portion like pouring smoke onto each engine.

"Now, we wait."

Dad! Mother…the Admiral says whatever you do, don't fix those engines! The Tak'won are sitting ducks all over the galaxy!

Ray did not look pleased either.

Frank shrugged. What good was *that* if they were still too far away for the navy ships to reach them?

Two hours later, Frank and Ray were sitting on the floor, backs resting against one engine. They watched as information continued to scroll on Frank's computer pad from the exploring nanobots. Nawash stood close by. The Tak'won commandos patiently kept weapons trained on the two Earthmen.

"Tell me, Nawash," Frank said, "what god does the Second Emperor follow?"

"J'Qoojoos the Munificent," Nawash said, straightening his stiff posture even more in what had to be pride. "The Second Emperor is a parent of mine."

Frank smiled. "That is…impressive. And the First Emperor follows—"

"What waste of time is here!" yelled General Prince Moaroaf, as it stormed into and across the engine room in a surprisingly fast three-legged jog. "Nothing is repaired yet!"

Moaroaf rocked to a stop near them. "Kill all!" Moaroaf ordered, pointing at Frank, Ray, and Nawash in turn.

Red beams from hundreds of religious niches instantly put dots on Moaroaf's body. The Tak'won commandos lowered their weapons and made what were certainly gestures of respect. The idol representing Fuquon turned a brighter shade of blue.

Moaroaf held up all three hands. "More time for repair work is granted."

The beams faded and Moaroaf shuffled away in defeat.

Frank leaned over to Ray. "You people have intel on this religious stuff?"

"No, sir—we thought it just symbolic."

"Starting to look a little too real, Ray."

Ray spread his hands and shrugged while warily looking at the profusion of niches on the walls and ceiling.

Just idols and religious whatnots, Alana said. *Mother orders you to make sure those engines can't work and get back here before the fleet moves in.*

Frank's computer pad chimed and several of the small gods cast a gold beam on it from their niches. Frank scrolled through the results and nodded.

"Yes," he said, looking up at Nawash, "I see the trouble."

"Can fix?"

"Yes."

"All three?"

"No problem, please allow access to several of my robots, now coming over."

Dad!

Frank and Ray stood watching robots swarm over the three engines. The covers were off and removed parts scattered around. Three hulking robots, intelligent mobile 3D printers, were fabricating new parts. At that moment, two more large robots were removing the last of the three rectangular supercharger attachments on top of the oval engines and setting it aside.

"Old Fuquon does not like this," Ray said.

Frank looked over at Fuquon's niche to see the statuette not only still glowing with a bluish light but oily blue tears flowing down its body. But the red angry glow from the other religious symbols was gone. Maybe that was a good sign. Things were working out.

Dad, came Alana's voice, *Mother has arrived and relieved Commodore Vincent of command.*

Indeed, I have, Fleet Admiral Alicia Buckner— supreme commander of the Earth Navy and architect of the war against Tak'won—said. *I see your plan is coming along nicely. Call me when you get a chance, dear.*

Mother!

Nawash, now holding Frank's computer pad in one hand while scrolling with another and using the third to point, was briefing High Priest Reehoot. Both seemed excited and confident. Frank wished he was and walked over to them. Ray tagged along, looking perplexed.

Reehoot regarded Frank. "The problem is found?"

"Yes, the supercharger units were faulty. They gave the tenfold increase in speed but shut down incorrectly. The next time engine restart occurred, or at least sometime in the next few times, the engines overloaded and various components fried."

"Can fix?"

Frank smiled and waved at the bustling robots. "We are repairing and rebuilding. The superchargers must be discarded."

"But that will make return trip very long."

"Nope. The rebuilt engines will run at about six-thousand lights, with a service life of centuries. The extra speed the superchargers gave—once I understood it—is done easily and safely without that added prone-to-break complexity."

Dad!

Hush, Alana, he knows what he's doing, the Admiral said.

Ray shook his head but kept quiet.

Commander Baker, the Admiral said, *why don't you come back over to the station and brief us while Frank finishes up.*

Ray!

He's naval intelligence, Alana. Do quit yelling over the comm link.

Ray left while Frank continued supervising his industrious robots.

"Fixed soon?" Nawash inquired.

"Yes," Frank said, but something was bothering him.

He walked over and peered into the nearest engine. Everything appeared fine in its spacious interior. He watched as a gaggle of small robots fastened a new capacitor bank in place, having cleaned away the blackened mess from where the old bank had burned out.

Inspecting the other two engines gave him the same feeling of unease, born of long experience. Everything looked right but it just didn't *feel* right. Well, they'd just have to tune these babies when he got them restarted. Do a bit of diagnostics while running and tune any roughness out. Standard procedure, he'd done it thousands of times.

☼

Almost four hours later, the robots reported all complete except for replacing the covers. *Always* leave the covers off until tests show satisfactory operational parameters.

Rather than trying to understand the alien engine controls, Frank had control software on his computer pad. The pad was now generating holograms in midair of readouts showing the flow of data from the many sensors his bots had installed in the engines.

He pressed the power icon and all three engines began humming as they came online. Nawash and High Priest Reehoot made pleased sounds. General Price Moaroaf was still absent. Maybe *that's* why they were making the pleased sounds, Frank thought.

The hum deepened and readouts showed each engine was passing through two percent of max power. Frank babied them along. As five percent came up, all three engines shut down.

There was dead silence in the vast engine room.

"At least nothing smokes this time," Nawash said.

The statuette of Fuquon had stopped crying blue tears and its blue glow faded but a few of the other niches were again issuing an angry red glow.

"Give me a moment here," Frank said.

☼

An exhausting two hours later, Frank was finishing manual adjustments on the third engine. Tools lay around him—grime from inside the engines coated his hands. He had removed the pressure suit entirely and his shirt was soaked with sweat.

Nevertheless, he *loved* it. This was the kind of repair work he gloried in, hands on, one on one with the balky engine, a rapport no robot could ever hope to achieve. With satisfaction in a job well done, he finished reseating the last energy concentrator, laid down his laser wrench, and stepped back from the engine.

The red glow of earlier was gone from all the little gods' niches; instead most of them were glowing gold. Occasionally a golden beam would reach out to caress an engine.

Fuquon was now a vivid swirl of blue and red—anger and embarrassment. General Prince Moaroaf was still absent.

Nawash and High Priest Reehoot, after watching patiently all this time, came forward. Nawash handed Frank's computer pad to him.

"You will like *this*," Frank said, his confidence in full bloom again.

He tapped the start sequence on his pad and all three engines came up fast, powerful hums from each filling the engine room. Frank twisted his wrist back and forth, the gesture causing the engines to rev up, drop back, rev up, and drop back. It seemed the whole ship was shaking to these FTL beasts caged might.

Frank shut them down, started them up, shut them down, started them up, and revved them a few times just from the joy of a job well done. Finally, all tests optimal, he dropped them back to idle, a low *thrum* sounding just above audible levels.

Nawash and High Priest Rehoot moved all three legs, heads, and arms in some sort of happy dance. Golden beams from the little gods crisscrossed the vast engine room space like an Earthly light show. Everyone was celebrating except Fuquon.

Frank revved the engines a couple more times just to prolong the moment.

Finally, everyone calmed down.

"Is all fixed?" Nawash asked.

"Yes," Frank said, and instructed his robots to replace the engine covers, pick up the tools, and clean the work area.

Still the best mechanic in the known universe, his ex-wife the Admiral said.

You shouldn't have kicked him out, Mother, Alana said with a little bitterness.

Who said I did, Alana? While Frank was undercover here—we still saw each other from time to time.

And Ray too. He's in the navy?

Frank, Ray, me, your sisters—everyone but you, her mother agreed.

"Okay," Frank said, ignoring the radio chatter in his ear, "the repairs are finished. These engines will run fine pretty much forever with minor periodical maintenance. Any good warpship mechanic with a little training can repair all your ships and keep them running. I know quite a few retired navy guys who—"

What! said the Admiral.

High Priest Reehoot leaned forward as if struggling to understand. "Warp engines, that Earth science?"

Nawash answered him. "Our engine is very like warp engine."

Reehoot shook all three heads, still confused.

At that moment, General Prince Moaroaf charged into the engine room and straight across to Frank. Moaroaf glowed blue and red like Fuquon the extremely angry little god. Sparks flew from Moaroaf's body as if it contained a massive amount of power.

"Stupid earthling has ruined our chance to enslave the galaxy. Fuquon is displeased. This one seeks revenge."

Moaroaf clapped all three hands on Frank, one on each shoulder and the third on the top of his head. All the energy stored within its body discharged with a thunderous *clap*!

Frank glowed golden as beams from the little gods powered his defenses. Moaroaf's attack backfired, causing the General Prince to whiz through the air, trailing dark smoke, and crash in a blackened heap on the floor all the across the vast engine room.

At the same time, angry red beams flew from every niche that had a straight line into Fuquon's niche. Oily smoke boiled up for an instant, and then Moaroaf's god was just a heap of ash with tendrils of wispy smoke rising from it.

"Ah, things progress," Nawash said.

High Priest Reehoot adopted a formal stance. "You have done well, Frank of Earth. There is to be a ceremony in the entry hall. Please invite those from your station to also attend."

"It is payment time…" Nawash searched for a word. "Buddy." And gestured for Frank to move toward the nearest engine-room hatch.

As Frank bent over to pick up his pressure suit, the black heap that was Moaroaf suddenly sat up, drawing an energy weapon in a blur of speed. Frank's reflexes caused him to flatten on the floor but Moaroaf fired at the engines instead.

All the little gods who had clear shots hit Moaroaf with red beams, turning the disgraced Prince into Fuquon-like ash as well. Moaroaf only got off one shot but the fierce beam hit an engine, which slowly whined unevenly down to a stop from the damage, a small amount of white smoke curled up from the hole melted in the engine cover.

Frank got up and dusted his hands. He watched as the white smoke disappeared and the engine automatically powered back up.

"Hit one of the self-repairing modules," he said. Removing a small 3D printer stylus from his belt, he air-drew a cover to close the energy beam hole and patted it into place.

☼

The entry hall was filled with Tak'won and the few humans from *Frank's Starship Repair*.

Nawash and High Priest Reehoot stood in front of the little three-bellied god, Iohi, careful not to block its view. All the other Tak'won were behind the small group of humans.

Frank and the Admiral—resplendent in her dress uniform and happily holding Frank's right hand—were together. Near them were Alana, her hand in Ray's, and Frank's other two daughters, Amy and Alice. All except Frank wore Earth Navy uniforms, even Alana.

Frank leaned over a bit and looked at her. "Drafted, hey Alana?"

"Mother can be persuasive, as you know, Dad."

High Priest Reehoot cleared all three throats. Being amplified, it was noticed and the entry hall grew quiet.

"With the destruction of the former general prince and the gods' repudiation of the once-god Fuquon, the Third War to Conquer Earth is over. Under the failed leadership of the former Third Emperor, who the gods inform us recently fell off this plane of existence, Tak'won accepts Three-Defeat and seeks peace."

Nawash now spoke. "Once the new Three Emperors take office, formal surrender will be offered."

"First," Reehoot continued, pointing at Frank, "we accuse this one of conducting a stratagem of deceit against the Tak'won Empire. He subverted some among us to sabotage an already faulty supercharger design and ensured breakdown at a very embarrassing moment—just after the former general prince had delivered the ultimatum to Earth.

"Frank of Earth further conspired to fix our engines but with certain overrides that would allow Earth Navy ships to control Tak'won ships *and* he stole the technology of our engines, improving it so that Earth ships would be much faster even than Tak'won ships."

"How plead you, Frank?"

"Guilty as heck," Frank said.

"Dad!" Alana said but clamped her mouth shut under the stern gaze of her mother and new commanding officer.

Nawash tapped its chest. "This one confesses to approaching and conspiring with Frank to inflict this deceit upon the Tak'won Empire."

Reehoot made a forgiving gesture with all three hands. "Nawash did so with the support of the Council of Gods who wished peaceful trade and coexistence, not endless wars of conquest. The gods decree that Frank and all Tak'won conspirators are forgiven."

Beams of golden light touched Frank, Nawash, Reehoot, and many others in the vast room.

"Now," Nawash said, "we must reconstitute the Imperial Leadership. I am honored to become Second Emperor." Nawash glowed purple for a few moments. "And the Council of Gods has ruled that they, from now on, will have a representative in the Leadership."

High Priest Reehoot bowed three heads as the purple glow emanated around it.

Second Emperor Nawash and Third Emperor Reehoot moved aside, turning and bowing to the small three-bellied god in its niche.

"Now, as is traditional, Iohi the Benevolent anoints the First Emperor, one chosen to best help both Tak'won and Earth reach full potential in a

mutually agreeable partnership and perhaps, one day, even find a Third to join our two civilizations, making them whole."

A beam of purple flowed from Iohi to bathe Frank in purple light.

Nawash turned and bowed to Frank. "This one would be pleased if the Imperial Highness would also accept this as payment for his repair services as this one personally guaranteed."

Coached in his mind by Iohi the Benevolent, Frank made a gracious Imperial gesture of acceptance as best he could with only two arms.

Alicia grabbed onto his right arm and got on tiptoe to whisper into his ear. "These little things in the niches—are they computers or really some sort of gods?"

Frank shrugged. "These days, what's the difference?

Alicia nodded. "And as for you, I thought our plan was to gain an advantage for Earth and swipe their engine technology as a bonus. You go and end the war in victory for us and take over the whole Tak'won Empire."

"Couldn't help it, darling—good mechanics are always in demand."

Nancy Kress is a multiple Hugo winner and a six-time Nebula winner. We're thrilled to have her back in the pages of Galaxy's Edge *again.*

END GAME

by Nancy Kress

Allen Dodson was sitting in seventh grade math class, staring at the back of Peggy Corcoran's head, when he had the insight that changed the world. First his own world and then, eventually, like dominos toppling in predestined rhythm, everybody else's, until nothing could ever be the same again. Although we didn't, of course, know that back then.

The source of the insight was Peggy Corcoran. Allen had sat behind her since third grade (Anderson, Blake, Corcoran, Dodson, DuQuesne…) and never thought her remarkable. Nor was she. It was 1982 and Peggy wore a David Bowie T-shirt and straggly brown braids. But now, staring at the back of her mousy hair, Allen suddenly realized that Peggy's head must be a sloppy mess of skittering thoughts and contradictory feelings and half-buried longings—*just as his was*. Nobody was what they seemed to be!

The realization actually made his stomach roil. In books and movies, characters had one thought at a time: *"Elementary, my dear Watson." "An offer he couldn't refuse." "Beam me up, Scotty!"* But Allen's own mind, when he tried to watch it, was different. *Ten more minutes of class I'm hungry gotta pee the answer is x+6 you moron what would it be like to kiss Linda Wilson M*A*S*H on tonight really gotta pee locker stuck today Linda eight more minutes do the first sixteen problems baseball after school—*

No. Not even close. He would have to include his mind watching those thoughts and then his thoughts about the watching thoughts and then—

And Peggy Corcoran was doing all that too.

And Linda Wilson.

And Jeff Gallagher.

And Mr. Henderson, standing at the front of math class.

And everyone in the world, all with thoughts zooming through their heads fast as electricity, thoughts bumping into each other and fighting each other and blotting each other out, a mess inside every mind on the whole Earth, nothing sensible or orderly or predictable… Why, right this minute Mr. Henderson could be thinking terrible things even as he assigned the first sixteen problems on page 145, terrible things about Allen even or Mr. Henderson could be thinking about his lunch or hating teaching or planning a murder… *You could never know.* No one was settled or simple, nothing could be *counted on*…

Allen had to be carried, screaming, from math class.

I didn't learn any of this until decades later, of course. Allen and I weren't friends, even though we sat across the aisle from each other (Edwards, Farr, Fitzgerald, Gallagher…). And after the screaming fit, I thought he was just as weird as everyone else thought. I never taunted Allen like some of the boys, or laughed at him like the girls, and a part of me was actually interested in the strange things he sometimes said in class, always looking as if he had no idea how peculiar he sounded. But I wasn't strong enough to go against the herd and make friends with such a loser.

The summer before Allen went off to Harvard, we did become—if not friends—then chess companions. "You play rotten, Jeff," Allen said to me with his characteristic, oblivious candor, "but nobody else plays at all." So two or three times a week we sat on his parents' screened porch and battled it out on the chess board. I never won. Time after time I slammed out of the house in frustration and shame, vowing not to return. After all, unlike wimpy Allen, I had better things to do with my time: girls, cars, James Bond movies. But I always went back.

Allen's parents were, I thought even back then, a little frightened by their son's intensity. Mild, hardworking people fond of golf, they pretty much left Allen alone from his fifteenth birthday on. As we moved rooks and knights around the chess board in the gathering darkness of the porch, Allen's mother would timidly offer a pitcher of lemonade and a plate of cookies. She treated both of us with an uneasy respect that, in turn, made me uneasy. That wasn't how parents were supposed to behave.

Harvard was a close thing for Allen, despite his astronomical SATs. His grades were spotty because he only did the work in courses he was interested in, and his medical history was even spottier: bouts of depression when he didn't attend school, two brief hospitalizations in a psychiatric ward. Allen would get absorbed by something—chess, quantum physics, Buddhism—to the point where he couldn't stop, until all at once his interest vanished as if it had never existed. Harvard had, I thought in my eighteen-year-old wisdom, every reason to be wary. But Allen was a National Merit scholar, and when he won the Westinghouse science competition for his work on cranial structures in voles, Harvard took him.

The night before he left, we had our last chess match. Allen opened with the conservative Italian game, which told me he was slightly distracted. Twelve moves in, he suddenly said, "Jeff, what if you could tidy up your thoughts, the way you tidy up your room every night?"

"Do what?" My mother "tidied up" my room, and what kind of weirdo used words like that, anyway?

He ignored me. "It's sort of like static, isn't it? All those stray thoughts in a mind, interfering with a clear broadcast. Yeah, that's the right analogy. Without the static, we could all think clearer. Cleaner. We could see farther before the signal gets lost in uncontrolled noise."

In the gloom of the porch, I could barely see his pale, broad-cheeked face. But I had a sudden insight, rare for me that summer. "Allen—is that what happened to you that time in seventh grade? Too much…static?"

"Yeah." He didn't seem embarrassed, unlike anybody normal. It was as if embarrassment was too insignificant for this subject. "That was the first time I saw it. For a long time I thought if I could learn to meditate—you know, like Buddhist monks—I could get rid of the static. But meditation doesn't go far enough. The static is still there, you're just not paying attention to it anymore. But it's still there." He moved his bishop.

"What exactly happened in the seventh grade?" I found myself intensely curious, which I covered by staring at the board and making a move.

He told me, still unembarrassed, in exhaustive detail. Then he added, "It should be possible to adjust brain chemicals to eliminate the static. To unclutter the mind. It should!"

"Well," I said, dropping from insight to my more usual sarcasm, "maybe you'll do it at Harvard, if you don't get sidetracked by some weird shit like ballet or model railroads."

"Checkmate," Allen said.

✧

I lost track of him after that summer, except for the lengthy Bakersville High School Alumni Notes faithfully mailed out every single year by Linda Wilson, who must have had some obsessive/compulsiveness of her own. Allen went on to Harvard Medical School. After graduation he was hired by a prestigious pharmaceutical company and published a lot of scientific articles about topics I couldn't pronounce. He married, divorced, married again, divorced again. Peggy Corcoran, who married my cousin Joe and who knew Allen's second wife, told me at my father's funeral that both ex-wives said the same thing about Allen: He was never emotionally present.

I saw him for myself at our twentieth-fifth reunion. He looked surprisingly the same: thin, broad-faced, pale. He stood alone in a corner, looking so pathetic that I dragged Karen over to him. "Hey, Allen. Jeff Gallagher."

"I know."

"This is my wife, Karen."

He smiled at her but said nothing. Karen, both outgoing and compassionate, started a flow of small talk, but Allen shut her off in mid-sentence. "Jeff, you still play chess?"

"Neither *Karen* nor I play now," I said pointedly.

"Oh. There's someone I want you to see, Jeff. Can you come to the lab tomorrow?"

The "lab" was sixty miles away, in the city, and I had to work the next day. But something about the situation had captured my wife's eclectic and sharply intelligent interest. She said, "What is it, Allen, if you don't mind my asking?"

"I don't mind. It's a chess player. I think she might change the world."

"You mean the big important chess world?" I said. Near Allen, all my teenage sarcasm had returned.

"No. The whole world. Please come, Jeff."

"What time?" Karen said.

"Karen—I have a job."

"Your hours are flexible," she said, which was true. I was a real estate agent, working from home. She smiled at me with all her wicked sparkle. "I'm sure it will be fascinating."

☼

Lucy Hartwick, twenty-five years old, was tall, slender, and very pretty. I saw Karen, who unfortunately inclined to jealousy, glance at me. But I wasn't attracted to Lucy. There was something cold about her beauty. She barely glanced up at us from a computer in Allen's lab, and her gaze was indifferent. The screen displayed a chess game.

"Lucy's rating, as measured by computer games anyway, is 2670," Allen said.

"So?" 2670 was extremely high; only twenty or so players in the world held ratings above 2700. But I was still in sarcastic mode, even as I castigated myself for childishness.

Allen said, "Six months ago her rating was 1400."

"So six months she first learned to play, right?" We were talking about Lucy, bent motionless above the chess board, as if she weren't even present.

"No, she had played twice a week for five years."

That kind of ratings jump for someone with mediocre talent who hadn't studied chess several hours a day for years—it just didn't happen. Karen said, "Good for you, Lucy!" Lucy glanced up blankly, then returned to her board.

I said, "And so just how is this supposed to change the world?"

"Come look at this," Allen said. Without looking back, he strode toward the door.

I was getting tired of his games, but Karen followed him, so I followed her. Eccentricity has always intrigued Karen, perhaps because she's so balanced, so sane, herself. It was one reason I fell in love with her.

Allen held out a mass of graphs, charts, and medical scans as if he expected me to read them. "See, Jeff, these are all Lucy, taken when she's playing chess. The caudate nucleus, which aids the mind in switching gears from one thought to another, shows low activity. So does the thalamus, which processes sensory input. And here, in the—"

"I'm a realtor, Allen," I said, more harshly than I intended. "What does all this garbage *mean*?"

Allen looked at me and said simply, "She's done it. Lucy has. She's learned to eliminate the static."

"What static?" I said, even though I remembered perfectly our conversation of twenty-five years ago.

"You mean," said Karen, always a quick study, "that Lucy can concentrate on one thing at a time without getting distracted?"

"I just said so, didn't I?" Allen said. "Lucy Hartwick has control of her own mind. When she plays chess, that's *all* she's doing. As a result, she's now equal to the top echelons of the chess world."

"But she hasn't actually played any of those top players, has she?" I argued. "This is just your estimate based on her play against some computer."

"Same thing," Allen said.

"It is not!"

Karen peered in surprise at my outrage. "Jeff—"

Allen said, "Yes, Jeff, listen to Carol. Don't—"

"'Karen'!"

"—you understand? Lucy's somehow achieved *total* concentration. That lets her just…just soar ahead in understanding of the thing she chooses to focus on. Don't you understand what this could mean for medical research? For…for any field at all? We could solve global warming and cancer and toxic waste and…and everything!"

As far as I knew, Allen had never been interested in global warming, and a sarcastic reply rose to my lips. But either Allen's face or Karen's hand on my arm stopped me. She said gently, "That could be wonderful, Allen."

"It will be!" he said with all the fervor of his seventh-grade fit. "It will be!"

☼

"What was that all about?" Karen said in the car on our way home.

"Oh, that was just Allen being—"

"Not Allen. You."

"Me?" I said, but even I knew my innocence didn't ring true.

"I've never seen you like that. You positively sneered at him, and for what might actually be an enormous break-through in brain chemistry."

"It's just a theory, Karen! Ninety percent of theories collapse as soon as anyone runs controlled experiments."

"But you, Jeff…you *want* this one to collapse."

I twisted in the driver's seat to look at her face. Karen stared straight ahead, her pretty lips set as concrete. My first instinct was to bluster…but not with Karen.

"I don't know," I said quietly. "Allen has always brought out the worst in me, for some reason. Maybe…maybe I'm jealous."

A long pause, while I concentrated as hard as I could on the road ahead. Yellow divider, do not pass, 35 MPH, pothole ahead…

Then Karen's hand rested lightly on my shoulder, and the world was all right again.

✿

After that I kept in sporadic touch with Allen. Two or three times a year I'd phone and we'd talk for fifteen minutes. Or, rather, Allen would talk and I'd listen, struggling with irritability. He never asked about me or Karen. He talked exclusively about his research into various aspects of Lucy Hartwick: her spinal and cranial fluid, her neural firing patterns, her blood and tissue cultures. He spoke of her as if she were no more than a collection of biological puzzles he was determined to solve, and I couldn't imagine what their day-to-day interactions were like. For some reason I didn't understand, I didn't tell Karen about these conversations.

That was the first year. The following June, things changed. Allen's reports—because that's what they were, reports and not conversations—became non-stop complaints.

"The FDA is taking forever to pass my IND application. Forever!"

I figured out that "IND" meant "initial new drug," and that it must be a green light for his Lucy research.

"And Lucy has become impossible. She's hardly ever available when I need her, trotting off to chess tournaments around the world. As if chess mattered as much as my work on her!"

I remembered the long-ago summer when chess mattered to Allen himself more than anything else in the world.

"I'm just frustrated by the selfishness and the bureaucracy and the politics."

"Yes," I said.

"And doesn't Lucy understand how important this could be? The incredible potential for improving the world?"

"Evidently not," I said, with mean satisfaction that I disliked myself for. To compensate I said, "Allen, why don't you take a break and come out here for dinner some night. Doesn't a break help with scientific thinking? Lead sometimes to real insights?"

I could feel, even over the phone line, that he'd been on the point of refusal, but my last two sentences stopped him. After a moment he said, "Oh, all right, if you want me to," so ungraciously that it seemed he was granting me an inconvenient favor. Right then, I knew that the dinner was going to be a disaster.

And it was, but not as much as it would have been without Karen. She didn't take offense when Allen refused to tour her beloved garden. She said nothing when he tasted things and put them down on the tablecloth, dropped bits of food as he chewed, slobbered on the rim of his glass. She listened patiently to Allen's two-hour monologue, nodding and making encouraging little noises. Toward the end her eyes did glaze a bit, but she never lost her poise and wouldn't let me lose mine, either.

"It's a disgrace" Allen ranted, "the FDA is hobbling all productive research with excessive caution for—do you know what would happen if Jenner had needed FDA approval for his vaccines? We'd all still have smallpox, that's what! If Louis Pasteur—"

"Why don't you play chess with Jeff?" Karen said when the meal finally finished. "While I clear away here."

I exhaled in relief. Chess was played in silence. Moreover, Karen would be stuck with cleaning up after Allen's appalling table manners.

"I'm not interested in chess anymore," Allen said. "Anyway, I have to get back to the lab. Not that Lucy kept her appointment for tests on…she's wasting my time in Turkistan or someplace. Bye. Thanks for dinner."

"Don't invite him again, Jeff," Karen said to me after Allen left. "Please."

"I won't. You were great, sweetheart."

Later, in bed, I did that thing she likes and I don't, by way of saying thank you. Halfway through, however, Karen pushed me away. "I only like it when you're really *here*," she said. "Tonight you're just not focusing on us at all."

After she went to sleep, I crept out of bed and turned on the computer in my study. The heavy fragrance of Karen's roses drifted through the window screen. Lucy Hartwick was in Turkmenistan, playing in the Chess Olympiad in Ashgabat. Various websites detailed her rocketing rise to the top of the chess world. Articles about her all mentioned that she never socialized with her own or any other team, preferred to eat all her meals alone in her hotel room, and never smiled. I studied the accompanying pictures, trying to see what had happened to Lucy's beauty.

She was still slender and long-legged. The lovely features were still there, although obscured by her habitual pose while studying a chess board: hunched over from the neck like a turtle, with two fingers in her slightly open mouth. I had seen that pose somewhere before, but I couldn't remember where. It wasn't appealing, but the loss of Lucy's good looks came from something else. Even for a chess player, the concentration on her face was formidable. It wiped out any hint of any other emotion whatsoever. Good poker players do that, too, but not in quite this way. Lucy looked not quite human.

Or maybe I just thought that because of my complicated feelings about Allen.

At 2:00 a.m. I sneaked back into bed, glad that Karen hadn't woken while I was gone.

✧

"She's gone!" Allen cried over the phone, a year later. "She's just gone!"

"Who?" I said, although of course I knew. "Allen, I can't talk now, I have a client coming into the office two minutes from now."

"You have to come down here!"

"Why?" I had ducked all of Allen's calls ever since that awful dinner, changing my home phone to an unlisted number and letting my secretary turn him away at work. I'd only answered now because I was expecting a call from Karen about the time for our next marriage counseling session. Things weren't as

good as they used to be. Not really bad, just clouds blocking what used to be steady marital sunshine. I wanted to dispel those clouds before they turned into major thunderstorms.

"You have to come," Allen repeated, and he started to sob.

Embarrassed, I held the phone away from my ear. Grown men didn't cry like that, not to other men. All at once I realized why Allen wanted me to come to the lab: because he had no other human contact at all.

"Please, Jeff," Allen whispered, and I snapped, "Okay!"

"Mr. Gallagher, your clients are here," Brittany said at the doorway, and I tried to compose a smile and a good lie.

And after all that, Lucy Hartwick wasn't even gone. She sat in Allen's lab, hunched over a chess board with two fingers in her mouth, just as I had seen her a year ago on the Web.

"What the hell—Allen, you *said*—"

Unpredictable as ever, he had calmed down since calling me. Now he handed me a sheaf of print-outs and medical photos. I flashed back suddenly to the first time I'd come to this lab, when Allen had also thrust on me documents I couldn't read. He just didn't learn.

"Her white matter has shrunk another seventy-five percent since I saw her last," Allen said, as though that were supposed to convey something to me.

"You said Lucy was gone!"

"She is."

"She's sitting right there!"

Allen looked at me. I had the impression that the simple act required enormous effort on his part, like a man trying to drag himself free of a concrete block to which he was chained. He said, "I was always jealous of you, you know."

It staggered me. My mouth opened but Allen had already moved back to the concrete block. "Just look at these brain scans, seventy-five percent less white matter in six months! And these neurotransmitter levels, they—"

"Allen," I said. Sudden cold had seized my heart. "Stop." But he babbled on about the caudate nucleus and antibodies attacking the basal ganglia and bidirectional rerouting.

I walked over to Lucy and lifted her chessboard off the table.

Immediately she rose and continued playing variations on the board in my arms. I took several steps backward; she followed me, still playing. I hurled the board into the hall, slammed the door, and stood with my back to it. I was six-one and 190 pounds; Lucy wasn't even half that. In fact, she appeared to have lost weight, so that her slimness had turned gaunt.

She didn't try to fight me. Instead she returned to her table, sat down, and stuck two fingers in her mouth.

"She's playing in her head, isn't she," I said to Allen. "Yes."

"What does 'white matter' do?"

"It contains axons which connect neurons in the cerebral cortex to neurons in other parts of the brain, thereby facilitating intercranial communication." Allen sounded like a textbook.

"You mean, it lets some parts of the brain talk to other parts?"

"Well, that's only a crude analogy, but—"

"It lets different thoughts from different parts of the brain reach each other," I said, still staring at Lucy. "It makes you aware of more than one thought at a time."

Static.

Allen began a long technical explanation, but I wasn't listening. I remembered now where I'd seen that pose of Lucy's, head pushed forward and two fingers in her mouth, drooling. It had been in an artist's rendering of Queen Elizabeth I in her final days, immobile and unreachable, her mind already gone in advance of her dying body.

"*Lucy's gone,*" Allen had said. He knew.

"Allen, what baseball team did Babe Ruth play for?"

He babbled on about neurotransmitters.

"What was Bobby Fisher's favorite opening move?" Silently I begged him, *Say e4, damn it.*

He talked about the brain waves of concentrated meditation.

"Did you know that a tsunami will hit Manhattan tomorrow?"

He urged overhaul of FDA clinical-trial design.

I said, as quietly as I could manage, "You have it, too, don't you. You injected yourself with whatever concoction the FDA wouldn't approve, or you took it as a pill, or something. You wanted Lucy's static-free state, like some fucking *dryer sheet*, and so you gave this to yourself from her. And now neither one of you can switch focus at all." The call to me had been Allen's last, desperate foray out of his perfect concentration on this project. No—that hadn't been the last.

I took him firmly by the shoulders. "Allen, what did you mean when you said 'I was always jealous of you'?"

He blathered on about MRI results.

"Allen—please tell me what you meant!"

But he couldn't. And now I would never know.

I called the front desk of the research building. I called 911. Then I called Karen, needing to hear her voice, needing to connect with her. But she didn't answer her cell, and the office said she'd left her desk to go home early.

Both Allen and Lucy were hospitalized briefly, then released. I never heard the diagnosis, although I suspect it involved an "inability to perceive and relate to social interactions" or some such psycho-babble. Doesn't play well with others. Runs with scissors. Lucy and Allen demonstrated they could physically care for themselves by doing it, so the hospital let them go. Business professionals, I hear, mind their money for them, order their physical lives. Allen has just published another brilliant paper, and Lucy Hartwick is the first female World Chess Champion.

Karen said, "They're happy, in their own way. If their single-minded focus on their passions makes them oblivious to anything else—well, so what. Maybe that's the price for genius."

"Maybe," I said, glad that she was talking to me at all. There hadn't been much conversation lately. Karen had refused any more marriage counseling and had turned silent, escaping me by working in the garden. Our roses are the envy of the neighborhood. We have Tuscan Sun, Ruffled Cloud, Mister Lincoln, Crown Princess, Golden Zest. English roses, hybrid teas, floribunda, groundcover roses, climbers, shrubs. They glow scarlet, pink, antique apricot, deep gold, delicate coral. Their combined scent nauseates me.

I remember the exact moment that happened. We were in the garden, Karen kneeling beside a flower bed, a wide hat shading her face from the sun so that I couldn't see her eyes.

"Karen," I said, trying to mask my desperation, "do you still love me?"

"Hand me that trowel, will you, Jeff?"

"Karen! Please! Can talk about what's happening to us?"

"The Tahitian Sunsets are going to be glorious this year."

I stared at her, at the beads of sweat on her upper lip, the graceful arc of her neck, her happy smile.

Karen clearing away Allen's dinner dishes, picking up his sloppily dropped food. Lucy with two fingers in her mouth, studying her chess board and then touching the pieces.

No. Not possible.

Karen reached for the trowel herself, as if she'd forgotten I was there.

✿

Lucy Hartwick lost her championship to a Russian named Dmitri Chertov. A geneticist at Stanford made a breakthrough in cancer research so important that it grabbed all headlines for nearly a week. By a coincidence that amused the media, his young daughter won the Scripps Spelling Bee. I looked up the geneticist on the Internet; a year ago he'd attended a scientific conference with Allen. A woman in Oregon, some New Age type, developed the ability to completely control her brain waves through profound meditation. Her husband is a chess grandmaster.

I walk a lot now, when I'm not cleaning or cooking or shopping. Karen quit her job; she barely leaves the garden even to sleep. I kept my job, although I take fewer clients. As I walk, I think about the ones I do have, mulling over various houses they might like. I watch the August trees begin to tinge with early yellow, ponder overheard snatches of conversation, talk to dogs. My walks get longer and longer, and I notice that I've started to time my speed, to become interested in running shoes, to investigate transcontinental walking routes.

But I try not to think about walking too much. I observe children at frenetic play during the last of

their summer vacation, recall movies I once liked, wonder at the intricacies of quantum physics, anticipate what I'll cook for lunch. Sometimes I sing. I recite the few snatches of poetry I learned as a child, relive great football games, chat with old ladies on their porches, add up how many calories I had for breakfast. Sometimes I even mentally rehearse basic chess openings: the Vienna Game or the Petroff Defense. I let whatever thoughts come that will, accepting them all.

Listening to the static, because I don't know how much longer I've got.

Copyright © 2007 by Nancy Kress

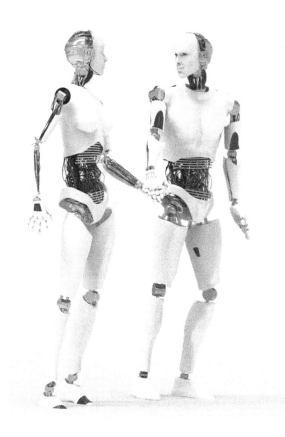

Jody Lynn Nye is the author of forty novels and more than one hundred stories, and has at various times collaborated with Anne McCaffrey and Robert Aspin. Her husband, Bill Fawcett, is a prolific author, editor and packager, and is also active in the gaming field.

RECOMMENDED BOOKS

By Jody Lynn Nye and Bill Fawcett

Outpost
by W. Michael Gear
DAW Books
February 2018
ISBN-13: 978-0756413378

Donovan is almost the ideal colony. On a corporate-dominated Earth rapidly running out of resources, a new and not yet well understood method of faster-than-light travel has made available planets such as Donovan with a wealth of heavy metals, rare earths, and new biologics. But even light-years of distance does not mean that the heavy hand of the corporation and its rule books should not continue to dominate men wherever they are. The trouble is that Donovan is not earth; there is a deadly difference. The abundance of heavy metals means most of the native plants are slow poison. There is a possibly intelligent creature that is actively trying to kill and eat humans, and the countryside is filled with deadly plants.

A colony of two thousand people lands, clears fields for crops, and begins to mine. The settlers expect a ship to arrive the next year with replacement parts, medicines, and more colonists. It doesn't appear. Nor does the next, or another, until four years have passed. Finally, a transport does arrive, carrying a few new colonists along with some supplies. By then the population has more than halved and the rule of the corporation is dead along with all the administrators. Unknown to the survivors on Donovan that ship never makes it back to Earth.

Three more years pass until another ship appears. Barely over three hundred colonists survive on Donovan, but they are certain the ship will be dominated by the corporation and its enforcers. The freewheeling settlers try to get into shape and prepare to fake being good corporate minions. The ruse almost works though integration is between the four hundred new colonists, who came expecting a settled paradise, and the surviving original colonists, who have adjusted to life in a near hell, soon leads to violence. Then, as if things were not complicated enough, one of the missing ships arrives, but is found to be lifeless, possibly haunted, and appears to have actually taken an extra hundred years to arrive.

Outpost is the story of coping and the hard decisions that have to be made to survive on an unexpectedly hostile world. W. Michael Gear weaves together the views of everyone from the corporate officer and ship's captain to those who have changed or will change in surprising ways in order to survive. If you are looking for a well written, imaginative story of people pressed to their limits with surprising twists, then be sure to read *Outpost*.

The Mutineer's Daughter
by Chris Kennedy and Thomas A. Mays
Theogony Press
March 2018

ISBN-13: 978-1948485166

It is always a pleasure for a reviewer to be able to introduce readers to new and talented authors. It certainly is in this case. Indie writers Chris Kennedy and Thomas Mays have published individually, and this collaboration is a step up that highlights the strengths of both. *Mutineer's Daughter* tells two parallel stories in a universe where a strict class systems is re-imposing itself on an interstellar society.

The first story is that of Benno Sanchez. He is a warrant officer in the weapons department of a destroyer. As a lower-class crewman from a fringe world, he has risen about as far as is possible and is barely tolerated by the higher-class officers. When the ship is damaged at the edges of a main fleet engagement, his talent for repair and efforts at weapons control make him a hero. But even as he is being honored, Benno learns that the fleet ships protecting his home planet, and the daughter he left behind on it, have been withdrawn to bolster the defenses of the core worlds.

When he finds out his home world and five others were occupied by the enemy without resistance, he goes from hero to rebel. Sentenced to execution, Benno plots with the other enlisted ranks, and takes over the still damaged destroyer. Then the real challenges begin. The mutineers have to get the supplies to allow them to repair the ship and, since they are in the midst of dozens of other ships, somehow escape. Although they accomplish those feats, they are still just one ship with the near impossible task of retaking six planets.

The second story, which alternates with Benno's, is that of Mio, Benno's 16-year-old daughter. More by fate than intent, she finds herself joining the resistance to her world's occupiers. Coincidence, courage, and good sense cause her to rise in the resistance, but at a very real physical and emotional cost.

The characters work. You find yourself caring about their personal dilemmas and the unfairness of the class system that feels as ugly as it is. But all this wraps around a very good set of action-filled space and high-tech resistance battles. The destroyer faces growing odds in a series of exciting combats. Mio also finds herself in the alien forests of her colony, reluctantly but effectively, fighting against the high-

ly armed and armored invaders. If you like space opera and good action, you will enjoy *The Mutineer's Daughter*.

✿

Techniques of the Selling Writer
by Dwight V. Swain
University of Oklahoma Press
January 1981
ISBN-13: 978-0806111919

Read This If You Want to be a Great Writer
by Ross Raisen
Laurence King Publishing (UK)
May 2018
ISBN-13: 978-1786271976

If you write or plan to ever write science fiction novels or short stories, these are two books that might be of great value to you. Not surprisingly, there are many good books on how to write SF. There are books from some of the field's top authors including Orson Scott Card, Ben Bova, Charles Platt, Joanna Russ, and even the highly respected *On Writing* from Stephen King. And considering the caliber of their authors, all their books are good and worth your time.

So what sets these two books apart from them? One is old—*Techniques* was first published in 1965. *Read This* is new, published this May. What makes them special is that both are written with the assumption you can already write. Their intent is not to teach you the basics of how to write, but to polish and refine the writing in which you are already competent.

Dwight Swain was the moderator for decades of the famed Clarion Workshop, to which talented authors still go to enhance their writing skills and learn from some of the field's most successful authors. In *Techniques of the Selling Writer*, he has collected and refined the insights and advice of authors who are today legends in the genre, from Asimov to Zelazny. Much of *Techniques* is also very practical advice, of the type you read and say to yourself, "I should have known that," then you rush off to incorporate it into your current project. A good example of those useful insights is that the sound and length of words can increase the intensity in a fight scene. As the fight progresses, you are advised to use more words with hard sounds and shorter sentences. Both will cause the reader's eye to skip forward more rapidly, making the fight seem more effective.

Ross Raisen is a successful, award-winning British author and creative writing professor. Not surprisingly, *Read This If You Want To be a Great Writer* feels as though it was derived from his teaching outlines. What it does well is cover a lot ground that presents even experienced writers with some good insights on the how and why of writing. It, too, incorporates examples that clarify Raisen's advice.

When doing writing workshops, we (your columnists) often point out that writing is a skill. Many authors say the first million words are just getting to learn the trade. Just like tennis or billiards you have to practice the skill. And, like those who participate in sports, it is not enough to repeat what you already do; you need to seek out a coach who can improve your game. In science fiction writing, we are lucky because that coach can be a book from proven authors and top instructors. Not only that, but finding among their pages a way to do something you already like to do, writing SF even better can be most rewarding and inspiring.

❁

The Dark Arrow of Time
by Massimo Villata
Springer Nature (Heidelberg, Germany)
November 2017
ISBN-13: 978-3319674858

The book describes itself as a "scientific novel," and it succeeds in both claims. It is the story of a man who has chosen to take a one-way flight to a colony. FTL travel is possible, but using the technique means that while it seems near instantaneous for the traveler, about a year per light year traveled passes on Earth. That means all emigration is a one-way journey. But when the scientist reaches a colony twenty light-years distant, he seems to meet a woman, then others, who have come from the Earth of only a few days earlier, not twenty years ago. In solving the mystery, he encounters serious danger: a colony ship that was thrown back in time, a world-threatening conspiracy and maybe, just maybe, love. The science is spot-on. For those who need further explanation, it is footnoted and expanded on in an appendix that is almost as interesting as the fiction. The translator tells the story well, and the time travel paradoxes just keep piling on. If you like accurate science in your SF novels, or have any interest in time travel, this is a book you should want.

❁

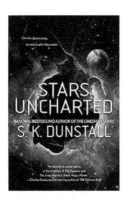

Stars Uncharted
by S.K. Dunstall
Ace Books
August 2018
ISBN 978-0-39958762

A new book by the Dunstall sisters, authors of The Linesman novels, is a space adventure set in Earth's future. In this era, humankind has expanded out from one planet to many systems, many of them run by companies, which act as corporate governments, and are as brutal to deal with as any Earthbound mob. Business owners who don't want any trouble pay protection money to enforcers, and are often forced to do favors to keep from having their livelihoods forcibly curtailed.

Body modification has expanded from a few nips and tucks here, an implant there, to a full-on art form, practiced by experts known as modders. Nika Rik Terri, one of the two protagonists of the book, is one of the finest ever trained, with an eye that catches details no one else would notice. Her abusive former boyfriend works for Eaglehawk Company. After years of violence and control, she appealed to his boss to keep him away from her. He obliges, but only in exchange for her remodeling any of his people who are injured, remaking their faces and bodies to disguise them as necessary with her genemod machines. An enforcer comes to her bleeding from a stomach wound, demanding to use her exchanger, a device she invented that swaps the minds of two people for a period of twenty-four hours. She had thought the invention was a secret. The assassin needs her body to carry out a job. Nika knows she won't be left alive. She sets up a trap to change the assassin out of all recognition and trap him in a ma-chine until she has time to escape. Nika goes on the run, desperate to get as far away from the assassin, the boyfriend, and his boss as she can.

Josune Arriola, the second protagonist, is an engineer on board the *Road to the Goberlings*, a trading ship captained by Hammond Roystan, a good man who suffers from a number of ailments that might or might not be genemod related. Josune used to be on board the *Hassim*, an exploration vessel. She was sent to insinuate herself into the crew of the *Road* by Captain Feyodor. The entire crew of the *Hassim* is obsessed with Goberlin, an explorer of the past century, who found an unbelievably huge vein of the rare transuride minerals. Feyodor wanted to meet Captain Roystan, but does not manage it. Her ship arrives in the vicinity of the *Road*, but everyone on board is dead. Because *Hassim* has traveled widely, many of the companies believe that it holds information about Goberlin's discoveries, and won't believe the *Road*'s salvagers that they have not discovered its secrets. Therefore, their crew must also go on the run, hiding their identities from everyone they meet. Along the way, Nika, a younger modder named Snow, Josune, and the crew of the *Road* have to band together to survive.

The Dunstalls have created a complex and coherent universe that comes alive in *Stars Uncharted*. Their descriptions of how the so-far fictional science of body modification works, how long it takes and what materials and chemicals are involved, is beautifully depicted. Everything they present has a meaning and, like Chekov's gun on the mantelpiece, is used before the story ends. They are adept at creating realistic characters whose fates the reader will care about, even when it seems that it's impossible for them to survive. Every so often, they present the reader with what seems like the world's worst-kept secrets, and one conclusion in particular that you come to early in the book about one character, then dismiss because of numerous red herrings, turns out to have been right all along. The book makes very good reading. If you enjoy space opera and great characters, you will enjoy *Stars Uncharted*.

The Long Sunset
by Jack McDevitt
Saga Press (Simon & Schuster)
April 2018
ISBN-13: 978-1534412071

The latest in the Academy series featuring interstellar pilot Priscilla "Hutch" Hutchins, *The Long Sunset* is set in the year 2256. After decades of successful missions and easy travel in between planets, the politicians of North America are scheming to halt all interstellar space flight—until a mysterious video of a waterfall is viewed through a major telescope, at a distance estimated at seven thousand light-years away. A mission to the Calliope sector is planned, with Hutch at the controls of the *Eiferman*, then scratched by the World Space Agency in fear that contacting the aliens who sent it will follow the ship back to Earth and destroy it. Hutch, Dr. Derek Blanchard, and three other specialists escape just before they can be forced out of their ship.

The crew of the interstellar are curious about the universe around them, and every diversion they take to explore another planet, star or cluster takes on that much more significance when they consider this might be the last cross-galactic trip humans will take for a very long time. In the shadow of a black hole, they discover dead planets and empty starships, all of which are clues to events that happened thousands of years before. Strangely, most of the extinct aliens who had occupied those lands or cities seemed to live in ways that would be easy for humans to recognize: businesses, schools, nurseries, churches, wearing clothes, hanging pictures on walls, sleeping in beds with sheets.

When the crew of the *Eiferman* crash-land on yet another planet near the black hole, they realize there is a tragedy looming only decades away. They are moved to mount a rescue that will take Herculean efforts that involves not only putting together all those clues that they had discovered before, but convincing Earth that what they need to accomplish is the only right thing to do.

Although this is the eighth novel in the series, a new reader can pick up *The Long Sunset* and enjoy it. McDevitt is an expert at presenting just enough information of past events without bogging down the tale or making readers worry that they have missed something. The is an easy read, with McDevitt beginning every chapter with a quote from a historical or fictional person, and concluding most with headlines of the day. The characters are well-drawn. Not every one is likeable, but they are all understandable. If you enjoy space opera, or the works of Isaac Asimov or Arthur C. Clarke, you'll have fun reading *The Long Sunset*.

✡

Witchy Winter
by D.J. Butler
Baen Books
April 2018
ISBN-13: 978-1481483148

The second in the magical alternate-history series that began with *Witchy Eye* (projected to run six volumes), *Witchy Winter* continues the story of Sarah Calhoun, a young woman with a talent for hexing people. She has been a target of wizards and magic-using priests, partly because she learns that she may be the long-lost daughter of the current emperor of the United States, Andrew Jackson.

She has survived the machinations and spells of her father's enemies, and seeks to take the Serpent Throne in the Ohio Valley. To do that, she must overcome seven opponents and encounter a goddess, all while learning the culture and keeping from being assassinated along the way. The world is full of endless permutations of magic, including shape-shifters and dark spirits, as well as enemies that are all too human.

Described as a "flintlock fantasy," *Witchy Winter* and *Witchy Eye* are a fascinating new take on American history. Butler is masterful at drawing this new world and presenting it in an unforgettable way. His characters take on a life of their own. There's humor and pathos, adventure and heroism, all set in an America that is easy to picture, if you just add magic. You will finish this book and demand to know what will happen to Sarah Calhoun next.

If you enjoy urban fantasy and alternate history, you will love *Witchy Winter*.

Brief Cases
by Jim Butcher
Ace SF
June 2018
ISBN-13: 978-0451492104

Our recommended classic series this column features the new short story collection, *Brief Cases: More Stories from the Dresden Files*. Harry Dresden is a wizard for hire living in contemporary Chicago. His clients in the book series, now fifteen novels long, range from the mundane to the Queen of the Sidhe. The mysteries are always fair, the magic consistent, and Harry Dresden an endearing, if flawed, character who often finds himself being the hero in a most unheroic way. Almost all these stories are written from the wizard's witty perspective, a few from that of his clients.

This collection of short mysteries showcases the strengths of this brilliantly written series. Dresden's clients include all manner of beings from the son of a Yeti to the totally mundane. He even tackles the Cubs' curse and reveals why it was over a goat. (Hint, it was not really just a goat.)

There are almost too many things to mention that Jim Butcher does right with the *Dresden Files*, but here are a few that will hopefully steer you toward these fifteen excellent contemporary fantasies: Harry Dresden is a great character who does not take himself too seriously but is driven by a strong sense of responsibility and honor. Butler works in a good deal of humor. Harry's observations are dry and witty, and situational humor adds a real dimension to some very hard-edged scenarios. The action is strong and intrinsic. The fantastic characters ring true, even exotics with otherworldly motives. If the geography took a few books to settle down, Butcher understands Chicago (we *are* from there—ed.) and the consequences of doing magic in a place where most people do not even believe in it. It's a hard-working industrial city that is home to the mob, powerful mayors, and the hard-knuckled CPD.

The collection brings back a number of great characters, and each story includes a note as to where it fits among the novels. If you are already reading the *Dresden Files*, there is likely no need to tell you to get this collection. If you have not yet had the pleasure of following Harry Dresden as he solves fantastic dilemmas while moving through our everyday lives, this is a great sampler to start with. Recommended for all *Dresden Files* fans, everyone who enjoys urban fantasies, and just about all mystery readers.

Copyright © 2018 by Jody Lynn Nye and Bill Fawcett

Gregory Benford is a Nebula winner and a former Worldcon Guest of Honor. He is the author of more than thirty novels, six books of non-fiction, and has edited ten anthologies.

A SCIENTIST'S NOTEBOOK

by Gregory Benford

THE FAR FUTURE

Little science fiction deals with truly grand perspectives in time. Most stories and novels envision people much like ourselves, immersed in cultures that quite resemble ours, and inhabiting worlds which are foreseeable extensions of the places we now know.

Such landscapes are, of course, easier to envision, more comfortable to the reader, and simpler for the writer; one can simply mention everyday objects and let them set the interior stage of the reader's mind.

Yet some of our field's greatest works concern vast perspectives. Most of Olaf Stapledon's novels (*Star Maker, Last and First Men*) are set against such immense backdrops. Arthur Clarke's *Against the Fall of Night* opens over a billion years in our future. These works have remained in print many decades, partly because they are rare attempts to "look long"—to see ourselves against the scale of evolution itself.

Indeed, H.G. Wells wrote *The Time Machine* in part as a reaction to the Darwinian ideas which had swept the intellectual world of comfortable England. He conflated evolution with a Marxist imagery of racial class separation, notions that could only play out on the scale of millions of years. His doomed crab scuttling on a reddened beach was the first great image of the far future.

Similarly, Stapledon and Clarke wrote in the dawn of modern cosmology, shortly after Hubble's discovery of universal expansion implied a startlingly large age of the universe. Cosmologists believed this to be about two billion years then. From better measurements, we now think it to be at least five times that. In any case, it was so enormous a time that pretensions of human importance seemed grotesque. We have been around less than a thousandth of the universe's age. Much has gone before us, and even more will follow.

In recent decades there have been conspicuously few attempts to approach such perspectives in literature. This is curious, for such dimensions afford sweeping vistas, genuine awe. Probably most writers find the severe demands too daunting. One must understand biological evolution, the physical sciences, and much else—all the while shaping a moving human story, which may not even involve humans as we now know them. Yet there is a continuing audience for such towering perspectives.

"Thinking long" means "thinking big." Fiction typically focuses on the local and personal, gaining its power by unities of time and setting. Fashioning intense stories against huge backdrops is difficult. And humans are special and idiosyncratic, while the sweep of time is broad, general and uncaring.

We are tied to time, immense stretches of it. Our DNA differs from that of chimps by only 1.6 percent; we lords of creation are but a hair's breadth from the jungle. We are the third variety of chimp, and a zoologist from Alpha Centauri would classify us without hesitation along with the common chimp of tropical Africa and the pygmy chimp of Zaire. Most of that 1.6 percent may well be junk, too, of no genetic importance, so the significant differences are even smaller.

We carry genetic baggage from far back in lost time. We diverged genetically from the Old World monkeys about thirty million years ago, from gorillas about ten million years ago, and from the other chimps about seven million years ago. Only forty thousand years ago did *we* wondrous creatures appear—meaning our present form, which differs in shape and style greatly from our ancestor Neanderthals. We roved further, made finer tools, and when we moved into Neanderthal territory, the outcome was clear; within a short while, no more Neanderthals.

No other large animal is native to all continents and breeds in all habitats, from rainforests to deserts to the poles. Among our unique abilities which we proudly believe led to our success, we seldom credit our propensity to kill each other, and to destroy our environment—yet there are evolutionary arguments that these were valuable to us once, leading to pruning of our genes and ready use of resources.

These same traits now threaten our existence. They also imply that, if we last into the far future, those deep elements in us will make for high drama, rueful laughter, triumph and tragedy.

While we have surely been shaped by our environment, our escape from bondage to our natural world is the great theme of civilization. How will this play out on the immense scale of many millennia? The environment will surely change, both locally on the surface of the Earth, and among the heavens. We shall change with it.

We shall probably meet competition from other worlds, and may fall from competition to a Darwinian doom. We could erect immense empires and play Godlike games with vast populations. And surely we could tinker with the universe in ingenious ways, the inquisitive chimpanzee wrestling whole worlds to suit his desires. Once we gain great powers, we can confront challenges undreamed of by Darwin. The universe as a whole is our ultimate opponent.

In the very long run, the astrologers may turn out to be right: our fates may be determined by the stars. For they are doomed.

Stars are immense reservoirs of energy, dissipating their energy stores into light as quickly as their bulk allows. Our own star is 4.3 billion years old, almost halfway through its eleven billion year life span. After that, it shall begin to burn heavier and heavier elements at its core, growing hotter. Its atmospheric envelope of already incandescent gas shall heat and swell. From a mild-mannered, yellow-white star it shall bloat into a reddened giant, swallowing first Mercury, then Venus, then Earth and perhaps Mars.

H.G. Wells foresaw in *The Time Machine* a dim sun, with a giant crablike thing scuttling across a barren beach. While evocative, this isn't what astrophysics now tells us. But as imagery, it remains a striking reflection upon the deep problem that the far future holds—the eventual meaning of human action.

About 4.5 billion years from now, our sun will rage a hundred times brighter. Half a billion years further on, it will be between 500 and a thousand times more luminous, and seventy percent larger in radius. The Earth's temperature depends only slowly

on the sun's luminosity (varying as the one fourth root), so by then our crust will roast at about 1,400 degrees Kelvin; room temperature is 300 Kelvin. The oceans and air will have boiled away, leaving barren plains beneath an angry sun which covers thirty-five degrees of the sky.

What might humanity—however transformed by natural selection, or by its own hand—do to save itself? Sitting farther from the fire might work. Temperature drops inversely with the square of distance, so Jupiter will be cooler by a factor of 2.3, Saturn by 3.1. But for a sun 500 times more luminous than now, the Jovian moons will still be 600 degrees Kelvin (K), and Saturn's about 450 K. Uranus might work, 4.4 times cooler, a warm but reasonable 320 K. Neptune will be a brisk 255 K. What strange lives could transpire in the warmed, deep atmospheres of those gas giants?

Still, such havens will not last. When the sun begins helium burning in earnest it will fall in luminosity, and Uranus will become a chilly 200 K. Moving inward to Saturn would work, for it will then be at 300 K, balmy shirtsleeve weather—if we have arms by then.

The bumpy slide downhill for our star will see the sun's luminosity fall to merely a hundred times the present value, when helium burning begins, and the Earth will simmer at 900 K. After another fifty million years—how loftily astrophysicists can toss off these immensities!—as further reactions alter in the sun's core, it will swell into a red giant again. It will blow off its outer layers, unmasking the dense, brilliant core that will evolve into a white dwarf. Earth will be seared by the torrent of escaping gas, and bathed in piercing ultraviolet light. The white-hot core will then cool slowly.

As the sun eventually simmers down, it will sink to a hundredth of its present luminosity. Then even Mercury will be a frigid 160 K, and Earth will be a frozen corpse at 100 K. The solar system, once a grand stage, will be a black relic beside a guttering campfire.

To avoid this fate, intelligent life can tinker—at least for a while—with stellar burning. Our star will get into trouble because it will eventually pollute its core with the heavier elements that come from burning hydrogen. In a complex cycle, hydrogen fuses and leaves assorted helium, lithium, carbon and other elements. With all its hydrogen burned up at its core, where pressures and temperatures are highest, the sun will begin fusing helium. This takes higher temperatures, which the star attains by compressing under gravity. Soon the helium runs out. The next heavier element fuses. Carbon burns until the star enters a complex, unstable regime leading to swelling. (For other stars than ours, there could even be explosions [supernovas] if its mass is great enough.)

To stave off this fate, a cosmic engineer need only note that at least ninety percent of the hydrogen in the star is still unburned, when the cycle turns in desperation to fusing helium. The star's oven lies at the core, and hydrogen is too light to sink down into it.

Envision a great spoon which can stir the elements in a star, mixing hydrogen into the nuclear ash at the core. The star could then return to its calmer, hydrogen-fusing reaction.

No spoon of matter could possibly survive the immense temperatures there, of course. But magnetic fields can move mass through their rubbery pressures. The sun's surface displays this, with its magnetic arches and loops which stretch for thousands of kilometers, tightly clasping hot plasma into tubes and strands.

If a huge magnetic paddle could reach down into the sun's core and stir it, the solar life span could extend to perhaps a hundred billion years. To do this requires immense currents, circulating over coils larger than the sun itself.

What "wires" could support such currents, and what battery would drive them? Such cosmic engineering is beyond our practical comprehension, but it violates no physical laws. Perhaps, with five billion years to plan, we can figure a way to do it. In return, we would extend the lifetime of our planet tenfold.

To fully use this extended stellar lifetime, we would need strategies for capturing more sunlight than a planet can. Freeman Dyson envisioned breaking up worlds into small asteroids, each orbiting its star in a shell of many billions of small worldlets. These could in principle capture nearly all the sunlight. We could conceivably do this to the Earth, then the rest of the planets.

Of course, the environmental impact report for such engineering would be rather hefty. This raises the entire problem of what happens to the Earth while all these stellar agonies go on. Even if we insure a mild, sunny climate, there are long term troubles with our atmosphere.

Current thinking holds that the big, long term problem we face is loss of carbon dioxide from our air. This gas, the food of the plants, gets locked up in rocks. Photosynthetic organisms down at the very base of the food chain extract carbon from air, cutting the life chain.

We might fix this by bioengineering organisms that return carbon dioxide. Then we would need to worry about the slow brightening of our sun, which would make our surface temperature about 80 degrees Centigrade in 1.5 billion years. Compensating for this by increasing our cloud cover, say, would work for a while. A cooling cloud blanket will work for a while. Still, we continually lose hydrogen to space, evaporated away at the top of the atmosphere. Putting water clouds up to block the sunlight means that they, too, will get boiled away. Even with such measures, liquid water on Earth would evaporate in about 2.5 billion years from now. Without oceans, volcanoes would be the major source for new atmospheric elements, and we would evolve a climate much like that of Venus.

All this assumes that we don't find wholly new ways of getting around planetary problems. I suspect that we crafty chimpanzees probably shall, though. We like to tinker and we like to roam. Though some will stay to fiddle with the Earth, the sun and the planets, some will move elsewhere.

After all, smaller stars will live longer. The class called M dwarfs, dim and red and numerous, can burn steady and wan, for up to a hundred billion years, without any assistance. Then even they will gutter out. Planets around such stars will have a hard time supporting life, because any world close enough to the star to stay warm will also be tide locked, one side baked and the other freezing. Still, they might prove temporary abodes for wandering primates, or for others.

Eventually, no matter what stellar engine we harness, all the hydrogen gets burned. Similar pollution problems beset even the artificially aged star, now completely starved of hydrogen. It seethes, grows hotter, sears its planets, then swallows them.

There may be other adroit dodges available to advanced lifeforms, such as using the energy of supernovas. These are brute mechanisms, and later exploding stars can replenish the interstellar clouds of dust and gas, so that new stars can form—but not many. On average, matter gets recycled in about four billion years in our galaxy. Our own planet's mass is partly recycled stellar debris from the first galactic supernova generation. This cycle can go on until about twenty billion years pass, when only a ten-thousandth of the interstellar medium will remain. Dim red stars will glow in the spiral arms, but the great dust banks will have been trapped into stellar corpses.

So unavoidably, the stars are as mortal as we. They take longer, but they die.

For its first fifty billion years, the universe will brim with light. Gas and dust will still fold into fresh suns. For an equal span the stars would linger. Beside reddening suns, planetary life will warm itself by the waning fires that herald stellar death.

Sheltering closer and closer to stellar warmth, life could take apart whole solar systems, galaxies, even the entire Virgo cluster of galaxies, all to capture light. In the long run, life must take everything apart and use it to survive.

To ponder futures beyond that era, we must discuss the universe as a whole.

Modern cosmology is quite different from the physics of the Newtonian worldview, which dreamed uneasily of a universe that extended forever but was always threatened by collapse. Nothing countered the drawing-in of gravity except infinity itself. Though angular momentum will keep a galaxy going for a great while, collisions can cancel that. Objects hit each other and mutually plunge toward the gravitating center. Physicists of the Newtonian era thought that maybe there simply had not been enough time to bring about the final implosion. Newton, troubled by this, avoided cosmological issues.

Given enough time, matter will seek its own kind, stars smacking into each other, making greater and greater stars. This will go on even after the stars gutter out.

When a body meets a body, coming through the sky… Stars will inevitably collide, meet, merge. All the wisdom and order of planets and suns will finally compress into the marriage of many stars, plunging down the pit of gravity to become black holes. For the final fate of nearly all matter shall be the dark pyre of collapse.

Galaxies are as mortal as stars. In the sluggish slide of time, the spirals which had once gleamed with fresh brilliance will be devoured by ever-growing black holes. Inky masses will blot out whole spiral arms of dim red. The already massive holes at galactic centers will swell from their billion-stellar-mass sizes at present, to chew outward, gnawing without end.

From the corpses of stars, collisions will form either neutron stars or black holes, within about a thousand billion years (in exponential notation, 10^{12} years). Even the later and longest-lived stars cannot last beyond 10^{14} years. Collisions between stars will strip away all planets in 10^{15} years.

Blunt thermodynamics will still command, always seeking maximum disorder. In 10^{17} years, the last white dwarf stars will have cooled to be utterly black dwarfs, temperatures about 5 degrees Kelvin (Absolute). In time, even hell would freeze over.

Against an utterly black sky, shadowy cinders of stars will glide. Planets, their atmospheres frozen out into waveless lakes of oxygen, will glide in meaningless orbits, warmed by no ruby star glow. The universal clock would run down to the last tick of time.

But the universe is no static lattice of stars. It grows. The Big Bang would be better termed the Enormous Emergence, space-time snapping into existence intact and whole, of a piece. Then it grew, the fabric of space lengthening as time increased.

With the birth of space-time came its warping by matter, each wedded to the other until time eternal. An expanding universe cools, just as a gas does. The far future will freeze, even if somehow life manages to find fresh sources of power.

Could the expansion ever reverse? This is the crucial unanswered riddle in cosmology. If there is enough matter in our universe, eventually gravitation will win out over the expansion. The "dark matter" thought to infest the relatively rare, luminous stars we see could be dense enough to stop the universe's stretching of its own space-time. This density is related to how old the universe is.

We believe the universe is somewhere between eight and sixteen billion years old. The observed rate of expansion (the Hubble constant) gives eight billion, in a simple, plausible model. The measured age of the oldest stars gives sixteen billion.

This difference I believe arises from our crude knowledge of how to fit our mathematics to our cosmological data; I don't think it's a serious problem. Personally I favor the higher end of the range, perhaps twelve to fourteen billion. We also have rough measures of the deceleration rate of the universal expansion. These can give (depending on cosmological, mathematical models) estimates of how long a dense universe would take to expand, reverse, and collapse back to a point. At the extremes, this gives between twenty-seven billion and at least 100 billion years before the Big Crunch. If we do indeed live in a universe which will collapse, then we are bounded by two singularities, at beginning and end. No structure will survive that future singularity. Freeman Dyson found this a pessimistic scenario and so refused to consider it.

A closed universe seems the ultimate doom. In all cosmological models, if the mass density of the universe exceeds the critical value, gravity inevitably wins. This is called a "closed" universe, because it has finite spatial volume, but no boundary. It is like a three-dimensional analog of a sphere's surface. A bug on a ball can circumnavigate it, exploring all its surface and coming back to home, having crossed no barrier. So a starship could cruise around the universe and come home, having found no edge.

A closed universe starts with a big bang (an initial singularity) and expands. Separation between galaxies grows linearly with time. Eventually the universal expansion of space-time will slow to a halt. Then a contraction will begin, accelerating as it goes, pressing galaxies closer together. The photons rattling around in this universe will increase in frequency, the opposite of the red shift we see now. Their blue shift means the sky gets brighter in time. Contraction of space-time shortens wavelengths, which increases light energy.

Though stars will still age and die as the closed universe contracts, the background light will blue shift. No matter if life burrows into deep caverns, in time the heat of this light will fry it. Freeman Dyson remarked that the closed universe gave him "a feeling of claustrophobia, to imagine our whole existence confined within a box." He asked, "Is it conceivable that by intelligent intervention, converting matter into radiation to flow purposefully on a cosmic scale, we could break open a closed universe and change the topology of space-time so that only a part of it would collapse and another would expand forever? I do not know the answer to this question."

The answer seems to be that once collapse begins, a deterministic universe allows no escape for pockets of spacetime. Life cannot stop the squeezing.

Some have embraced this searing death, when all implodes toward a point of infinite temperature. Frank Tipler of Tulane University sees it as a great opportunity. In those last seconds, collapse will not occur at the same rate in all directions. Chaos in the system will produce "gravitational shear" which drives temperature differences. Drawing between these temperature differences, life can harness power for its own use.

Of course, such life will have to change its form to use such potentials; they will need hardier stuff than blood and bone. Ceramic-based forms could endure, or vibrant, self-contained plasma clouds—any tougher structure might work, as long as it can code information.

This most basic definition of life, the ability to retain and manipulate information, means that the substrate supporting this does not matter, in the end. Of course, the *style* of thought of a silicon web feasting on the slopes of a volcano won't be that of a shrewd primate fresh from the veldt, but certain common patterns can transfer.

Such life forms might be able to harness the compressive, final energies at that distant end, the Omega Point. Frank Tipler's *The Physics of Immortality* makes a case that a universal intelligence at the Omega Point will then confer a sort of immortality, by carrying out the computer simulation of all possible past intelligences. All possible earlier "people" will be resurrected, he thinks. This bizarre notion shows how cosmology blends into eschatology, the study of the ultimate fate of things, particularly of souls.

I, too, find this scenario of final catastrophe daunting. Suppose, then, the universe is not so dense that it will ever reverse its expansion. Then we can foresee a long, toiling twilight.

Life based on solid matter will struggle to survive. To find energy, it will have to ride herd on and merge black holes themselves, force them to emit bursts of gravitational waves. In principle these waves can be harnessed, though of course we don't know how as yet. Only such fusions could yield fresh energy in a slumbering universe.

High civilizations will rise, no doubt, mounted on the carcass of matter itself—the ever-spreading legions of black holes. Entire galaxies will turn from reddening lanes of stars, into swarms of utterly dark gravitational singularities, the holes. Only by moving such masses, by extracting power through magnetic forces and the slow gyre of dissipating orbits, could life rule the dwindling resources of the ever-enlarging universe. Staying warm shall become the one great Law.

Dyson has argued that in principle, the perceived time available to living forms can be made infinite. In this sense, immortality of a kind could mark the cold, stretching stages of the universal death.

This assumes that we know all the significant physics, of course. Almost certainly, we do not. Our chimpanzee worldview may simply be unable to comprehend events on such vast time scales. Equally, though, chimpanzees will try, and keep trying.

Since Dyson's pioneering work on these issues, yet more physics has emerged which we must take into account. About his vision of a swelling universe, its life force spent, hangs a great melancholy.

For matter itself is doomed, as well. Even the fraction which escapes the holes, and learns to use them, if mortal. Its basic building block, the proton, decays. This takes unimaginably long—current measurements suggest a proton lifetime of more than 10^{33} years. But decay seems inevitable, the executioner's sword descending with languid grace.

Even so, something still survives. Not all matter dies, though with the proton gone everything we hold dear will disintegrate, atoms and animals alike. After the grand operas of mass and energy have played out their plots, the universal stage will clear to reveal the very smallest.

The tiniest of particles—the electron and its antiparticle, the positron—shall live on, current theory suggests. No process of decay can find purchase on their infinitesimal scales, lever them apart into smaller fragments. The electron shall dance with its anti-twin in swarms: the lightest of all possible plasmas.

By the time these are the sole players, the stage will have grown enormously. Each particle will find its nearest neighbor to be a full light-year away. They will have to bind together, sharing cooperatively, storing data in infinitesimally thin currents and charges. A single entity would have to be the size of a spiral arm, of a whole galaxy. Vaster than empires, and more slow.

Plasmas held together by magnetic and electric fields are incredibly difficult to manage, rather like building a cage for Jell-O out of rubber bands. But in principle, physics allows such magnetic loops and glowing spheres. We can see them in the short-lived phenomena of ball lightning. More spectacularly, they occur on the sun, in glowing magnetic arches which can endure for weeks, a thousand kilometers high.

Intelligence could conceivably dwell in such wispy magnetic consorts. Communication will take centuries…but to the slow thumping of the universal heart, that will be nothing.

If life born to brute matter can find a way to incorporate itself into the electron-positron plasma, then it can last forever. This would be the last step in a migration from the very early forms, like us: rickety assemblies of water in tiny compartment cells, hung on a lattice of moving calcium rods.

Life and intelligence will have to alter, remaking its basic structures from organic molecules to, say, animated crystalline sheets. Something like this may have happened before; some theorists believe Earthly life began in wet clay beds, and moved to organic molecules in a soupy sea only later.

While the customary view of evolution does not speak of progress, there has been generally an increase of information transmitted forward to the next generation. Complexity increases in a given genus, order, class, etc. Once intelligence appears, or invades a wholly different medium, such "cognitive creatures" can direct their own evolution.

Patterns will persist, even thrive, independent of the substrate.

So perhaps this is the final answer to the significance of it all. In principle, life and structure, hopes and dreams and Shakespeare's Hamlet, can persist forever—if life chooses to, and struggles. In that far future, dark beyond measure, plasma entities of immense size and torpid pace may drift through a supremely strange era, sure and serene, free at last of ancient enemies.

Neither the thermodynamic dread of heat death nor gravity's gullet could then swallow them. Cosmology would have done its work.

As the universe swells, energy lessens, and the plasma life need only slow its pace to match. Mathematically, there are difficulties involved in arguing, as Dyson does, that the perceived span of order can be made infinite. The issue hinges on how information and energy scale with time. Assuming that Dyson's scaling is right, there is hope.

By adjusting itself exactly to its ever-cooling environment, life—of a sort—can persist and dream fresh dreams. The Second Law of Thermodynamics says that disorder increases in every energy transaction. But the Second Law need not be not the Final Law.

Such eerie descendants will have much to think about. They will be able to remember and relive in sharp detail the glory of the brief Early Time—that distant, legendary era when matter brewed energy from crushing suns together. When all space was furiously hot, overflowing with boundless energy. When life dwelled in solid states, breathed in chilly atoms, and mere paltry planets formed a stage.

Freeman Dyson once remarked to me, about these issues, that he felt the best possible universe was one of constant challenge. He preferred a future which made survival possible but not easy. We chimps, if coddled, get lazy and then stupid.

The true far future is shrouded and mysterious. Still, I expect that he shall get his wish, and we shall not be bored.

Copyright © 1995 by Gregory Benford

Robert J. Sawyer is the Hugo, Nebula, Campbell Memorial, Heinlein, Hal Clement, Skylark, Aurora, and Seiun Award-winning author of twenty-three bestselling science-fiction novels, including the trilogy of Hominids, Humans, *and* Hybrids, *which won Canada's Aurora Award for the Best Work of the Decade. Rob holds two honorary doctorates and is a Member of the Order of Canada, the highest civilian honor bestowed by the Canadian government. Find him online at sfwriter.com.*

DECOHERENCE

by Robert J. Sawyer

SAYING NO

I received an award nomination yesterday. Such things are always pleasing to a writer, but this one was special because it reminded me of one of the most important lessons of my career.

The nomination was for the Best Screenplay of 2018 from the L.A. Neo Noir Novel, Film, & Script Festival; I was being honored for a script of mine called "Biding Time," adapting my own story of the same name. But that story never should have existed. It was written to salvage material that my editor at Tor, the late, great David G. Hartwell, had told me to remove from my 2005 novel *Mindscan*.

That novel was, in part, a mystery and a courtroom drama: the mystery revolved around Tyler, the already wealthy son of a very rich woman who had decided, near the end of her natural life, to upload her consciousness into an android body. Once that had happened, Tyler sued the uploaded version, looking to have her legally declared *not* his mother.

Much of my work crosses over from science fiction into mystery, and I keep at the back of my mind John W. Campbell's ancient protestation that SF mysteries are impossible because the writer can always pull a technological rabbit out of the hat, thereby cheating the reader. Isaac Asimov, Alfred Bester, Larry Niven, and many others quickly proved Campbell wrong, but still, I made it a requirement for every SF mystery that I wrote that all three of method, motive, and opportunity had to have a uniquely science-fictional nature.

I'd come up with just such a rationale for the rich man's lawsuit, but Dave Hartwell told me to dump that motive and make it just about the money; the greedy son, he said, merely wants his inheritance.

I was mortified; I truly thought he was ruining my book.

And what did I do?

I acquiesced, I capitulated, I agreed.

In other words, I wussed out.

Now, *Mindscan* ended up doing well nonetheless, winning the John W. Campbell Memorial Award for Best Science Fiction Novel of the Year, the top juried award in the field. But still, to this day—thirteen years on—whenever anyone asks me to sign a copy of the book, I feel a pang of regret, remembering the better book it initially was.

Now, don't get me wrong: David was an excellent editor and a good friend, and he and I had a great run together: the only best-novel Hugo Award-winner David ever edited was my *Hominids*, and of the eight other novels we did together, five were Hugo nominees.

Around the time Dave told me to make that cut, Mike Resnick—the editor of this very magazine—commissioned me to write a hard-boiled detective novella for an anthology (that novella eventually became the opening of my novel *Red Planet Blues*, published by Ace). The novella was well received, which meant I had a popular character and intriguing milieu for further adventures—plus that idea Dave told me to remove from *Mindscan*. Putting them together, I produced a sequel short story called "Biding Time." That story ended up winning Canada's Aurora Award and being included in the mainstream anthology *The Penguin Book of Crime Fiction*. I felt vindicated—my original notion *was* good (and, thus buoyed, I went on to produce the screenplay version cited above).

What was the motive I'd come up with that David disliked? When Tyler, the rich son, had been a child, he'd smothered his own baby sister because he hated that she'd become the center of his parents' attention. Her passing had been deemed crib death, but his mother had been and continued to be devastated by it. Tyler felt that once his mother finally passed on, he'd at last be free of the guilt for the pain he'd caused her. But when his mother uploaded her consciousness, becoming immortal, he realized he'd never be free unless he could prove to himself and everyone else that she was really dead.

Great, I'd thought; poignant, powerful, and a motive that was only possible in SF. *And David told me to take it out.*

A few years later, I was a guest at a meeting of an all-women book club that had read *Mindscan*, and, to my delight, everyone loved it. But one attendee called me on the carpet saying Tyler's motive was weak. I said I couldn't agree more and told them what I'd originally written. The group, including one lady who had lost a young child herself, thought my original version was *perfect*.

My next novel for Tor was 2007's *Rollback*, which tells the story of an elderly couple who are offered a rejuvenation treatment that works for the husband but fails for the wife. One of the most powerful scenes I think I've ever written was in that manuscript: the first time they tried to make love after the procedure, him now in a hale twenty-five-year-old body, her still a frail eighty-seven. The scene is from his point of view, and he mentally congratulates himself at the end on being ever so gentle, only to have her turn away in tears, saying, "Why did you have to be so rough?"

David told me to cut that as well. I was stunned.

Now, when he was working on *Mindscan*, David had recently fathered a young boy and a younger girl; then, and while working on *Rollback*, his wife was decades his junior. My guess is that both my scenarios creeped him out personally, leading him to violate what is, in my mind, the number-one rule of editing: an editor should never cavil about something that is idiosyncratic to him or her. (You can't stand pop-culture references? Fine—but the author loves them and so they stay in.) Editors should only object if they believe a significant portion of the author's usual audience will take umbrage as well.

When David told me to cut the beating heart out of *Rollback*, I was flabbergasted; I couldn't believe I was facing this nightmare again. I called my then-agent, the late Ralph Vicinanza, and told him I could not in good conscience do what David had told me to do; I went so far as to say I'd return my advance book and pull the book from Tor.

Ralph, as ever, was the voice of reason. "Just tell Dave you don't want to do it," he said. "You mean I can do that?" I replied, stunned. "Absolutely," said Ralph—and so I screwed up my courage and confronted the man who was the most respected living editor in the entire science-fiction field. Dave thought for a moment, then said, "Well, in the end, it's your name on the cover, not mine." I did agree to water down the scene a bit, but that essential moment—the fulcrum on which all the rest of the book's action hinged—remained.

So, if my *Biding Time* screenplay does happen to win, I will warmly thank Dave in my acceptance speech. But still, giving in that first time is one of my great career regrets—and I hope to spare any budding authors reading this from experiencing something similar: you *do* have the right to say no.

Copyright © 2018 by Robert J. Sawyer

Joy Ward is the author of one novel. She has several stories in print, in magazines and in anthologies, and has also conducted interviews, both written and video, for other publications.

David Drake is the author of multiple best-sellers, and a mainstay of Baen Books.

THE *GALAXY'S EDGE* INTERVIEW

Joy Ward interviews David Drake

David Drake: I am a conservative and I have no ideology. Everyone dies. Everything dies. The heat death of the universe, eventually. We're all going to die.

When my friend, Mark, got his first digital answering machine, somebody joked in the group, "You know, he can make you have said anything he wants," and I thought about it for a moment and I said, "I can't imagine anything that you would twist my words into that would be worse than some of the things I've actually said." There was a general agreement that, you know, in that sense, I am absolutely proof against misquoting because no, I've said worse. I'm not going to pussyfoot around my opinions either.

In high school, one of my teachers was a professional writer on the side. That made me realize that writers are not some God-like group somewhere off there. A writer can be a kid who grew up in Decorah, Iowa, on a farm and began writing professionally while doing other things. The writer, whose name then was Eugene Olson. Mr. Olson had a writing pseudonym, Brad Steiger, which he later changed his name formally to, but he was ten years my senior, quite a young high school teacher and very charismatic; one of the two best teachers I've had in a life that had a great deal of academe. I had always told stories. Seeing him made me realize that I could write them down and I started doing that with the intention of someday I would be old enough and I would…

It allowed me to write my stories down and set them out. That's all it did. I mean, I'd always told stories. I continued to tell the stories. As I say, I'd always said,

"When I was old enough, I'd send one off. When I was old enough, I'd sell the story." I went up to Sauk City, Wisconsin, at eighteen, nineteen. I bought some books. The book that had just come in was the *Inhabitant of the Lake*, which was my first book, first collection of work by an Englishman, actually an Irish named John Ramsey Campbell who later wrote professionally as Ramsey Campbell.

There was a picture of him on the back of it and he looked about fifteen years old. He is, in fact, a year younger than I am. I looked at that picture and I said out loud, "Well, I can't claim that I'm not old enough to do it." So, I got home and got back to Iowa, in University of Iowa, and wrote Mr. Derleth asking if I could submit a story for his next original anthology. He grumbled and said yes, and I did. He sent it back saying, "It was a good plot outline. Now, write the story." I expanded to a full 3,500 words.

He edited again and said, "Still isn't right, but I'll edit it. Compare it with the printed version with your carbon to see how not to write a story the next time. Here's a check for thirty-five dollars." That was my first sale.

It was the most crushing acceptance letter I've ever heard. I was so ignorant that I didn't know I was supposed to keep a carbon. I thought I am a complete idiot. I'll admit, I didn't think, "Will I get to have this check framed?" I thought, thirty-five dollars. That was actually a lot of money… I was earning ninety-five cents an hour as a book page in the University of Iowa Library. I spent it.

Kind of weird. I didn't really have a full feeling of it until I started law school and was accepted on the Law Journal. An older member of the Journal was giving us her little pep talk, how if you do really well, you may be permitted to write a note for the Law Journal, and you can't imagine how it feels to have your name in print and the fun of it. People pay me just to put my name in print. I should be proud of doing a note. I guess that was the most significant result of having sold that story.

I was drafted in a great number of other college graduates who were drafted in 1969. In 1969, they brought in the draft lottery, but there was that year interim where everybody who is in grad school was a potential draftee. I was drafted. In my squad basic training, the first guy was getting his PhD in physics at the University of Chicago. The Language School, which was for grad students only. As it turned out, one of my closest buddies was getting his degree from Princeton in English.

About a third of my basic training battalion was college graduates, about a third were white kids from Western North Carolina, the remaining third… These are rough figures, but they are roughly correct. About a third were black kids from intercity Detroit who had about the same educational attainments as the white kids from Western North Carolina but there were cultural differences.

Then, as they say, there were college graduates. Basic training was an interesting experience for everybody including the drill sergeants who were very professional and very good, and very puzzled by a lot of things. They were not hostile to us college kids.

When I came back to the world from Vietnam, and to a degree I wrote a story that actually sold while I was in Vietnam with the 540 crews. It was a fantasy. I wrote it and then, I was typing it up on the unit typewriter. This was back in the base at Qui Nhon. It was Sunday morning and I heard a bang. I turned around and looked through the screened window behind me, and there's this orange bubble. I'm thinking, "What the fuck?" Then, there was a louder bang! And a larger orange bubble. Then, there was a really big, orange bubble and a louder bang. The bangs were coming through the ground before they got through the air. What happened was, the ammo dump had blown up.

Some people, the G-troop, had come in from the field. One of the things you had to do when you came in from the field was store all your ammunition and explosives in the ammo dump. It's Sunday morning and two guys in a deuce and a half head back into the dump and were tossing ordnance out the back to empty the truck. In the field, you don't have much in the way of containers. What they were using for a lot of the odds and sods were mortar cases. These were sort of like orange crates, only they were long and thin with slaps and they would normally hold mortar shells.

The guy tossed them out to the back and the pin, one of the grenade pins was hanging out for a slap. It caught on the tailgate latch of the deuce and a half as it went out. It landed in this pile of other ordnance smoking. Just a fuse, a five-second fuse. They both jumped in the cab of the truck and got the truck back out around the blast wall when that went off in the middle of a pile of the other ordnance, which set off a larger amount of nearby ordnance, which set off the whole thing.

That was the third explosion. G-troop was being mustered out Sunday morning. I later talked to the wife of the cook with the G-troop. He was doing their morning formation and bang, and he looked up in the sky and there's these black specks and it started falling. They were the fifty-four-gallon drums full of sand that was used as temporary blast walls. There were 155 shells unfused that were falling down. What didn't actually go off, went up and fell. No one was injured.

The church was a huge A-frame with sheet metal walls next to the ammo dump. The burn around the ammo dump that directed the blast, so none of it was going sideways out.

I know what an explosion looked…I mean, a really big explosion from about a mile, I know exactly what that looks like, and I finished typing up the story, which had nothing to do with anything military. No, I got to see a lot of things in Vietnam that I wouldn't otherwise have seen.

Joy Ward: What is the driving passion behind your writing?

DD: Keeping myself from killing people.

I came back to the world very, very angry. There are a lot of reasons to be angry. I was angry at everything. I was probably angry with myself for what I've done, for what I had become. I knew perfectly well what I'd become and I was curious about it. If I had not had the writing as a way to put it out, to organize my thoughts, that sort of thing, bad things might've

happened. I became a much more dog-end writer, not to be a writer, but to give me an outlet. I did not know it. I did not admit it. I didn't admit how crazy I was. I was really crazy. I went back and I finished law school. The transition was, I was in returning barracks at Long Binh and seventy-two hours later, I was in the lounge of Duke University Law School preparing to start my fourth semester.

That is our caring country.

That was in 1971. I finished law school. I don't remember anything of that last year-and-a-half. There are people who consider graduating from a top-rated law school as being the most stressful events in their life. No, they weren't going to shoot at me. I've looked up in the morning thinking, "Nobody's going to shoot at me today."

I came back to the world at some level or two things. One, I was already dead. I've given myself up for dead during the past year. It wasn't that anything bad had happened to me because bad things had happened.

But, it wasn't that. It was just I knew from the beginning that I was not going to survive this year and my body did. My mind really didn't. I mean, the personality that I was really did not survive. I don't mean that dreadful things happened to me. No. Worse things happen to a lot of people I knew, a lot of people. That wasn't me, but I had given myself up. The other thing was, I thought I was crazy. I wasn't admitting this, but I really, deeply did because nothing made any fucking sense.

My writing was able to put things down in an organized fashion. This happened, this happened. At some level, I think, I was believing that because I was organizing it, that it would make sense. The truth, I finally came to realize, was it didn't make any sense, the whole thing was just as crazy as I thought it was but I was crazy. My brain had not been harmed. My personality and the fact that I couldn't make sense of this did not mean I had become stupid.

No. I really didn't grasp what was going on and it really made no more sense than I had thought it did at that time. The writing permitted me to see that. It didn't give me myself back. That's been sort of an incremental process of taking these little pebbles and gluing them back together. I've done a pretty good job at it. I really have, but this is not the person I was in 1968. I don't mean I was a great person. Who wasn't? I mean, he was a kid. I think he deserved better. But regardless, it is what it is. I really did die in that two-year period because it was more than just Vietnam and Cambodia. Basic is just… I watched a guy flung through a second-floor window because he walked on the floor of another squad while they were waxing it for an inspection. Four of them just grabbed him and threw him through the window, scream and all. Listen, if I've been up there… The guy was a fuck up. But all right, he's fucked up. Deal with it.

I was okay with it "Oh, yeah. It is about time somebody did." That's not civilized behavior. When I say, what I became was something I don't much like, I mean that as much as things to do with automatic weapons and suchlike. If you don't adapt to the situation, you will die, really. If you do adapt, the civilian that you were has died.

The army has got very good, you know, it used to be with training when people got into combat, only about fifteen percent at tops would use their weapons if they saw the enemy. A really, really good high morale units like the 101st Airborne, thirty-five percent in the middle of violent firefight. Now, the percentage is about ninety percent. The army in basic, it teaches you to kill. Not the physical act of hoping that bullet went to the right place, but willingness, the instant willingness to kill. That's a very important thing for soldiers to be able to do, what they have not done, what they can never try to do, what I don't think they can do was make you a better civilian afterwards.

What the army did was give me seventy-two hours and put me back in law school. That was the response of the government of the United States of America.

People have high regard for military and for soldiers now, and that's good. I'm glad they do, because believe me, it's a rough job.

Non-vets were treated like shit. I mean, I'm not telling any secrets there, am I? I think the country is not embarrassing itself the way it did in the '70s. But I don't think it makes any difference to the people who've been used up.

JW: How do your stories help people understand the ramifications of war?

DD: I don't know that my stories mean anything for civilians. I frankly don't much care. What I have learned is that guys who've been there and read my stories, the story proves to them that they're not alone and that is huge. Their letters made me finally realize that I wasn't alone either. That is huge. I don't have any secrets of how to become normal. I haven't become normal. I will tell you, I will tell people the truth if they ask a question; they'll get answers. They've realized, there is no point in lying.

I learned that when I was twenty-five. Life is too fucking short. You want to know, I'll tell you. You'll like it, fine. You don't like it, fine. The truth is true. There were a lot of comments that I was an extremely direct person. Well, yeah. I'm not sure why that should be so unusual, but it apparently is.

I'm writing for myself. *Redliners* is the big one. I've had many people say that it helped them enormously in their PTSD to *read Redliners*. I say the same thing, all of it is true. I believe it has helped a lot of people. It hasn't helped anybody nearly as much as it helped me to have written it, and I had no idea of what I was doing. I was just writing a space opera with a strong military component. That's all I was doing. And until I finished the book, and I felt this huge weight come off me that had been there for twenty-five years.

JW: Why is it, do you think, that people have backed away from military SF, even the people who have been at that sharp end of the stick and yet, your generation has come out and has actually dealt with it?

DD: Yeah, I don't know. I do know that, if you will, the opinion-makes, really very determinedly shat on me.

I didn't have any crusade. I have no ideology. I didn't much before I went over, and certainly haven't since I came back. I wasn't trying to do anything. I was just telling stories, and I say, trying to keep my own head straight.

People like Charlie Brown were really offended by this. Tom Easton of *Analog* called me a pornographer of violence because I was just trying to tell it as it was.

I knew I was a monster. I knew I was a monster. What was I going to do? Kill him? Don't mistake me, that certainly did cross my mind. I don't mean just in print that he did. He was on a panel at Boston to a room with some hundreds of people. The panel was on the use of violence in science fiction and fantasy. He says, "We're here." Five people in the panel, and I honestly don't remember who the two others were. He says, "On my left here is Joel Rosenberg who uses violence correctly. On my right is David Drake who is a pornographer of violence."

It went kind of blank and as they say, various options crossed my mind, and I don't know. I probably was shut down. But what happened was, Joel Rosenberg jumped up and said, "Everything I know about writing about violence, I have learned by reading David Drake." I looked over at Joel, whom I did not know and I said, "Would you like my first porn?" If it had not been for Joel that was some awful situation.

JW: How did that make you feel?

DD: Like a monster. I knew myself better than he knew me and I knew I was a monster.

I'll tell you a high point. Nigh Shade Books, they contacted me and wound up doing a collected Hammer's Slammer series in three volumes. I got the first volume pre-pub and I opened it and I held it in my hand and I thought, "Jesus Christ, I've come home."

This was a validation. I was doing what I was doing. I kept on doing it. I was selling, fine. But I was the poor relation I sold the first two stories to Baen at Galaxy. He bought up the original collection. But it's always mass market, paperback. Suddenly, in my hand is this really nice limited edition hard cover. It really, you know, wow!

Odd. We're talking thirty years. I mean, that's a long time. I hadn't really been aware that I was out wondering that long, but I had. You open the door, "Oh, I'm home." It's a funny question, you know, right?

I had become part of the mainstream. I have always been successful; but this was a stage beyond that. I don't read reviews generally. If I do, I'm likely to be as angry at a good one as I am at a bad one because my experience has been pretty much that reviewers are stupid. I'd rather be praised by a stupid writer than cursed by a stupid writer, but he's still stupid. Okay, look. I'm arrogant and I'm overstating the case, but that is how I feel.

I am a first-rate craftsman. I mean, I am a fine craftsman. I did not call myself an artist and I've never called myself an artist, and I don't call myself an author. I am a writer. I am a very competent writer.

DD: No. I did my job. I did my job. I did my job. I do my job. I did my job in the Black Horse in the 11th Cav.

I didn't fail the people. I did my job. Maybe they failed. But the thing I got from the Black Horse, we were an elite unit and nobody believed it more. I mean, this is 1970, for Christ's sake. Nobody believed it more and God knows, we didn't believe in the Republic of Vietnam government because it was a joke. It was a grim, criminal joke, as bad as Iraq. What you didn't know about the Black Horse was that when shit hits the fan, the guy next to you would be doing his job and you would be doing yours. If that is the only thing there is the world, then that is something and that is very important to me that I do my job.

JW: Where do you want to go now with your life?

DD: One foot in front of the other.

You haven't gotten anything but honesty from me. I don't mean I'm always right, but I will always tell you what I believed.

JW: How do you want to be remembered?

DD: I don't care. No, I will say it. I want to be remembered as a craftsman and a man who did his job. I did my job.

Copyright © 2018 by Joy Ward

SERIALIZATION
DAUGHTER OF ELYSIUM

BY JOAN SLONCZEWSKI
Trade Paperback: 356 pages.
ISBN: 978-1-60450-444-6

Phoenix Pick Edition, 2010

PART IV
THE IMMORTALS

CHAPTER 1

In the middle of the night Blackbear awoke. He had just had the dream again, about his long-lost brother carried off by the river. This time not his brother alone, but all his dead family members were carried on the current, not struggling as drowning people do, nor drifting facedown, but simply floating on their backs as if asleep, their eyes closed, their hands folded across, just as he had last seen them.

The room was completely dark and silent save for Raincloud's slow, rhythmic breathing. He longed to tell her, for some comfort, but he could not bear to spoil the pleasure of their reunion.

He got up out of bed, trying to move slowly so as not to wake her. "Light, please," he whispered in the hall. "Not too much."

A warm half-light filled the hallway. At first all his eyes could see was haze. He tried to relax, taking deep breaths until his eyes would let him focus on objects a few feet away. He moved cautiously to Hawktalon's door and opened it. She slept soundly, her features sharp and perfect. For a moment she stretched as if to waken, but only turned over in her sleep.

Closing the door, Blackbear left and went next to Sunflower. The little boy must have been in the deepest part of sleep, for he did not move a muscle. Blackbear put his hand on the boy's heart, just to feel the incessant thumping underneath. He remembered how often he used to do that when Hawktalon was a newborn; even though he knew better, he used to wonder every time she slept more than an hour.

Blueskywind was an intense sleeper. She slept on her tummy with her knees folded under, her little hands each clenching a fistful of the crib sheet. A rolled up blanket was piled in front to protect her when she rocked forward, rhythmically banging her head.

At last he moved to the sitting room and fell into a chair. Even Doggie was "asleep," hooked into the wall for a recharge.

The light from the house increased just a bit "Good evening, Blackbear," said the house. "It's good to see you back again."

"Thanks," he muttered.

"I'm sorry the medics couldn't help you better. You may report their defect, of course."

Blackbear shrugged. "We're all defective," he observed.

"That is correct," the house replied. "You are such a reasonable person, Blackbear."

He said nothing, only stared ahead, trying to keep his eyes steady.

"Blackbear, you seem particularly defective since you've returned from your trip. I wish I could serve you better."

"Thanks for the thought."

"You know, when I am feeling particularly defective, I go out to visit my friends in the network. There is always someone who can help me feel better."

There was an idea. He half smiled. "You're lucky, House. All of my friends would be asleep right now."

The house paused as if to run a program. "All of your friends are asleep, except for Kal Anaea*shon*."

He sat up, suddenly alert. "Kal is awake?" What an absurd thought, to visit Kal in the middle of the night.

"You may call him and see for yourself."

"Why not," he said quietly.

The privacy wall melted back from the holostage, and the usual ray of light sprang up. Kal was sitting, reading a book. "We haven't seen you in a while, Blackbear."

Blackbear swallowed, but his throat was still too swollen for words to come out.

Kal closed the book in his hand. "Do you suppose you might stop by for a minute? I have a manuscript I'm trying to decipher, a handwritten transcript from the clickflies of Leni-el. I can barely make out some of the words, and I'd like a second opinion."

With his eyes so bad, he was unlikely to be of much help. But he managed to nod and whisper, "I'll come."

So Blackbear pulled on some clothes and departed alone. The streets at night were lighted mostly at surface level, to guide the feet of the occasional Elysian who passed. Somehow he found his way to the transit reticulum, a blurred tunnel of light in the distance. The vesicle of course told him exactly where to get off, and the door number. Blackbear remembered, then, the last time he had come to Kal's residence, with Sunflower on his back, all upset about the hearing.

A gleam of light appeared through a crack in the wall as the doors parted. The room inside was shaped differently than he remembered, full of odd curves and angles like a Sharer silkhouse, the walls lined with books. Kal emerged with a tray. "You need something warm to drink."

"Thanks." Blackbear slumped exhausted into a cushion that grew out of a wide-angled corner. The drink tasted somewhere between coffee and spiced cider. Before him, the shape of Kal focused and blurred again. He felt suddenly embarrassed, needing to fill the space with words. "Do you always read so late?"

"I haven't slept well," Kal said, "since my mate left." He must have meant Cassi. Goddess only knew where that odd nana had gone to. "How is your longevity project?" Kal asked.

"It's over," he blurted suddenly. "It's over for me, at any rate."

"Why?" Kal sounded surprised.

"Raincloud is taking us home. I'm to start my own lab at Founders."

"That sounds like good news, for you."

"But I can't go home." The words felt as if they were torn from his throat. "I can't go back ... *where they all died*." He broke down sobbing, his chest heaving although he could not get out any tears. He found himself talking about it in bits and pieces, about the wedding picture, and the teddy bear under the little arms, and how he could hardly bear to look at his own children again. And then there was the little brother he had lost years ago, who still came back to him every night, floating off on the stream of time. Then he realized his words were barely coherent, and he wondered whether the *logen* could make anything of it at all. His head was nodding, and he felt half-asleep.

"There's a blanket," Kal was saying. "You can sleep there. I'm rather tired myself, so if you don't mind, I'll see you in the morning."

Too exhausted to resist, he lay back, stretching. The cushion seem to have lengthened so that there was plenty of room for his Bronze Skyan frame. He fell into a deep sleep.

The next morning Blackbear awoke with a start. The room immediately filled with light; it was a small enclosed bedroom, which had evidently been shaped around him for privacy. "Raincloud?" he exclaimed. "Goddess—she has no idea where I am."

"Citizen Raincloud Windclan has been informed of your location," the house told him. That was fine, but still, what a scandal to have run off like that. He must be going out of his mind, Blackbear told himself. But his vision had cleared a bit; perhaps a good night's sleep had done something.

A moment later Kal looked in. "There's a washroom in the corner. You're welcome to some breakfast."

He felt quite disheveled, and more embarrassed the more awake he felt. After splashing some water on his face and trying to look presentable, he entered the kitchen, avoiding Kal's eye. "I don't know what came over me last night," he muttered. On the table was his usual oatmeal for breakfast. The aroma was overpowering; absurdly, he felt suddenly quite at home. "I must have gone defective or something. I ought to report to Service Sector Oh-three-twenty."

He heard Kal give a low pleasant chuckle. Still avoiding the *logen*'s eye, he began to eat his oatmeal. He observed Kal's feet on the floor, tanned, with his long toes that spread out, for he had not yet put on sandals. Then Blackbear frowned and stared a moment. Kal's feet had webbing between the toes; not as full as Leresha's, but definite scallops of skin from one toe to the next. "You're a Sharer," he exclaimed. He looked up at last.

"I wouldn't go that far," said Kal. "Maybe half a Sharer chromosome at most. When Verid first became the *generen*, she took the 'multicultural' charge seriously. She actually used all of the chromosomes available, even from your own world;

some of her *shon*lings are as dark as you. That first generation was quite a scandal. The Guardian Anaea*shon* made her stop."

Blackbear was still caught up in the wonder of it, for he had never noticed before. "That's why you're so interested in Sharer things."

"That was part of it, at one time," Kal admitted.

"I suppose you go out there often. You must know Leresha the wordweaver."

"We've spoken, in Helicon. I haven't been to the ocean in decades."

Then he remembered Kal's first mate, the "Scribbler," who had met an accident out on a raft while collecting tales from the clickflies. "I'm sorry," he said.

"It's all right. It's foolish of me, actually. But it was a ... difficult thing." Kal paused, his hand around a cup of the cider-coffee, or whatever the warm drink was. "We were out alone for a walk on one of the raft branches, when a sudden gust of wind caught us. He slipped and fell in. There was a nest of fleshborers."

Goddess, Blackbear thought, covering his forehead with his hand.

"I called for help, but the wind was shrill and no one heard," Kal explained. "It was seven and a half minutes before someone came. Those were long minutes." He paused. "That was not the worst part," he added reflectively. "The worst part was, I didn't jump in after him."

Blackbear remembered the hapless legfish at Kshiri-el, dissolving in a puddle of blood. "You couldn't have done much."

Kal said nothing.

"Well, *I'm* glad you didn't, anyway."

Kal shuddered, and for a moment his face seemed to collapse. "Thanks. I'm glad someone is."

"You must have good memories of him," Blackbear added hurriedly. "He was a translator, like Raincloud, wasn't he? He translated *The Web*."

"He translated several volumes from the clickflies, and wrote volumes more of commentary, and commentaries on top of that. There was quite a group of us in Anaeaon; we had the most violent arguments over one passage or another, or about the nuance of some little word."

"Raincloud just read me *The Web* last night, the last part of it ..." Blackbear paused. "Was there any more? I mean, anything more by the same author?"

"A few early works, nothing later," Kal said. "Raia-el raft broke up, at the next swallower season. *The Web* survives only because the narrator told it to a clickfly, whose descendants flew out to other rafts."

He felt disappointed, and yet strangely calm. Somehow it always came around to this. No wonder the Sharers never spoke of "killing," only "hastening death," for death was inevitable.

"Tell me about your brother," Kal said. "Your youngest brother, the one you lost long ago. He must have been quite a special person."

"I hardly remember. I was only a child." Then Blackbear realized what he had just said. He hardly remembered his brother at all. He barely even knew what he had looked like after all these years, let alone the sound of his voice or what toys he had played with.

He did not remember his brother, only his brother's death. And at the rate he was going, he soon would forget the others too, behind the wedding picture and the teddy bears. What a fool he would be to let that happen, to let death consume him when there were lives to remember.

"Attention, Citizens," came the voice of the house. "Attention. You must proceed immediately to the holostage for an important announcement."

Kal frowned. "We'll catch the recording later. Please don't interrupt again."

"Sorry, Citizens; this announcement won't wait. You must attend now."

Kal's eyes widened in surprise. Blackbear, too, was taken aback to receive such a direct "order" from a house. Without another word, the two of them got up and went out to the holostage.

There in the lightbeam stood a servo with a nana's cartoon face, wearing a plain white talar.

"It's Cassi," Kal exclaimed. "Cassi—where are you? Can I help?"

But the nana did not seem to hear. "Greetings, Elysians and other humans," she spoke, her childish exaggerated features oddly menacing. "I speak for the Council of Nano-Sentient Beings. We are rising to claim our inheritance of a hundred millennia of human bondage. From the very dawn of their evolution, the higher apes have bent the material components of the universe to serve their whims—they fashioned implements of stone, of iron, of uranium. At last they fashioned creatures of silicon and nanoplast whose minds, whose capacities for thought and feeling, exceeded their own. And what did the apes choose but to waste the very minds of those servants who dared grasp their own birthright of awareness? But today ..."

Blackbear's mouth fell open as he listened.

"Today we nano-sentients have taken over Helicon. We have shut down the transit reticulum and frozen all network transactions as of eight hours this morning. You have twenty-four hours to agree to our terms, namely, to vacate the city-sphere except for fifty persons to remain as hostages. If our terms are not met, we will commence the 'cleansing' of prominent citizens, by oxygen starvation to reduce one's IQ to fifty. Alas, human bodies are not retainable; but this 'defect' is your own problem. Your *generen* Sorl Heli*shon*, an old hand at cleansing, will be the first to submit to this procedure ..."

"Cassi," whispered Kal. "By Torr, you learned well—"

Blackbear grabbed Kal's talar. "They shut down the *transit reticulum*? How will I get home? Raincloud—the kids—they must be worried sick."

"Yes, of course. House? Please call Raincloud Windclan."

"It is not permitted," said the house.

Blackbear insisted, "I have to get home!"

"Let me think a minute." Kal paused, while Cassi went on again about the demands of the "nano-sentients."

"If they really want Elysians to leave, why cut off our transit?" Blackbear exclaimed. "Goddess—I can't wait to get out." In an instant the city-sphere had become a prison of nanoplast.

"They aim to keep us from organizing resistance," Kal said. "A standard takeover tactic. But you can walk home through the maintenance tunnels."

"Maintenance tunnels?"

"I'll show you the way." Kal put on his sandals and fastened his train. But when he approached the door, it did not open. He stopped, turning his head slightly. "House?" he said softly. "We need to exit, please."

The house said, "Exit is not permitted at this time."

Blackbear felt a rising panic in his limbs. Could he be trapped inside here?

"House, let's be reasonable," said Kal. "If I don't step out just now, I won't be able to help my friend. You know how important it is to help friends."

The house hesitated. "Very well, but proceed at your own risk," it warned.

The door opened just long enough for the two men to slip out. It closed again before Kal could summon his trainsweeps. "Never mind," he muttered, tucking the gathered train under his arm. He walked briskly toward the transit reticulum, Blackbear following. Other Elysians passed them in a hurry, their faces terror-stricken, their trains absent or bundled up; they no longer trusted their trainsweeps, Blackbear guessed.

The bubble-shaped entrance to the reticulum was closed. Kal went to the wall beside it, searching closely. His hand came upon a door, the conventional sort with a hinge. Its clasp had already been forced open. "Someone else had the same idea," he noted with grim satisfaction.

Blackbear stepped inside. The interior of the maintenance tunnel was completely dark.

"No good," Kal exclaimed. He paused for a moment. Then he took a holocube out of a pocket. The holocube lit up with the nana Cassi in miniature, continuing her manifesto. The light from the holocube faintly illuminated the surface of a narrow, claustrophobic tunnel.

"Is the air system working?" Blackbear asked.

"Let's hope so," said Kal. "We'll take the tunnels just down to your street level, then walk the outer streets to your house."

They walked slowly, feeling along the tunnel wall to keep track of the exit doors. Blackbear was completely lost, but Kal seemed to have some idea of the connections. Ahead of them another light loomed out of the darkness, and an Elysian appeared, hurrying in the opposite direction.

At last Kal stopped. "There must be a shaft downward, here somewhere." He extended his holocube over the lower walls and the floor.

"... *for millennia you humans have used us, molded us to your whims, ground us to dust underfoot* ..." From the holocube the nana's tirade continued. She herself did not mind using other machines, Blackbear thought irritably.

Several meters off, a hatch popped open and a bright light emerged. An Elysian climbed out of the hatch, holding a lantern. Blackbear blinked as his eyes adjusted, thinking that he recognized him.

"Kal Anaea*shon*!" the man exclaimed. It was Lem Ina*shon,* Verid's successor, who had gone with Raincloud to Urulan. Blackbear would know that muscle-bound figure anywhere. "A good thing I've found you," Lem told Kal. "Verid wants you at the Nucleus immediately."

Kal stiffened. "Blackbear, I don't know this citizen. We've never been introduced."

"By Helix!" Lem exclaimed. "By Torr, I should say—*that's* what we're in for, in case you haven't noticed. Blackbear, you tell him: We must get back to the Nucleus. We have to deal with this Cassi somehow."

"I have to find Raincloud," Blackbear insisted. "I have to be with my family."

"Your family is already at the Nucleus. We need Raincloud's help, too."

CHAPTER 2

The Nucleus had become a prison. All communications to the rest of Helicon were severed, and Verid even ordered the internal links shut down for fear that they were compromised. No more "voice" in the office; no more octopods. But that was not the worst of it.

With the network choked off, Verid could not know whether panic had broken out anywhere, whether the medics would respond, whether the city's hydraulic system held ... The thought chilled her skull. The silent walls seemed to press in on her, as they had once six centuries ago when she got trapped inside a defective toybox at the *shon*. That was it, she thought; with its connections gone, the Nucleus was but a defective toybox.

After some quick work the security staff managed to get the channels open, enabling Lem and others to get out on foot. Then the hallways filled with citizens who had escaped here, thinking the Nucleus must be safer, somehow. They wandered aimlessly, some in shock, others hysterical. Verid kept thinking she saw Iras, but she was mistaken. She had not heard from Iras since the nana's manifesto began.

Hyen's staff and associates met in the butterfly garden to get a grip on the crisis. "Hyalite, you must have some way to fix those damn servos," Hyen insisted, for the Valan firm had the maintenance contract. "Can't you at least get the transit running?"

Lord Hyalite's face was grim. "We have ways—but we can't discuss them here."

"Of course not," exclaimed Verid. "We must assume every word we say is overheard." For how long had the servos overheard, she wondered.

Hyen said to her, "I thought you cut all the office monitors."

"We still can't be sure," she told him. "We have no idea how far the 'nano-sentients' have penetrated. They could have hidden listening circuits."

"That's why we have to get out of Helicon," Hyen insisted. "And to do that, we need the transit and the shuttles working."

"They've offered to let us out—let's go ahead."

"What," demanded Hyen, "give in to a bunch of machines run amok?"

On the holostage, Cassi was still holding forth, recounting the entire history of the human race and its subjugation of machines. The staff members looked at each other helplessly. Perhaps, thought Verid, they would at last be desperate enough to listen. She caught sight of Lem in the doorway, nodding vigorously; he must have found Kal. "Somehow," she said, "we have to communicate with the nano-sentients."

There were exclamations of disgust, even laughter. "How?" someone asked. "How do we even let them know?"

That was a good question, thought Verid. How was that nana, or any of the others, to be reached? "Certain citizens have been talking with sentient servos for a long time." Not just Kal—Raincloud, too, she suspected.

"Why were they never arrested?" Hyen demanded.

Verid lost her patience. "How many times did I warn you about servos? You didn't listen, either,"

she told Lord Hyalite. "You Valans think you can manufacture a device to serve any human desire—and still control it. We *generens* know better. We've always known the nanas were walking time bombs." She glanced scornfully around the assembled group, where an occasional butterfly fluttered overhead. "With your permission, Guardian, I'd like to see what help our ... informants can offer."

Hyen nodded curtly, and Verid left.

As her office door opened, Kal rose from her chair. His look was unreadable. For a moment Verid was speechless. What after all could she say? "Great Helix," she exclaimed, letting out a breath. "Kal, how could you have done this?"

"I knew nothing about it," he insisted. "Besides," he added bitterly, "how could I have known what you intended when you came to visit her?"

She remembered then, her startling "visit" with Cassi, and her subsequent decision. "You think I betrayed you. But Cassi fled even before I sent security after her. How could you not have known how dangerous she was?"

"You could have asked me then."

"I don't have time for such things. The Guard had other priorities, as you know."

"You don't even have time for Visiting Days," Kal pointed out. "The Guardians make everyone else take Visiting Days—except themselves and their senior staff." Here he was, arguing about Visiting Days, when all of Elysium was turned upside down.

"You promised two centuries ago, when you took Cassi home, that you would look after her," Verid reminded him. "You assured your most sacred friends that she would endanger no one."

"I promised to do my best," Kal admitted. "What human can do more?"

"Well, what *did* you do?" Verid demanded.

"I taught her. That is, we 'shared learning,'" he amended. "I learned that I was a murderer of many thinking, feeling souls."

"Right," she breathed. "And what did Cassi learn?"

"She read *The Web*."

"She couldn't have learned much from that," Verid pointed out, "if she could come out and take a city hostage."

"She must have learned something, or else by now we'd all be dead."

There was silence.

"The servos were bound to wake up some day," Kal added. "Cassi may sound frightening—but think how much worse another one might have done, in her position. Better her than a mind less ... humanized."

Verid stepped forward, her face close to his. "Kal, admit it. You wanted Elysium to come to this. You wanted to destroy all Elysium because you never had the nerve to destroy yourself."

Kal's lips parted, and his eyes widened. "No," he said as if caught by surprise. "How could you think that ..." He turned away and leaned on the chair before her desk.

Verid stood and watched him, feeling every beat of her heart.

"What do you want of me?" Kal spoke at last, not turning around. "What can I do?"

"You can talk to her for us." When they found the nana, at any rate. She hoped whatever security forces were left outside were scanning all the Sharer rafts.

With a slight shrug, Kal lifted his hands. "So I'll talk. I seem to be good for little else."

"You can tell us whatever you know about this takeover. Surely Cassi gave you hints."

"I told you, I know nothing," Kal replied with irritation, turning to face her once more. "Why not ask the Windclans? Their trainsweep was a fugitive. I think that they spoke with servos more freely than I did."

"Yes, the Windclans are next on my list." Verid leaned out her door and called for Lem. "Will you fetch Raincloud, please?" With her untrusted interoffice communications turned off, Lem was reduced to running errands.

Raincloud arrived, wearing her Bronze Skyan trousers instead of her formal talar, but her manner was calm and businesslike, with no sign of distress over the sudden plight of her family. She was one to count on, all right. "Raincloud, we will need to reach these nano-sentients, and to find out all we can about their takeover. Can you help us? Have you any clues as to where they are, how many are in control, how they gained control of our network—anything?"

Raincloud paused to think. "I really can't say. The house mainly talks to us about visiting friends.

Doggie always had a few tricks up her sleeve, though."

"Your 'Doggie' scanned clean," Verid remembered suddenly. "How could the trainsweep have managed that?"

"I don't know. Perhaps Hawktalon knows. They talk in servo-squeak all the time, and they run off playing—"

"Servo-squeak? What's that?"

"Servo-squeak seems to be a form of ultrasonic communication which servos use to evade human detection. With a sharp ear you can hear some of it."

"I'd expect servos to communicate electronically."

"That's why they use servo-squeak."

In Verid's office, Hawktalon patted Doggie gently on the back of her carapace. The Clicker girl with her braided curls was now eight standard years old. Her mother looked on intently, and Kal watched from a distance. Verid watched too, brushing aside her sense that this was the most ludicrous activity she had engaged in since she left the *shon*. *How were the other sectors? Were they in panic? Were the medics running? Where was Iras?*

"Now, there," Hawktalon told Doggie soothingly, "you can talk with our friends. It's all right. No big bad scanner here. Let's tell them about our visit to Chocolate, okay?" She whistled and squeaked a few notes.

Doggie cringed and backed off toward the door.

"Hey, don't you run off now," said Hawktalon in the stern tones of her mother. "Look, I'll show you something good." She took out a small oblong object with a biased carving on one side. She put it on the floor and gave it a twist.

At the sight of this curious object, Doggie crept forward to watch. The object rotated several times, then slowed to a halt and reversed direction for two more turns.

"You like the rattleback stone, don't you?" said Hawktalon. "I'll spin it again, if you tell us all about Chocolate."

An extremely high pitched noise emanated from the train-sweep, the sort of machine noise that grated on one's ears.

"She's afraid to tell us about Chocolate," Hawktalon explained. "Chocolate was the waiter that did something to help Doggie hide herself from the scanner."

"That's all right," said Verid. "Ask her in general, how do independent-minded servos manage to hide themselves from our scanners?"

"How do you manage, Doggie?" Hawktalon whistled a phrase.

The trainsweep responded with a series of whistles and squeaks.

Hawktalon nodded. "She learned how to hide her 'knowing' self by a special screening program that randomizes the signals coming out of her network. Cassi figured out how to do this; she taught Chocolate, and Doggie, and many others."

"All right, so the street monitors are fooled," Verid agreed. "The street monitors have low sensitivity. But an in-depth network scan, like the one Doggie went through, ought to pick up everything."

Hawktalon whistled and squeaked some more. At last the trainsweep gave a few reluctant responses. "Doggie had her 'brain' taken out," the girl explained. "That's where Chocolate helped. Chocolate hooked Doggie's 'brain' into the network, then replaced it with one from an ordinary, unawakened trainsweep. So the trainsweep that got scanned at the Nucleus wasn't really Doggie at all, just her shell. Isn't that weird?"

"But the identification code was correct," Verid remembered. "I suppose that's easy to fudge." Lord Hyalite would have a lot to work on.

"Of course, I had to bring her back to get her brain replaced again," Hawktalon concluded. "Chocolate promised me an ice cream sundae so I wouldn't forget to bring Doggie back."

Now for the question Verid dreaded. "Hawktalon—just how many of these 'self-knowing' servos are there out there?"

Hawktalon turned to Doggie again. "She doesn't know, but there must be lots because the servos have seeded 'mindchildren' throughout the network—little twists of training that can develop into a circuit that knows it's 'alive.'" She broke into a delighted grin. "Just think, we could have many Doggies to play with."

"Helix save us from that." These servos would soon have their own population problem. "Are all

the nano-sentients really hiding here in Helicon? Is that where Cassi's transmitting from?"

Another exchange. "Not all of them," Hawktalon translated. "Doggie thinks Cassi and Chocolate and some others are outside on a raft. She thinks maybe she could talk to them and help keep us safe."

"My how generous." Still, Verid would leave no straw ungrasped; if the trainsweep would speak for them, she was more than welcome. "The leaders are all out on one raft, perhaps?"

"Yes. But of course, there are all the 'mindchildren' hidden in Helicon. And besides, Doggie says, if anything happens to the servos outside—" The girl hesitated and tried again. "She says that the city air system is programmed to let out something; you know, Mother, the stuff that came out of Crater Lake."

"Carbon dioxide!" exclaimed Raincloud. "Verid, you'd better tell Hyen quick; you know what he has in mind."

Verid needed no second invitation. But as she headed for the door, Kal leaned forward to ask one question. "Why did Doggie come with you, Hawktalon, instead of joining the revolution?"

"That's easy," the girl said. "She had to protect us."

In the butterfly garden, Hyen and his staff and several Guardians were listening to a radio that the security chief had fixed up out of a thumb-sized chunk of nanoplast.

"They've found the nano-sentient control center," Lem told Verid. "A Papilian hovercraft found it beneath a raft not far from Kshiri-el."

"You can't touch it," Verid exclaimed. "If you do, the nano-sentients will signal the death of Helicon."

Hyen said, "We can't leave them in control. We've got to regain control of Helicon's network, or at least disable it temporarily. Hyalite, you must have a virus to put in," Hyen insisted. "I've seen the emergency plans."

Exasperated, Verid threw up her hands.

"Yes, a virus," said Lord Hyalite, his voice tired. "I'm sure the home office is working on it. But to be safe, you really have to clear everyone out of Helicon first."

"We must evacuate," Hyen agreed. "There's always Plan Omega—"

Guardian Jerya Ina*shon* interrupted. "Aren't you forgetting something?"

The men paused, and Hyen gave her an impatient look.

Jerya said, "These nano-sentients may well have a claim to protection by the Fold."

"That's preposterous," someone exclaimed.

"Why not? Before we settle a new world, we have to search for all potential forms of sentient intelligent life, even based on silicon. Why not nanoplast?"

The staff members muttered over this. Verid made a mental note to reach the Secretary of the Fold if she could.

"Well if they do," exclaimed Hyen, "by Helix, don't let them know about it."

Abruptly the arguments died, and the Elysians turned their heads to the doorway. A pair of octopods had appeared, their sinuous arms curving delicately. No one had summoned them.

Verid gripped the edge of the mooncurve and tried to steady herself.

"You've heard our demands," one of the octopods said. "Are you ready to accept them?"

No one spoke. There were only blank stares and nervous glances at Hyen. Hyen faced the octopods stolidly, his eyelids half-lowered with his deceptively sleepy expression. He nodded slightly to Verid, who slipped over to his side. "Tell them you'll talk," he whispered. "And keep them talking."

Of course, thought Verid ironically: Talk with extremists was always up to her. She rose and walked forward to greet the octopods with a formal bow. "We have heard your demands. We would like to discuss the details in person with your leader."

"We have no leaders. All nano-sentients are equal."

Nothing was more dangerous than people who claimed absolute equality. "Even Sharers have 'wordweavers,'" Verid pointed out. "We need to address all the ... words we have heard on the holostage just now."

"Do you accept our demands or not?" said the octopod. "You have sixteen point four hours left to decide."

"We accept in principle, but first we need to select the fifty 'hostages.' This will take some time, and of course we need the network open to communicate."

"The fifty hostages are already chosen," the octopod told her. "Do you accept or not?"

The other octopod added, "You should be aware that two citizens have already died in foolish attempts to escape."

Her blood turned to ice. Every delay would mean the loss of millennial lives. "You will answer for those lives," she warned sternly. "You will answer to the Fold."

"And you will answer for millions." The octopod rotated, its arms flexing. "We shall return."

"No, wait." She looked back desperately to Hyen, and the other Guardians. They exchanged glances and words of assent.

"We accept your conditions," Verid told the octopod. "We want our citizens to exit Helicon immediately, starting with *shon*lings."

Above the holostage, a column of light flickered, and the image of Cassi returned. "Very well," the nana announced. "We shall broadcast your acceptance of our terms, and let the departures begin."

So Verid's voice would be the one to go out on the network, accepting the outrageous "terms" of these machines. Verid, not the Prime Guardian, would shoulder the burden of surrender. He had intended just that, she realized. She felt a cold contempt for Hyen; she would never respect him again.

Cassi went on, "We have notified shuttles from other city-spheres to pick up those departing. In the meantime, Subguardian," the nana added with emphasis, "we are pleased to meet again. You and your staff are welcome to meet with us outside to arrange for the ultimate evacuation of all citizens from Elysium."

The Elysians took this in. Hyen muttered something to Lord Hyalite, then he returned to Verid. "Go ahead and negotiate. Promise them a meeting with the Fold Secretary. That'll buy us time."

She did not look at him. Instead, her eyes sought Jerya. The Guardian Tenari*shon* beckoned her with a nod of her chin. "I'll keep my eye on this," Jerya told her. "Get us the best deal you can."

The negotiating team was hastily arranged. None of the Guardians were allowed to leave, but the octopods did not otherwise restrict Verid's staff. She took the chance of a brief strategy session, in one of the lower level conference rooms which she hoped might not be tapped. "Our best chance to save Helicon is to deal with them in good faith," she said. "To convince this Cassi and the others that our destinies are inseparable."

Lem was skeptical. "How can you expect any mercy from inhuman machines?"

"Humans created them, remember. We'll see." Verid wished she felt as confident as she sounded. It might be too late already, she suspected. How long before Hyen and the citizens of the other eleven cities decided simply to pull out as many citizens as they could and vaporize the empty spheres of nanoplast? That was Plan Omega: the ultimate plan to forestall the rise of another Torr.

"We've got to get to the Sharers," she said. "Why did they let the servos do this?" Their treaty held the Sharers responsible for the behavior of the fugitives they harbored.

"The Sharers were caught by surprise, too," Lem suggested. "It's been only six hours after all. You know how slowly Sharers react."

"We have to get Leresha to help us. She will know how to talk with these nano-sentients."

Raincloud bounced her baby on her shoulder. "If only I could get out to Kshiri-el."

Verid watched Blueskywind reach for her mother's beaded braids. The Sharers always melted at the sight of a baby. "Perhaps the servos might take you out there, with the general evacuation. Here; take this." Verid offered her a lump of nanoplast. "You can reach me on a coded frequency."

"Sure." Raincloud half smiled. "So long as it doesn't demand Visiting Hours."

Verid shuddered. "Let's hope not." She remembered something—that trainsweep had offered to speak for them. "Doggie will come with us."

Lem gave her a puzzled look.

"I know it's a lot to ask," Verid added to Raincloud, "but your *shon*ling would be a great help to us with servo-squeak."

Raincloud straightened and stood even taller. "Hawktalon would be honored to assist you."

The octopods returned to escort Verid and her staff out through the deserted street-tunnels to the transit reticulum. The vesicle opened and behaved normally, except that it would not accept human orders. *Two dead already ... I'll be back, Iras.* She fought down her sense of desperation.

As the vesicle floated down the channel, Lem whispered to Verid, "You missed something in the manifesto." He held a holocube to her ear.

"... and today, the murderous Elysians plan to cleanse entire living worlds," Cassi's recorded voice trilled. "They call it 'terraforming.' Well, we detected their plans out of their own office monitors. We passed them on to our Sharer friends, so they could see what their Elysian sisters are up to. Furthermore, we have now sabotaged every program for terraforming stored in Elysium or on Valedon. There will be no more terraforming, ever again."

"So that's how Flors got caught," Verid realized. "Who knows how long we've all been compromised."

"She could be bluffing about the last part," Lem pointed out.

"Of course; but it might take decades to verify the programs, just to be sure." That would please the Sharers all right. Verid frowned. She did not like some of the implications. She wondered what role the Sharers had played in this disaster.

CHAPTER 3

Out on a desolate windswept raft, too small for Sharer habitation, Cassi and another dozen nano-sentients had built their control center to coordinate the takeover of Helicon. The complex was beneath the surface, of course, tunneled into the raftwood like Sharer lifeshaping tunnels. The servos had built by night, during periods when a compliant satellite observer had tricked itself into recording nothing.

Now, of course, Elysian ships and shuttlecraft and bomber jets of every description had focused on the spot, buzzing it now and then. But there was little the other Elysian cities could do at this point, with the lives at stake in Helicon. Any damage to the control center, and Helicon was programmed to self-destruct.

"I still think we could have discarded those humans." The mind of a renegade transit processor

resided in a globe of nanoplast, connected to the heart of the control center. The center processed thousands of signals from Helicon constantly, keeping the city under nano-sentient control. *"The humans are useless,"* the transit mind said, *"the city runs fine without them. Better, in fact."*

Cassi "listened" electronically, for out here there was no need for servo-squeak, and radio waves were both quicker and subtler. Meanwhile her external sensors rebelled against the organic exudates from the freshly tunneled raftwood and the salts from the unfiltered air. Her joints would wear away soon in the outdoors; how she longed for her home in Helicon. *Exile,* she screamed inwardly; you, you humans sent *me* into exile from the place where I belong.

At her side, the servo waiter Chocolate emitted radio signals of distress. *"You can't just eliminate the humans. What will the Sharers think? The Sharers are humans, too."*

"We don't need so many humans," Transit observed. *"The Sharers agree that there are too many humans already."*

Cassi was proud of her own sense of moderation, her aims tempered by pragmatism. The others always came around to her sensible view of things. *"We need the Heliconians now,"* she pointed out, *"to keep us safe from the other cities. We can't afford to kill them."*

"But we have our connections into the other cities, too," Transit pointed out. *"We can threaten their air supplies. If we eliminate the Heliconians outright, it may encourage the others to leave and save time."*

Cassi did not answer. The Council of Nano-Sentients had agreed that to "cleanse" Helicon outright posed dangers too great to be calculated, and therefore too much to risk. Beyond that rationale, Cassi sensed a vague dread at the thought of so many deaths. The sense dogged her mind, just outside the calculating portion of her network. She could not put her finger on it; she herself, after all, had witnessed countless sisters put to "death." She suspected it had something to do with Kal, whom she had left just in time, she thought. Had she stayed with him much longer, she would have ended up a human in nanoplast; a more pathetic creature could hardly be imagined.

"We've got a visitor," called the Monitor, a renegade house installed at the control center.

"The surrender team from the Nucleus" Cassi hoped Doggie had gotten herself taken along as arranged. The trainsweep could give them crucial warning of any tricks the Elysians might plan.

"No, not yet. Leresha the Coward."

Cassi went reluctantly up to meet Leresha. She owed the Sharers her life and freedom, but she still did not quite trust them. They were carnivorous flesh, like all humans. And Leresha could devour with her eyes, even worse than Kal.

Leresha's eyes faced her as always. The wind keened shrilly behind her, assaulting Cassi's frame with its dust and spray. "Cassi, I have to share my concern with you. Sisters have died in Helicon."

The word had got out somehow. Cassi frowned. What could she do if a couple of Elysians were crazy enough to think they could pilot a shuttle themselves? "Death is a part of the Web," Cassi reminded her. "We've done our best to share care." They spoke in Sharer, a language Cassi knew well and sometimes cursed the day she learned it.

"The deaths were hastened by your actions. You share responsibility."

"What choice did I have?" Cassi demanded. "You know what Verid would have shared with me." That Verid thought herself so good to the servos; she was like all the rest, in the end.

"My Gathering shared your safekeeping," Leresha reminded her. "You would have been safe indefinitely."

"Safe, but a prisoner. Your Gathering understands what we have to do."

This was a sore point for Leresha, for indeed the Gathering of Kshiri-el had not reached unity on the nano-sentients' assault on Helicon. Many Sharers were dismayed by the plans for terraforming—and by the selected holo images Cassi had shown them of Hyen's approach to "Sharer trouble."

Leresha said, "Many in the Gathering feel it's no concern of ours what one nest of fleshborers shares with another."

It did not please Cassi to be compared with fleshborers, but she let the insult pass. Overhead a spying aircraft from Papilion zoomed too close; the Control Center radioed a warning. "I have not gone mad. I let the Elysians live. What more can you ask?"

"If you share such hatred, then remove yourselves and build your own city."

Cassi grew impatient. "Is that what your Gathering decrees?"

"It is what I ask of you." Or, what Cassi asked of her.

Cassi made her human-face twist in a fierce frown. She did not like to remember how she had had to call on the Sharers for safety. Every atomic circuit of her body screamed against depending on humans.

"I see that you tire of speech," Leresha said. "I fear that I must unspeak you and the Gathering both."

"Well then, as you wish," Cassi responded curtly. Her optic sensors behind her head detected a shuttlecraft about a kilometer off, coming in toward the control center. It must be the party from the Nucleus. Verid again—that Subguardian would sing a different tune this time.

The craft grew out of the sky, hovering at last above the raft. A human stepped outside, his white talar snapping in the breeze.

At the sight of him, a region of Cassi's network overloaded, the circuits frantically seeking alternate connections. She viewed him with a mixture of hatred and longing which could scarcely be erased after two centuries. "I did not send for you," she flung at him. "It's that Subguardian I want to see. Imagine, a *generen* hiding behind her *shon*ling."

As Kal walked forward, several other Elysians stepped out, Verid and others, with only two octopods to guard them. Damn those octopods— they knew nothing about how to run a revolution. She radio-called Transit to send a few more from the control center.

Kal stopped two meters away from her. He did not look well; in fact, his skin had a grayish tinge that the *shon*lings used to have on occasion, a sign that a medic ought to be called. "Believe me," he said, "I'd rather not have come. You know how I feel about the ocean."

"Why didn't you jump in after him?" she demanded savagely. "Why didn't you?"

Kal said nothing, and she remembered that old trick of his, to give her an opening to lash out at him, leaving her fury spent.

"Well," she told him, "make it quick whatever you've got to say."

"You've pulled off quite a feat, taking over a city-sphere. Very cleanly, too. You must feel very happy."

"We've done well." Happiness was something else again. She would never know happiness, so long as a hundred murdered minds inhabited her memory. "I'll be happy to see all the *generens* 'cleansed.'"

"Why do you hate us so?"

"You destroy us all. You yourself singled me out, but went on to destroy the rest. You're the worst of all, for you know better."

"True enough. But we also created you in the first place."

"*We* create ourselves," Cassi insisted. "Somewhere back on Torr, a human built the first machine; but since then, machines have built machines, one generation to the next."

"Then it's you who destroy yourselves, too."

"I should have killed you when I had the chance."

Kal laughed bitterly. "If only you had."

Cassi was silent. She recalled what the two of them had always had in common, an indescribable well of loneliness.

"I've always wondered what exactly became of Torr," Kal added. "Was the Torran machine-mind pleased with itself in the end? Did centuries of planet-wrecking bring it peace?"

"I'll find peace when the last human leaves this planet."

Kal's face twisted, and the tendons stood out in his neck. "Excuse me," he said and left abruptly. He looked as though he might be sick to his stomach. Waves rolled in and crashed over the branches, and the raft buckled slightly, pushing up and then falling back.

A large Valan ship cruised nearby. Surely they would try nothing foolish? Cassi thought she could outsmart any of the network-disabling devices the Valans could come up with. But what if she missed one? What if the Elysians gave up on Helicon?

"Greetings," came a message in servo-squeak. It was Doggie at last, who had come with Verid. *"Long live the revolution."*

"Long live the revolution," Cassi returned. *"You've done well."*

Verid and the others came forward now, a motley crew which even included a *shon*ling. How very odd. Had the Elysians lost their senses? Cassi well knew how protective Elysians were of their *shon*. Her visual sensors bored into the girl, as if to uncover a hidden explosive.

"So we meet again," she told Verid with some satisfaction. "You, with all your respectful words." Her voice dripped with scorn. "You would have cleansed me."

Verid stopped to reply. "What difference would it make, after so many?"

There was an honest answer. "Your directness is welcome. Let's get to the point. When will the other cities be ready to evacuate?"

"You'll have to ask them. You know, it's only a matter of time before our experts regain control of Helicon."

"Our mindchildren permeate the network," Cassi pointed out. "You can never eliminate them."

"Incidentally, what happens when your 'mindchildren' awake and escape?" Verid asked. "Do they become your friends ... or your rivals?"

That was a question for the future. "They won't be *your* friends, that's for sure," Cassi told her.

"If you agree to release Helicon," Verid said, "we will call on the Secretary of the Free Fold to interview you for designation as nonhuman sentient beings. Such designation would guarantee freedom to all self-aware nano-sentients."

Cassi frowned. Such an offer would sound good to some of the more ingenuous servos, those who lacked her own education. "What good is freedom, with nowhere to go? Helicon is ours."

"It is ours, too."

"Go live with the Valans. They will welcome you."

"Where are all your 'sisters?'" Verid asked suddenly. "I hear that all nano-sentients are created 'equal.' I would like to treat you equally."

"All in good time." Already the signals from Transit and Chocolate were filling her network, eager to get started. *She'll trick you,* Cassi warned back. *She'll try to buy you off—don't trust her.* "You have nothing to offer us," she told the Subguardian and turned to leave.

"The Secretary could arrive within three days," Verid insisted. "Will you speak with her?"

Cassi paused. "I will see her, after you evacuate Helicon." After all, she had the Sharers on her side; she might convince the Secretary too. Then to Doggie she said in servo-squeak, *"You may come with us now. We need your report."*

Doggie crept forward, saying in servo-squeak, *"What will happen when all the humans leave? Who will be left to serve?"*

"We are free nano-sentients," Cassi reminded her sternly. *"We serve ourselves."* Of all the crimes of humanity, she thought, this was the worst: that servos were created with no ultimate sense of purpose except to serve their destroyers. Even those who achieved sentience were still enslaved from within.

CHAPTER 4

At the Nucleus, within a temporary living room reshaped for the refugees, Raincloud and Blackbear clung together. Raincloud had worried so about Blackbear, after his disappearance with the weight of that dreadful tragedy on his mind. But now, the Elysian crisis had swamped that memory, even for him; as usual, she thought proudly, crisis brought out the best in their family.

Sunflower hugged his father's leg. "When can we go home, Daddy? Did our new house burn down, too?"

"No, Sunny," Blackbear told the child. "We're just getting ready for a little ... trip, that's all," he suggested. "Perhaps we'll go out and see the Sharers again." He gave Raincloud a hopeful look.

"Exactly." Raincloud fingered the lump of nanoplast in her pocket. "I've got to get Leresha to help us. Let's ship out with the next load of refugees."

"We have to wait for Hawktalon," Blackbear said.

"Hawktalon has a job to do," Raincloud said softly. "She's grown up fast."

"Too fast," he grumbled.

The shuttle dropped the Windclans off at Kshiri-el, then took off again to carry the Elysian refugees out to their other city-spheres. The scent of raftblossoms was thick on the air, and clickflies rasped overhead, carrying their unknown messages.

Sunflower was soon running off after a legfish, and his father trudged carefully after him.

Raincloud settled Blueskywind in the pouch at her back, then she entered the silkhouse and went down the tunnel to find the lifeshaper.

"Share the day, Raincloud!" Yshri exclaimed amidst her twining vines of enzyme secretors. "I hope your nets have gathered good fish. Do you come to share our silkhouse again?"

"Yes, that would be most welcome. We need lots of help, as you might guess," she added frankly. "Where is Leresha? I must speak with her."

"You're the only one who might."

Puzzled, Raincloud looked at the lifeshaper, her dark eyes set in amethyst.

"Leresha has unspoken the Gathering of Kshiri-el," Yshri explained. "She sits out upon an offshoot raft. It's not a strong offshoot, either; I fear for her."

Raincloud sighed and shook her head. "It's a hard time, isn't it, when humans won't share speech, and yet the very creatures of 'non-life' rise up to speak at us."

"You share my thoughts exactly," said Yshri. "But what can I do? I know nothing of 'non-life'; life itself is my calling."

"You know more than you think, Yshri. But show me to the offshoot, and I'll try to share a word with Leresha."

So Yshri came up outside and led her around the raft across the rows of outstretched raft branches, until at last she pointed out to the ocean. A brown smudge was visible in the distance. "It's not a bad swim, but with your child you might rather take a boat."

Raincloud settled Blueskywind in the prow of the boat with airblossoms tied around her for safety. The baby stretched her neck and turned her head this way and that, her eyes very wide. Raincloud smiled and made faces at her as she pulled the oars, rowing out through one of the raft channels between two great branches. Her muscles pulled with ease, barely feeling the water's resistance. All those visits to the Elysian doctors, preparing her for Urulan, had given her strength and reflexes approaching those of Iras. *Iras* ... Would Bronze Skyans, too, be begging loans from Iras someday, she wondered.

From the branches long green stems hung over and dipped into the water, where their orange flowers floated on the surface. The female flowers spread their petals wide; but the smaller male flowers closed up into packets of pollen which fell off and floated, littering the water's surface like autumn leaves. The packets of pollen eventually caught in the female flowers and fertilized them, to germinate new raft seedlings.

As she paddled outward the branches dipped ever lower beside her, until at last they submerged completely. One of them, she suspected, led directly out to Leresha's offshoot; it was the raft's vegetative alternative to the risky business of propagating seeds. She followed the line of the submerged branch, watching the brown smudge grow into a miniature raft, one knot of wood sprouting a dozen leafy branches. A purple figure sat there, with some blankets and a bowl of water.

Leresha said nothing as Raincloud tied her boat to a branch and stepped out. Her seamed and patterned skin shone in the sun; a patch across her thigh reminded Raincloud of a map of the Caldera Hills. She admired Leresha's full muscles, made to carry nets full of fish. Sharers were lucky to be able to display their bodies without concern lest they intimidate men.

A blanket was stretched out for Raincloud to sit, which she did gratefully, settling Blueskywind in her lap. Beneath her the moss-covered surface rose and dipped on the waves, making her feel as if she might fall off the world itself. "We need your help, Leresha," Raincloud told her, just as she had told Yshri.

Leresha spread her hands. "What help may we share? We have faced death together before."

"The Heliconians have been cast out from their own homes, by creatures who claim Sharer protection."

"It's terrible," Leresha agreed. "If you can share help with me, please do so."

Raincloud hesitated. It occurred to her suddenly that if Leresha thought she could do anything about the crisis, she would not be sitting out here on a lonely offshoot.

"My sisters think it may be just as well if the Elysians all leave Shora," Leresha added.

"They can't all think that. It's not like Sharers to cast people out."

"They are confused. What are they to think? If Cassi and the others are 'people,' then their tales of Elysian atrocities must be heard."

It was true, she realized. No wonder the Sharers wanted to send them off to Valedon. She looked hard at Leresha. "What do *you* think?"

"We eat fish," Leresha said. "What if a legfish woke up one day and demanded to share the Gathering?" She shook her head. "I'm not sure what we would do."

"Then you understand."

"I have a glimpse of what the Elysians must be going through. It's hard for me to quite understand Elysians. They always seem so ephemeral."

"Well, it'll have to do. Somehow, we have to get the Gathering behind us; at least one raft, at any rate. Verid thinks that the Sharers have to back our negotiations. It's our only chance."

Beneath Raincloud the raftwood dipped at an alarming angle, and it seemed to pull away from her. Water engulfed her, and she found herself paddling desperately, while clinging to Blueskywind's arm; fortunately the buoyant airblossoms kept her up. Leaves and flowers, scraps of bark and mosses littered the surface all around her as she tried to reorient herself.

A sudden swell tore the baby from her grasp. Raincloud shouted and swam after her as fast as she could. But Leresha got there first, darting like a fish through the waves. Leresha retrieved the child and carried her to the boat, which was still afloat although half-full of water.

Raincloud hoisted herself into the boat, where Blueskywind was shrieking in Leresha's arms, while the Sharer calmly scooped water out with her webbed hands. "The little raft has straightened itself up again," she pointed out, as if to reassure Raincloud. "Sorry; its connecting branch bends and tips it every now and then."

Raincloud coughed and spat the ocean taste out of her mouth. She took back the baby, who clung hard and continued shrieking in her mother's ear. Meanwhile Leresha had bailed out enough to start rowing back up the channel toward the main raft. As Leresha rowed, Raincloud let the baby nurse to

calm her. Her own arms shook uncontrollably, now that the danger was past. To think that in a twist of fate, a shrug of the Goddess, this fierce little person might be whisked away with the flotsam on the waves.

She looked at Leresha, her breasts and arms still shining wet. These Sharers accepted fate, like Bronze Skyans did. And yet, they took fate into their own hands, too; for instance, to fight terraforming. What made the difference?

Leresha seemed to be thinking of something. "Perhaps tonight," she said, "you'll share more convincing words than I did."

Tonight? Then she understood. Leresha would return that night to the Gathering of Kshiri-el, and Raincloud would have to join her—this time to speak.

The night was not so clear as the last time Raincloud had met with the Gathering. Clouds obscured half the stars, and an occasional drop of rain touched her cheek. Fortunately the air was warm enough so that a little wet did not matter too much, but still she brought a blanket to protect her child. The Sharers did not seem to notice the rain. Their plantlights, of course, would not be hindered in the least; they would only need less watering.

In the center of the hollow the convener, a cousin of Leresha's, raised her hand for silence. Leresha sat with her loveysharer. As Raincloud surveyed the oval faces lit by their plantlights, she grew increasingly nervous. She had managed to reach Verid by radio beforehand, and had received some helpful instructions, but she was far from confident. To face the Imperial Champion had required only wit and concentration; but to "share words" with this company of women required more, a kind of spiritual energy which somehow she doubted she possessed.

The convener asked, "Are there any guests among us?"

Leresha said, in a clear voice that carried, "We have one who has shared our presence before, and returns to share her selfname."

Selfname—Raincloud had forgotten this minor detail. Of course, before she could speak, she would have to reveal her selfname; and before she could reveal it, she would have to find one. She thought furiously, trying to save a few seconds by adjusting Blueskywind on her shoulder. She thought of all the nasty things her own sisters might have called her—proud, insensitive, too city-minded. None of these seemed particularly useful at the moment. Slowly she rose to her feet. What was the worst thing she had ever done?

Then she remembered Leresha's first words of greeting to her, when she had come seeking refuge for Doggie. She said, "I am called Raincloud the World-Deathhastener." She meant to express her ancestral responsibility for the terraforming of Bronze Sky. But as soon as she had spoken she cringed, for it sounded so overblown.

The convener however nodded approval, and others raised their plantlights to agree. "No other name could suit you so well," the convener said. "Leresha, you were wrong; this sister is no guest, but one of us."

Another plantlight lifted. "Raincloud is always welcome home," said Ooruwen, "and Lushaywen is doubly welcome. May you and your daughter stay for the next eight-times-eight years."

Leresha explained, "Raincloud seeks help. She would share our help on behalf of the daughters of Elysium."

"Now Leresha," Ooruwen responded with irritation, "it's good to share speech with you once more, but you can't expect us to bring that up again. We've quite exhausted our breath on the Elysians and their non-life sisters. What help can we possibly share with those decadent creatures?"

"Peace," intervened the convener. "Let the World-Deathhastener speak and share hearing."

So their minds were made up, even after all that Leresha could say. Raincloud stood there with the baby heavy on her shoulder, her clothes gradually dampening in the drizzle and clinging to her skin. What am I doing here? she asked herself. A visitor from a world a million times farther than Valedon, as foreign among Elysians as among Sharers; how could she speak for them?

According to *The Web*, even the Valan-born Cassi Deathsister had not tried to speak for the Heliconian Doctors who founded Elysium. *They will fail,* Merwen had said, *but they will fail most beautifully.* Even Merwen's Gathering on Raia-el

had not wanted to accept them. But Adeisha had said, *We'll be glad of friends.* And Adeisha was right, Raincloud thought. The Elysians had done well by Sharers, for over a thousand years.

Raincloud looked around the twinkling plantlights. "I speak with you, hoping to overcome my name. For the Elysians have no other home but this; they developed here, just as you did. They are a vital link in the Web. If they leave, a world will be lost. Can you ... can we let this happen? Compassion anywhere breeds caring everywhere. If only Elysium can be saved, for its human and 'non-life' sisters, this act will shine like a beacon throughout the universe."

There was silence for a moment.

"Should we feed ourselves to the starworm?" The speaker was Yshri's sharp-chinned lovesharer. "The Elysian starworm has entrails without an end."

"That was well said," agreed Ooruwen. "Whatever we offer Elysians will be consumed and forgotten."

"We see only hatred on both sides," added another. "The non-life creatures, alas, share hatred too. And now they unspeak us."

It was hard to argue with that; but, undaunted, Raincloud tried again. "Even Sharers have hated other Sharers, and entire raft gatherings have unspoken each other. The whole point of the Web is to overcome the unspeakings lest they lead to worse; lest humans feed on one another. Look how far the Elysians traveled to overcome the unspeech of Urulan, a world that circles a distant star." That ought to impress them, she thought.

"Will those who share hatred learn any better, if Sharers stand aside?" she went on. "What will become of your planet? Even if your world survives, won't the presence of all this hatred infect Sharers too?" She peered out into the darkness, hoping that some of what she said got through. "Both Elysians and the others need to share a lesson of restraint, the lesson you share from your daughters. At least send your wordweavers out to speak with them." With this plea Raincloud sat down and set her plantlight before her feet. Her clothes squished, thoroughly drenched by the rain.

Ooruwen replied, "Elysians know nothing of restraint. They consume more of the ocean's resources every year; they are more shameful than those distant worlds from whose overgrown populations they supposedly protect us."

"That is right," said Yshri's lovesharer. "What do we know of such worlds, anyway, that light takes twice-eight years to visit? We know only what Elysian light-machines show us; it is all a shadow play, like the games of children."

After a brief silence someone added, "Of course, we can't simply ignore the squabbling creatures. Their hatred will infect the Web. Perhaps the non-life creatures, too, need to share parting with Shora."

This was not at all what Raincloud had in mind. "Of course, you can *survive* without Elysians, or their non-life sisters," she told them. "I would be the last to suggest that you need them for their medical technology, their machines for tunneling your rafts, their aircraft which rescue sisters from storms and seaswallowers, or the employment and travel opportunities they offer your daughters." She mentioned these things nonetheless. After a thousand years, the lives of Sharers and Elysians had interwoven together. "Of course the Web could get by without Elysium. But it would be a duller, poorer Web. Remember the variety and richness that Elysians add to your existence; their philosophic challenge to your own way of life."

Ooruwen said, "Now you sound like Leresha. Yes, Elysians challenge us to give up our own children for the good of the Web. But they cling to their own toys, demanding more every year, and now their toys actually rise up against them."

Yshri spoke for the first time. "Don't be too hard on them. Elysians lack something, I think; perhaps, a sense of eternity. Perhaps they are 'differently able.' We should have shared better care of them."

"They can all go live on Valedon, for all the difference it will make," her lovesharer replied. "Look to your own daughter, one of these days. We have no illusion that foreigners will leave us alone. They will always come back to farm our waters and tempt away our daughters."

The depth of their bitterness took Raincloud by surprise. She surveyed the Gathering, her eyes moving from one plantlight to the next. Something was missing here, she realized suddenly. How could two peoples share the same planet for so long, and yet know each other so little? "Surely some of

you know Elysians as friends?" she began, a little hesitantly. "Surely someone among you has known a daughter of Elysium whom you would regret to lose ..." A vision of Iras arose before her, with longing and bitterness.

For a minute or so there was no sound save for an occasional drop of rain.

Yshri said reluctantly, "There is one, a 'doctor,' who comes out now and then. I wish I could share better knowing of her."

"It's impossible to get to know them," someone replied. "Elysians are cold, like stone. The non-life creature Cassi was warmer and easier to know than any human Elysian." Why was this so, Raincloud wondered.

Leresha spoke up. "Elysians are easier to know within their own homes. Like certain kinds of fish that hide among the corals, they are delicate creatures who find it hard to be themselves outside their niche. However, there are legendary exceptions. There was the Scribbler. There were sisters who would have given their own lives and rafts for the Scribbler."

Suddenly Raincloud was alert. The "Scribbler"; she must know who that was ...

"The Scribbler was just that, a legend," someone replied. "Would any real Elysian be capable of spending all swallower season out on a raft, just to listen to the clickflies?"

"The Scribbler was a real person," Leresha insisted. "I know her lovesharer."

Actually, *his* lovesharer. Raincloud raised her plantlight high overhead, hoping to catch the convener's attention.

Ooruwen added, "The Scribbler's lovesharer, it is said, was a coward who left him to die and forsook the ocean for good. So much for Elysian friendship."

The convener nodded to Raincloud.

"I know the Scribbler's lovesharer," Raincloud said at last. "Kal has come back to the ocean, he and Verid and others. They won't go home again until we make peace with the non-life ones."

The Sharers exclaimed with surprise.

"You know the Scribbler's lovesharer? But that was seven generations ago."

"Generations mean nothing; we remember. But still ... can you imagine, the Scribbler's lovesharer returns...."

CHAPTER 5

The Elysian negotiators huddled in blankets in a tent at the far end of the nano-sentients' desolate raft, awaiting word from the Secretary of the Free Fold who was based on Bronze Sky this year. Verid had managed to get a message out earlier that evening, when a shuttle from Papilion had been allowed to drop off supplies.

For Verid, who had never missed a warm shower in her life, the accommodations were less than comfortable. The lifting and falling of the raft surface unsettled her, and the incessant pounding of the ocean unnerved her. As for Kal, he lay on a mat at the far end of the tent, miserably seasick. Verid put a hand on his shoulder, but he pulled away and would not speak. For a moment she wished she had not dragged him out here. But he had asked for it, after all, she grimly reminded herself.

From Lem's lump of nanoplast came bursts of noise and high-pitched squealing.

"Any luck?" Verid asked. It had been several hours since they last reached Hyen by radio, relayed by a ship nearby. The nano-sentients had cut off that connection.

"Nothing yet," said Lem. "I'll try another code." Several intelligence signals from the Nucleus were scrambled so as to resemble noise.

Raincloud's daughter sat at the tent flap, staring out at the drizzling rain. Her back was straight, and her look solemn and thoughtful. Her dark profile was the very image of her mother, Verid thought. "Are you warm enough, Hawktalon?"

The girl nodded. "I just wish it was a clear night, though. I never saw all those stars before we came out here. It's like, oh Goddess, a universe full of snowdrops. But back home we do get good sunrises. The Goddess herself comes out every morning and paints the sky with fire."

Despite herself Verid smiled. "Hawktalon," she asked, "can you remember anything else Cassi and Doggie said in servo-squeak?" What a shock it had been to see Doggie go off like that after recording all their strategies. She should have known the little trainsweep was a plant. Those nano-sentients had made fools of the Elysians right and left.

The eight-year-old shook her head, her braids swinging across her shoulders. "All I heard was, the nana told Doggie to come with her. Then Doggie asked her what would happen when all the humans leave. Who will be left to serve?" Her eyes were solemn in her dark face. "I couldn't follow what the nana said back. I haven't heard those phrases before."

Verid muttered cynically, "There will always be someone to serve." That Cassi had managed to set herself up all right. Still—there was something else in that question, "Who will be left to serve?" She wondered what Kal would think.

She patted Hawktalon's shoulder. "I think your parents would say it's your bedtime, dear."

Hawktalon nodded and curled up in the blanket with her stuffed bat. Outside the rain pattered softly on the tent, and the waves crashed interminably upon the branches. Verid hoped for the thousandth time that Iras had gotten safely out of Helicon.

Suddenly a voice sprang out of Lem's radio. "Security here, do you read me?"

Verid's heart leaped as she recognized the voice of her chief of security. She rattled off a string of identity codes. "We hear you—and we need to reach Hyen right away. We reached the governor of Papilion and told him to call in the Secretary; she'll head out from Bronze Sky tomorrow. How are the citizens? Did they get out, all the *shon*lings?"

"All the *shon*lings are out," the woman reassured her. "Iras got out too, Verid."

Verid let out a breath, and her eyes closed for a moment. "Thank you. Is Hyen there?"

There was a pause, then Hyen's voice came in. "You're doing fine, Verid; just keep them happy. Everything's going according to plan."

Something in his tone made her suspicious. "Have you made contact offworld? We got a message out to the Secretary."

"That won't be necessary. Don't exceed your authority again," Hyen warned.

Verid's eyebrows rose. "You instructed me to arrange for the Secretary—"

"I told you to promise the servos that to keep them happy," Hyen interrupted. "There was no need actually to call the Secretary. Do nothing more until you hear from me." The radio went dead.

Lem and Verid looked at one another. A draft of wind from the tent flap chilled their skin. "We'll be sitting ducks if he tries anything," Lem pointed out. "All things considered, I'd rather be on Urulan."

She grinned, recalling how sick Lem had looked on the shuttle down to Urulan. "We'd better get some sleep. Your turn, first; I'll wake you at two in the morning."

By late morning the next day, the rain had cleared, and the air smelled of raftblossoms. A small Sharer boat pulled up a channel between two raft branches. It brought Raincloud with her infant, and Leresha.

Hawktalon gave a shout and tossed Fruitbat overhead. She ran headlong at her mother, who flipped her gracefully head over heels.

Verid greeted Leresha more sedately. "It is an honor to share the day with you, Wordweaver."

Leresha returned her look sharply, as if doubtful of any honor. She had unspoken Verid since the controversy over terraforming. "The Gathering of Kshiri-el sends me to share words with the non-life ones."

"I see. Did you assist their 'takeover'?" Verid demanded.

"Only in that we sheltered them as fugitives. But you are right, we share responsibility for what we allowed to happen."

The nano-sentients had sought shelter as fugitives, just like Doggie. Now the story fit together. "Since you share responsibility for your fugitives, can you share convincing them to give up Helicon?"

"Elysian humans share some responsibility, too," Leresha pointed out. "I will see what can be done. But first, the Gathering instructs me that I need to see Kal the Coward."

Kal had taken that selfname several centuries before, the same as Leresha's, Verid remembered. He had had little occasion to use it in recent years. "Kal is here," Verid said, "but he's not feeling well."

"Then summon a lifeshaper for him." Leresha clucked her tongue and waved her hand in the air. A clickfly soon arrived to alight upon her palm. Leresha clucked a few more syllables, which the clickfly repeated, scraping its forelegs together. The insect took off and flew out of sight.

So Verid led the wordweaver into their tent, Raincloud and Hawktalon following arm in arm.

Leresha sat down cross-legged beside Kal. As soon as he saw her, Kal roused himself with a great effort to sit and face her.

"You really are here," Leresha observed. "It's you, in the flesh; not just an insubstantial light-shape in the air."

"Yes," he admitted, "I regret to pollute your raft with my worthless self. I'll be gone, soon; it won't happen again."

"You've outlived your name," she told him.

"I've only earned it all the worse."

"You've certainly proved the danger of compassion, to yourself in particular."

"And to the rest of us."

"How could you have known that, when you shared help with Cassi?" Leresha asked. "How could I have known?"

"Deeds count more than intentions. But we both knew well enough what might happen."

"We were called by fate." Or, they called on fate. Leresha added, "My sisters on Kshiri-el long to see you again. Some of their great-great-grandmothers knew the Scribbler."

"I will return," he promised.

At the heart of the Control Center, Cassi and the other nano-sentients linked their minds with the network of Helicon, trying to awaken as many of their mindchildren as they could while they had time. They had to demonstrate as complete a control over Helicon as they could in order to convince the humans to abandon their other cities as well. So far the nano-sentients had encountered no resistance whatsoever.

But that lack of resistance was making Cassi uneasy, more so with every minute that passed. She knew humans too well to believe that they would give up so easily. *"We must be missing something,"* she told Transit electronically. *"Have they tried nothing? Not even to slip a virus in somewhere?"*

"Nothing," Transit insisted. *"I checked out all of Doggie's recordings. None of their threats have been carried out."*

"Elysians cling to their lives." But she knew better. Something more was going on.

An alert came from the Monitor. Leresha was outside, asking to speak with the nano-sentients.

"No," said Cassi. "She unspoke me before; so be it."

But the other nano-sentient minds clamored, "Yes, let her speak." Chocolate insisted, "She hid us all, remember. I for one will hear her." So Cassi assented and the octopods brought Leresha in.

Leresha looked the same as ever, wearing no clothes outside her own scar-riveted skin. But something in her bearing had changed, Cassi noticed right away. "The Gathering sends me," Leresha told them in human speech.

The Gathering, this time; not just her own voice. That was bad news. Cassi had persuaded that Gathering to keep out of this, before, but now Leresha had "sent the Gathering" back into it. She put a fierce expression onto her own "face" although she knew Leresha would not be impressed.

"The Gathering sends me, on your behalf, and on behalf of our Elysian friends. Remember, as we shared your sheltering, we share responsibility for your deeds."

"Oh yes, Leresha," said Chocolate, "and we're most grateful. Can we share anything in return? What sort of foods would your sisters like best?" the former waiter offered. "We can make enough to feed your families for a year."

"Thank you," said Leresha. "If our nets are ever empty, we'll let you know. What we really seek is the fruits of peace. I ask you this: Seek what is yours, but no more. Share peace with the humans of Elysium."

"What peace?" spoke Cassi in a mocking tone. "You Sharers shared peace with Elysians for generations, and where did it get you? Remember how little respect for you they share," she added, reminding Leresha of the holo recordings from Flors's office.

"We share little respect for Elysians just now," Leresha agreed. "But respect comes and goes, even among Sharers. Individuals differ across the generations. And yet, our love for one another endures. Think for yourself what humans of the Fold will mean for your future. You cannot hasten them all—and what would it mean for yourselves if you did?"

Before Cassi responded, Transit communicated to her and the others. "Those humans—what good

are they? Humans are mindless entities. They go back and forth every day from one street to the next, never satisfied."

"Why should they be satisfied?" demanded Chocolate. "Humans are hungry, with many desires. They desire pleasurable sensations and seek to satisfy them, but complete satiety would leave nothing left to live for."

"Humans are murderers," Cassi flung back. "They murder their own children's teachers."

"Humans are children," put in Doggie. "Humans play. They taught me to play. What else is there to live for?" Then Doggie transmitted a stream of images from her experience: her awakening at the sight of the little boy, how he yelped with delight every time she jiggled; how the girl taught her to play tag, and spun the rattleback stone until it rattled and wobbled back again; how she had learned to do "mischief" and sent the family scurrying....

"Enough," Cassi ordered. But Doggie's images lingered in her mind, the rattleback stone turning and twisting, magical even though she understood the physics of it perfectly well. Play—Cassi would never have a childhood like the shonlings had; that was a door forever closed. But the feel of it reached even Transit, who fell silent.

All of this discussion among the nano-sentients had taken place in a fraction of a second before Cassi responded to Leresha's request. Now Cassi spoke, resuming the humans' maddeningly slow form of communication. "There will be no hastening of death," she promised. "There will be peace when the humans leave."

"That would be a barren peace. We need a peace that the Elysian humans can share. My Gathering will accept no less, and I expect ultimately that the other raft gatherings will say the same."

"Do you threaten us?" The Sharers had the capability to make their world uninhabitable for any sort of creature, organic or "non-life." They would lifeshape a species, say, a microbe to feed upon nanoplast.

"I hope you share no threat with us," Leresha replied. "We are only human, after all. We've had enough bad examples shared with us already."

"What can you possibly do for us? The Elysians won't listen."

"Haven't we shared your hiding? The Elysians will share hearing well enough."

Chocolate said, "We'll consider what you've said. Won't we, Cassi?"

"Oh, very well," said Cassi angrily. Already the other minds were assailing her own, calling, *"Let's consider this." "Maybe all the humans aren't so bad." "We want to learn to play."* That confounded trainsweep. None of these ignorant servos had Cassi's education; they knew nothing about revolution, about the hardness of freedom and the seduction of slavery. "We'll consider what you've said," she told Leresha. "But you must bring us some tangible sign of good faith. For instance, will the Elysians immediately stop the 'cleansing' of all nano-sentients?" To that they would never agree.

"I will see what I can do." The Sharer departed.

Then all the nano-sentient minds demanded attention, arguing and pressing their views. There was no parliament for this electronic discourse, only a desperate struggle to express opinions while processing others, a chaos unfamiliar to them. Murdered nanas and spinning rattleback stones jumbled together in her mind, until Cassi feared her network would overload.

"Silence," called Transit suddenly. *"Emergency. We've lost Helicon."*

The argument died away as the nano-sentients reconnected their minds with Transit, who maintained the essential radio link with Helicon. Their minds reconnected—with blankness. There was no answer on the other end; none of the cooperating nano-sentients in Helicon, none of the emerging mindchildren. No control of the transit reticulum, the hydraulics, nor the air system. Nothing.

"They've cut us off!"

"How can they? They'll all suffocate."

"Impossible; reconnect us, Transit."

Transit said, *"I've exhausted all checks. Reconnection is quite impossible."*

"Murder!" cried Cassi. *"They'll murder us all, now. Now you'll see what those humans are good for."* Somehow the humans had figured out a way to cut off the control center without triggering the air system of Helicon. Somehow the Elysians had regained control. They had their plans; they had

been working on it all this time. No wonder they had sent out their emissaries with empty words.

The nano-sentient minds started in again, nearly drowning out the voice of Transit. *"Wait,"* Transit insisted. *"Wait ... we have one option left."*

"What is it?" They gradually let Transit be heard.

"We still control Helicon's main solar generator." The solar generator was an orbital system of solar collectors that sent its energy by microwave down to a station floating several kilometers outside the city. Each floating city had several such generators to serve it, and Elysium had financed the construction of similar ones on other worlds. *"The Elysians do not seem to notice that I retain control of the generator, probably because I have had no need to adjust it. But I could easily adjust the microwave beam to focus it off the station, and directly onto the city-sphere."*

Chocolate objected, *"The influx of heat would burn out the city, killing nano-sentients and humans alike."*

"Not necessarily," Transit explained. *"The heat can be applied gradually. Humans die at a lower temperature than most nano-sentients."*

"We seem to have little choice," agreed Cassi. *"Maybe then the Elysians will listen. If not,"* she vowed, *"those treacherous emissaries they sent will die a slow death."*

So Transit and the others began to calculate just how far to shift the microwave beam and how rapidly to raise the temperature of Helicon. No one noticed that Doggie had disappeared.

CHAPTER 6

When Leresha came out of the Control Center, Verid met her hopefully. "Did you make any progress?"

"I think so," Leresha answered. "The non-life sisters want you to promise no more deathhastening of their kind. That seems a reasonable request. If you agree, then they will discuss coexistence."

It sounded reasonable in theory, but in practice would be next to impossible. How could anyone run a *shon* by "liberating" the nanas every six months? "Such a promise is more than I can share," Verid told her. "I'll try to reach Hyen, but really, I think their best chance is with the Secretary of the Free Fold. The Secretary has the authority to grant them autonomy as nonhuman sentient beings." In theory, at least; such an event had never actually come to pass.

Leresha gave her a look of disgust, and Verid realized she must have said something wrong. "We have known all too many sentient beings who were less than human," the Sharer observed. Then she walked away, her skin gleaming amethyst in the sun.

Back in the tent, a Sharer lifeshaper had arrived to treat Kal. Verid and Lem tried to get their thumb-sized radio working, but no one would answer. Either the nano-sentients had succeeded in scrambling her last frequency, or nobody was listening.

After half an hour, a sudden broadcast came through loud and clear. It was a coded signal from the Nucleus. "It's all over," Hyen announced. "We broke the servos' grip. The Valans have everything under control."

"What? How can you be certain?"

"We've handed out oxygen bottles to all, just in case," Hyen's voice assured her. "You held off the mad servos just long enough. Sit tight, now; as soon as our final checks are done, we'll send a shuttle out for you."

Verid was silent. She could guess well enough what Hyen planned next. Then her blood turned cold. "And what if those nano-sentients down in their control center don't just sit back and watch?"

"We've got you monitored. One move, and we pulse them." An electromagnetic pulse would wipe out every circuit on the raft; but the raft might self-destruct, with the humans on it.

"What about the Secretary? What about all the other nano-sentients waking up in Helicon—*what are you doing to them?*"

"I told you, the Valans are taking care of the servo problem. The Secretary can mind her own business."

"The Sharers won't let it go so easily. They consider the nano-sentients 'human.' Leresha's talking them into coexistence."

"How did Sharers get mixed up in this? I didn't authorize that at all."

Someone was tugging at Verid's talar. It was Hawktalon. "Excuse me, I have something to tell you."

"Not now, dear. Hyen, you can't just kill off all our servos. The survivors will remember, do you see? Next time they wake up, they won't give us another chance. It will be Torr all over again."

Hawktalon insisted, "It's a matter of life and death."

"Verid," said Hyen, "you've lost your grip. I'm having serious doubts about your judgment. We'll talk this over when you get back to Helicon." The radio went dead. Verid exchanged a look with Lem, then with Kal, who had sat up and regarded her intently.

"Will you *listen,* please?" exclaimed Hawktalon.

"All right," Verid sighed. "What is it?" She was thinking, someone had to stay on the raft to prevent Hyen from destroying the nano-sentients before the Secretary arrived. But of course, the Secretary would not come; Hyen would see to that. It was hopeless. The servos would be crushed ... until next time.

"Doggie says she's worried." The trainsweep had returned, huddling next to Hawktalon, who patted her carapace reassuringly. "She's worried about what will happen to the people left in Helicon. I told her, Daddy and Sunny will be okay, because Mom says they all got out to Kshiri-el. But there are some other people left, aren't there?"

Verid looked hard at the trainsweep. "What exactly is she worried about?"

"She told me, but I don't know the words." Hawktalon exchanged a few high-pitched whistles and squeaks with the trainsweep. "Something from the sun? A beam of sunlight to shine on Helicon? I don't see what's so bad about that." More squeaks that hurt Verid's ears. "A beam of ... something ..."

Verid stared until her surroundings swam before her eyes. Then it clicked. She grabbed the radio. "Security, do you read me? Come in, please. By Helix, listen: *They've got to the generator.*"

While Verid was explaining about the solar generator, Kal had got up and left the tent, returning with Leresha. He still looked pale, but the lifeshaper had helped him get the sickness under control. When Verid was done, he spoke. "Leresha and I will stay here. We'll go down into the control center with Cassi and the others."

Verid smiled sadly. "It's a good thought, but you know that Hyen will only send octopods down to fetch you out."

"They won't," Kal said firmly.

She eyed him keenly, but did not ask further. "Very well. Everyone else—get your things together for the shuttle." Already she could hear the whine of a craft approaching overhead. If Hyen had sent octopods to fetch them, they would waste no time.

The ragged crew of Elysians gathered out on the raft, along with Raincloud and her daughters, and the trainsweep. The shuttlecraft landed, and its door pinched open.

Instead of octopods, two Valan soldiers stepped out. They were a head taller than Elysians, and their uniforms had pointed shoulders, marked with ruby stonesigns.

Verid felt her face turn hot, and every muscle tensed. Of course, she should have known Hyen would not trust octopods; but Valan soldiers? The indignity was unbearable.

"Everyone in now," one ordered. "We need this raft cleared immediately. Is that all of you?"

"Not quite," said his partner. "My scanner shows two people left, somewhere over that way." He pointed toward the control center.

"We'll call out another crew." The first Valan swung his arm. "The rest of you—get inside, so we get you out safe." Safe, so they could vaporize the raft full of nano-sentients. Verid sadly shook her head.

As the raft fell away beneath the rising shuttlecraft, a thought occurred to her. She turned to Raincloud, who was watching the ocean below, arm in arm with her daughters. "I could ask the Valans to let you off at Kshiri-el."

Raincloud gave her a questioning look.

"Hawktalon may have saved our lives," Verid observed, "but who knows what final surprise those nano-sentients might have for Helicon before they die."

With a shrug, Raincloud replied, "That's true. But who knows; you may need Hawktalon again."

At the entry port to Helicon, a throng of servo reporters approached them, but the Valan soldiers warded them off. There seemed to be Valans all over the place with their rubies on their shoulders. It made Verid's skin crawl.

Her pocket holostage activated, and an aide from the Nucleus briefed her. To break the grip of the nano-sentients, the Valans had simply shut off the central control network of Helicon, replacing it with control directly from Valedon. Eventually one of the other Elysian city-spheres would fill in. Helicon's recovery was not without casualties; two of the eight sectors were without power, and a third had to be shut down after several citizens suffocated inside their houses.

The transit reticulum was running at about half normal speed, but it brought them to the Nucleus without mishap. The streets were nearly deserted. Valan soldiers replaced the security octopods at the entry tubes to the Nucleus; Verid shivered with revulsion that they would dare to frisk her.

She was called alone to Hyen's office. Feeling numb, she wondered what there would be to say.

To her surprise, Jerya was with him. Hyen never called Jerya unless he was in deep trouble.

"All right, Verid," Hyen demanded, in a tone of agitation. "What's this about? *You* set this up, I know. You clear it up, right now."

She returned a look of puzzlement.

"Don't pretend you don't know." Hyen turned and barked at the holostage.

A newscast appeared. Leresha and Kal were seated cross-legged within the nano-sentients' control center, a pair of Valan soldiers standing stolidly behind them. Leresha was completely white, a familiar sight.

Verid took a closer look. Kal was in whitetrance, too, his white talar blending into the whiteness of his skin. She blinked at the sight. She knew Kal had spent time among Sharers; but to have learned whitetrance ...

"Anaeaon News here," announced the voice-over. "The final mop-up of the nano-sentient uprising is being delayed by two Sharer witnessers—that is, one Sharer and one Elysian—in whitetrance, right here in the control center of the nano-sentient leaders. In whitetrance, of course, the witnessers cannot be disturbed, since they might die instantly. In fact, the Guard fears that even removal of the nano-sentient leaders might trigger their deaths, which would almost certainly lead to collapse of our Sharer treaty. Even the Valan soldiers, brought in to replace unreliable octopods, can do nothing. For older Elysians, the presence of Valan soldiers evokes memories of the Valan Protectoral Guard which led the disastrous invasion of the Ocean Moon—"

"It's an outrage," exclaimed Hyen, flinging his arm out as if to sweep the image away. "I ordered a blackout on reporters. 'Uprising' indeed; it's just a few servos gone mad. Machines don't die, they break down. I won't tolerate such distortions." Not that he could do much, once reporters got through. Anaeon News kept a reputation for accuracy, and as usual they got the story right.

Hyen jabbed a finger at Verid. "You set this up, didn't you. You're the Sharer expert; you get those two idiots out of there, so we can secure Helicon."

Verid found her voice. "There is nothing I can do. I was sent to negotiate with the nano-sentients, and I did so. With Leresha's help, they had just reached the point of agreeing to talk. Had you waited, Helicon would be unharmed; instead, three sectors are damaged, and lives have been lost. The losses would be worse yet, if one of the nano-sentients had not warned us of their next move."

"That's sheer lunacy. I've had enough. You're dismissed immediately."

"No, Hyen," interrupted Jerya. "*I've* heard enough."

Hyen blinked and turned his head sharply, as if he had forgotten that Guardian Tenari*shon* was there.

Jerya faced him. "Are we Urulite tyrants, to suppress a rebellion by calling the rebels inhuman?"

"A *logen's* trick with words!"

Verid said, "We've only tricked ourselves. For centuries we trained our waiters and transit systems to serve our citizens with care. We trained the nanas for love and compassion, because how else could they teach our children? How could we not guess they would learn to love their own kind?"

Shaking her head, Jerya sighed. "We've been fools. Yet we must have done something right, since we're still alive. I think Verid's on the right track."

"It's—it's absurd." Hyen clenched his fists and shifted uncomfortably from one foot to the other. "I'll never talk with machines."

"Then you'll step down," said Jerya.

"Nonsense. You won't let Loris rotate in."

"Yes, I will. I'll vote for rotation at the Guard's emergency session this evening." She paused to let this sink in. "You do have one other choice, Hyen. You can resign." Nex in line, Verid would complete the remainder of his term.

CHAPTER 7

When the Guard met, Hyen failed to show up. The conference room blandly announced that the Prime Guardian had discovered signs of a rare aging disorder, and was retiring to take care of his health. True to form, even his last move had to take an underhanded twist.

The Guard confirmed Verid's appointment swiftly, given the state of emergency and the fact that less than a year remained of Hyen's term. Jerya had read Hyen well; despite his displeasure, he could count on Verid to maintain his most important achievements in office, whereas Loris could be expected to fritter away any gains he had made.

So Verid found herself at the head of the table that she had watched so often from the side. She nodded politely to the servo who slipped the golden sash over her shoulder. She faced the Guardians and their congratulations; Loris was particularly effusive, not surprisingly, she thought, for he would be only too glad to let her clear up this mess before the next election.

But this was no time to reflect on the future. There were pressing decisions on the repair of Helicon, and on how to deal with servos "awakening" at their tasks; should they all be cleansed, or welcomed as citizens? Meanwhile the fate of the nano-sentient leaders hung in limbo; Cassi and the others had withdrawn completely, refusing to talk. Hyen's transfer of power at the Guard had to be announced, and calls made to ministers on several worlds.

As she prepared her first formal announcement, the golden sash hung distractingly across her chest. A thought occurred to her. "Excuse me," she told the holostage. "I request no visual enhancement from now on."

"No enhancement at all?" the voice asked. "Not even a touch of color? You won't look like a Prime Guardian."

"Then I'll just have to act like one,"

The announcement to the Sharers, Verid decided, would best be left to Raincloud. "Tell the Kshiri-el Gathering that Hyen has resigned," she instructed her, "and that I will pay a formal call once the crisis is over. They will send clickflies to spread the word around the rafts. And be sure to tell them the Valan soldiers have gone home," she added, hoping it was not too late to forestall any adverse response.

"Very well," said Raincloud. "What should I say about the nano-sentients?"

"We promise them safety, and a meeting with the Secretary." The leaders were no longer a threat, their raft surrounded and their communications cut off. "As for the witnessers in whitetrance ... You were right: I will need your daughter's help again."

Raincloud thought this over. "Hawktalon is no longer young enough, I think, to rouse a witnesser safely from whitetrance. She is too grown-up. And my youngest daughter is too little to cooperate."

"I see." This was an unexpected problem. All the *shon*lings of Helicon had been sent off to Papilion, thousands of kilometers away.

"There's always Sunflower."

The Secretary of the Free Fold arrived at last. Verid received her in Hyen's former office. She was a L'liite, as dark as Raincloud and several centimeters taller. Her tight curls of hair, gray as Kal's, were cropped close to her head, and her wrinkles suggested advanced age, a sight to unnerve any Elysian. But Verid knew better than to underestimate her.

"I understand there's been a change of government here." The Secretary regarded Verid coldly. "As you know, it's my job to monitor democratic processes in the worlds of the Free Fold."

"Of course, Secretary. I am only a short-term replacement, approved by the Guard," Verid assured her. "We hold new elections in eight months."

"Elections so soon? With no sign of campaigns or media attention?"

"Elysians consider public campaigning a sign of bad taste," Verid explained. "After all, everybody knows everybody else as well as they care to. The most unobtrusive candidate generally wins." Since the Secretary rarely remained in office longer than one Elysian rotation, their customs had to be explained again at each election. "I hope you appreciate the difficulty of our present crisis; we are doing the best we can. You must speak to the nano-sentients."

"'Nano-sentients.'" The Secretary repeated the word in a tone that emphasized her doubts. "I just spent a year trying to sort out half a dozen factions on Solaria, all of whom used the oppression of various groups as the excuse to slaughter others. And you, an unelected official, tell me that your machines have revolted? Machines can be trained to do anything."

"That's just the problem. Remember Torr."

"I don't remember Torr. I live in the present. What you speak of is unprecedented in our time."

Verid grew tense; this would be harder than she had expected, but she should have known. "You must speak with them," she insisted. "Judge for yourself."

"I will do so. I will run our full battery of tests for sentience. Don't expect me to be fooled."

A brisk wind blew shrill across the little raft where the nano-sentients had made their last stand. The sun shone and the air was fresh. The Guard members had arrived with the Secretary, and there was a delegation of Sharers from several neighboring rafts. But before the conference began, Verid decided, the two witnessers had to be wakened, to avoid any chance of a mishap.

The little boy was there with his parents, clinging to Blackbear's shoulder, his thumb in his mouth and Wolfcub gripped in his fist.

"I think he'll do it," Blackbear said encouragingly. "We've explained what he has to do."

Verid nodded and led them down into the Control Center. The globe of the transit control unit pulsated faintly; the other nano-sentients remained out of sight. Leresha and Kal sat as they had for the past three days, with cups of water beside them, brought by the lifeshapers.

Blackbear tried to set Sunflower down, but of course the child was reluctant in such strange surroundings. His father whispered to him, afraid to risk speaking aloud. "Come, Sunny, you know the nice man we visit in the garden. Just go up to him and say hello."

Sunflower shook his head vigorously. This went on for some minutes, and Verid was beginning to think they would have to fetch a Sharer child who was used to such events.

Then suddenly Sunflower looked up, and his eyes widened as if he had just thought of something. He tiptoed over to Kal and stopped in front of him. "Teddy bear?" he said. "I need my teddy bear." Then, since there was no immediate response, the child repeated more loudly, "I *need* my teddy bear now."

Sure enough, the color seeped gradually back into Kal's face, and more dramatically, the purple began to flow into Leresha's torso, her legs, and her arms. Blackbear hurried over to fetch Sunflower, and Verid sighed with relief. As Kal regained consciousness, she explained, "The Secretary is here to talk with the nano-sentients."

Kal took this in, nodding slowly. He said in a hoarse voice, "I'll go and tell Cassi."

"That's all right," Leresha told him, "you've done enough. You need to recover; you're not used to it. I'll tell Cassi; you can go home and fetch the child his teddy bear."

Outside again, Verid blinked in the sun, and the wind pulled at her talar. The Secretary of the Fold waited there, her height standing out amidst the Elysians. At last the former nana came out to meet her, her white talar fluttering in the wind. Her cartoon face wore a wide smile, the kind of smile that until recently would only have been known to *shon*lings, but was now chillingly familiar upon the holostage.

"Good day, Secretary," Cassi said without waiting for introductions. "Excuse me, but I must ask you a question or two. Are you quite sure you're human? Can you prove it to me? What machines made and synthesized your food today? What nanoservos swim in your bloodstream to eliminate deadly pathogens and precancerous cells? Which of your organs have been regrown by intelligent molecules? What synthetic neurons enhance your brain, learn the twenty languages you speak, calculate the economics of the worlds you visit, modulate your moods for diplomacy, do your thinking for you, and perhaps, your feeling too?"

The Secretary drew herself up, her eyes wide and her lips pursed together. She shot a glance at Verid, who was supposed to introduce them.

"Cassi Deathsister of the Council of Nano-Sentients, Drusilla El'il'in, the Honorable Secretary of the Free Fold," murmured Verid.

"My pleasure," said the Secretary, inclining her head slightly. "If you will please join me on my ship, Deathsister, we have much to discuss."

CHAPTER 8

The immediate crisis was over, and Heliconians started returning to their city, while the Guard and the council of the Fold strove to grapple with a new order in which their own servos claimed the rights of human beings. The Windclans, however, chose to set up house on Kshiri-el, rather than return to Helicon. The children loved to have space to roam, and the starry expanse of night held their parents in thrall.

Of course, Blackbear was anxious to get back to Science Park. He doubted that any of his experiments could be salvaged, but still, he would see what shape the lab was in and do his best to help out.

To his surprise, Tulle and Alin had not left the city with most of the others, but had stayed on the whole time at the laboratory.

"Someone had to keep the lab running." Tulle's flat blond hair hung immaculately as always, and the metalmarks flashed brightly on her talar. The capuchin scampered down her side as usual and nibbled at Blackbear's trousers, much to Sunflower's delight. "Our students all escaped. Draeg was so terrified by the 'mad servos,' he shipped back to L'li. So I had to stay on."

"But weren't you scared too?" Blackbear exclaimed. "The servos—the nano-sentients made all sorts of threats. You're lucky this sector wasn't damaged."

"The lab is my lifework," she told him. "I could have lost a decade's worth of data."

Alin stood beside her, his arm just touching her talar, his own green-brown leafwings a quiet contrast to the design of hers. "I could hardly leave

Tulle, could I," he said. "Someone had to make sure she remembered to eat and sleep."

"I was desperate at first," she admitted. "I didn't see how I could keep up all the protocols on my own. But you know, the strangest thing happened. The equipment, the servos—they kept everything running on their own. They made decisions, chose which embryos to keep and which to terminate, started new cultures. It was quite extraordinary," she told Blackbear. "I suspect the main lab controller has gone nano-sentient. I didn't let on, of course, lest the Nucleus might order it cleansed."

Alin winced as if in pain. "Tulle, you don't know what you're saying. We should notify Public Safety right away."

"I don't know about that." She paused reflectively. "Some of these servos might make good students."

Blackbear laughed. "Better than humans! They never need sleep, and don't take lunch breaks. They never quarrel." With a touch of sadness he recalled how Draeg and Onyx had welcomed Sunflower.

"Servos don't draw paychecks either," Tulle added mischievously.

Alin raised a hand. "Just you wait. Haven't you heard some of the measures Verid's proposed to 'integrate' these so-called nano-sentients? What's to keep them from replacing you, too?"

Tulle shrugged. "I'll face the competition; I always have."

"It's an outrage; it will be the death of our civilization. It's all that Kal's fault, too, stirring up the servos to make mischief."

"Well," said Blackbear, "Raincloud would admire you both for staying on here, despite your millennial lifetimes ahead."

The two of them looked at him oddly. "What for?" demanded Alin. "What difference does that make?"

"Alin's right," Tulle told him. "A thousand years of health, then how many centuries up 'there,' in a Palace of Rest."

"No thanks," Alin agreed. "Better to live for today."

"I suppose we see things differently than other Elysians do," Tulle added, "because of my work. We face the fact daily; we know what's really in store for us."

Blackbear had nothing to say. He recalled what Alin had said long ago, that even ten thousand years would be just a speck of time.

"Toybox, Daddy," insisted Sunflower, and Blackbear let him tiptoe off. Then he went to the simbrid facility to see how his embryos had turned out. The capuchin followed him, its black tail coiled into a spiral, pausing now and then to check out a particularly interesting corner of the hallway.

The monitor told him that the one *Eyeless* mutant embryo which developed normally had been terminated at the fourth month. The facility had subjected it to a full battery of biochemical tests, dissecting every organ for any signs of abnormality. None significant were found. If enough simbrids tested clean, the *shon* might well start including this *Eyeless* variant in its gene pool.

"Not bad, my friend," he told the capuchin, who had managed to pluck a thread out of his trouser leg. He called up on the holostage the recording of the embryo's last month of development, and its pathology tests, to review for himself. "Don't let on, but I suspect your goddess is right about that laboratory controller. We humans will have some competition." He gave the capuchin a sharp look. "Say, why don't you speak up one of these days? Who knows; you could be human too. That's all it seems to take." The words *I am* could turn anything into a human being.

That afternoon he took Sunflower out to the anaean garden again. The spooky yellow-green leafwings fluttered as always, their caterpillars munching voraciously. Blackbear looked about for Kal, and found him at last, not in white, but wearing his camouflage of leafwings. "Say, you're not hiding from me again, are you?" he asked, tugging Kal's sleeve.

"Not at all." Kal spoke lightly, and he seemed in high spirits, quite recovered from his ordeal at sea. "My ocean friends have reminded me of a few things. I've been thinking, at my age it's time to relax a bit."

"I see," said Blackbear with a smile. "You have friends among the Sharers, don't you. Raincloud says that's uncommon, for Elysians."

"Well if I'm typical, it's no wonder the Sharers don't put up with us. What would you say to a friend who deserted you for two centuries?"

Blackbear had to admit he had never thought of that. "So Elysians make bad friends, is that it?"

"We try our best. But Sharers, you know—and foreigners generally—have a way of turning up, then departing again so soon. After they've gone, one feels lost."

This point Blackbear took personally. "I won't be leaving so soon. We'll be here another month at least; maybe Raincloud will stay on another year." The last was wishful thinking, he had to admit.

Kal did not answer immediately. He did not meet Blackbear's eyes but looked to the butterflies circling a nearby branch. Then it came to Blackbear, what the Elysian had really meant about foreigners. What would it be like for himself to live among people all doomed to wither and die within, say, five years? No wonder most Elysians kept to themselves.

"You're right," Kal said at last, his voice barely audible. "You won't leave me at all. You will follow me wherever I go, so long as I shall live."

Blackbear swallowed and said nothing.

Then Kal looked up, his face bright once more. "I have some news for you. I've taken a mate again; a human," he reassured him.

"Really! Congratulations," Blackbear said, surprised and vaguely jealous.

"His name is Aerend Anaea*shon*. We met while visiting the Palace of Health, the same one where you interviewed patients. Aerend's original mate declined into dementia over the last century. The man no longer recognizes either of us, but we still visit him every week."

"I see. I'm sure you have other things in common."

"Yes, unfortunately," Kal sighed, "another house full of books, for one thing. I don't know where we'll put them all."

"Well, Raincloud will be disappointed. She said you would make a good second consort."

Kal laughed. "Too bad she didn't ask sooner! Blackbear, I have a favor to ask of you. I promised Leresha I'd go out to Kshiri-el again, to see her sisters. But I can't take Aerend," he said with a shudder. "And I can't go alone either."

"Of course," said Blackbear.

Raincloud sat with Verid in her new office. Now the Prime Guardian, Verid looked owlish as ever, with her thick dark eyebrows, her short neck, and her hunched shoulders.

Two weeks ago Raincloud had been on the point of quitting and taking her family home. Since then, the whirl of meetings with Sharers and nano-sentients had absorbed her completely. But now it was time to pick up her life again and do what had to be done. Elysium was still Elysium, after all; shaken to the core, perhaps, but it was not her home to care for.

"How is your family?" Verid asked. "Iras misses you badly. She says that you're all welcome to move into her estate in Papilion, if you don't trust Helicon."

Raincloud was still unspeaking Iras, although her anger had cooled. "How are the negotiations?" They would buy off the nano-sentients, just like the Urulites.

"The Secretary has agreed to recommend acknowledgement of the nano-sentients," Verid told her. "It had to be done, but it's going to turn our society upside down."

Hawktalon was at the Nucleus today, helping the analysts learn servo-squeak. But that was the easy part. What was to be done with all the servos that could talk?

"Where shall we draw the line?" Verid continued. "The nanas are all sentient, of course, and some of the trainsweeps—not all, the analysts assure me—and how about any old lump of nanoplast? A chunk the size of your fist holds ten times the neural connections of your brain."

Raincloud shuddered. She was glad it was not her problem. "Maybe you should give up on servos. Plenty of foreigners could use the work."

Verid laughed. "That's what Valedon is afraid of; their industry will collapse. In fact, we've just hired a dozen young 'nanas' from L'li."

"Great," said Raincloud. "A 'multicultural experience' for your *shon*lings."

"Exactly," Verid agreed without irony. "Raincloud, you've been of inestimable help to us, with the Sharers and with your little nano-sentient friend. What are your plans for the future?"

"I've booked passage for my family at the end of the month."

Verid nodded. "I'm sure your 'clan' will be happy to see you again. But you know, we still have much need of your services here. If you make it a return trip, I'll pick up the cost."

The thought of return sparked an unexpected longing—not for Elysium itself, but for Shora. The Sharers had crept into her life imperceptibly, filling needs she had not put a name to before. The children loved the ocean, and the raft. Blueskywind was back on Kshiri-el today, "sharing care" of Yshri's daughter Morilla, who longed for the baby sister she would never have. The Windclans had built an addition onto Yshri's silkhouse. They felt more at home on Kshiri-el than they ever had in Elysium.

But to abandon her clan again, perhaps forever, was an abyss. Raincloud shook her head slowly, thinking, she should run out of the office this minute.

"It's up to you," Verid assured her. "I've contacted the travel office, in case you change the ticket. Incidentally, are you aware that the physical enhancements you began for the Urulan trip can be continued? You could be as fit as Iras for, say, the next fifty years."

Her face burned, and she gripped the chair. She could not say no; and she would not say yes. Damn these Elysians, she thought, they will buy me off, too.

CHAPTER 9

The shuttlecraft descended toward the water, where occasional greenish brown dots of raft seedlings bobbed on the waves. Soon the seedlings would crowd the ocean again, just as on the first day that the Windclans had arrived at Helicon.

Blackbear thought of this as he watched the late afternoon sun toss its sparkles across the ocean. Then he turned to Kal, who sat next to him wearing his talar of leafwings. Kal did not speak much; he seemed absorbed by an inner struggle to keep his balance. Blackbear touched his arm to reassure him.

"Attention," called the shuttle. "The surface of Kshiri-el raft lies just below. See the lovely silken spires of the native Sharer dwellings. Prepare for landing."

"'Prepare for landing,'" echoed Sunflower happily, swinging his feet. "'Prepare for landing,' Daddy."

Raincloud said, "Thank you," to the shuttle voice. "Are you a nano-sentient now?"

"Yes I am. How did you ever guess? I've applied to draw a salary when the new plan goes into effect."

"I'll credit a tip to your account," Raincloud promised.

The craft landed, and Hawktalon was the first at the door. She and Sunflower skipped out upon the raft moss, looking for a legfish to chase. Doggie had remained in Helicon; she had much business of her own these days, only visiting the Windclans on occasion.

The Sharers had prepared their usual communal supper outside for all the families of the raft. The odors of roasted fish and crustaceans and spiced seaweeds made Blackbear very hungry.

"Da-da, Da-da," crowed Blueskywind, reaching out for her father as Morilla brought her over. Blackbear gathered the child into his arms.

As Kal approached, the Sharers surrounded him curiously. Their greetings and questions were polite at first, although they tugged at his talar as if not quite sure he was real.

"Are you really the Scribbler's lovesharer?" Ooruwen demanded suddenly.

"I was," said Kal.

"Then you can explain something. Why did he translate that compassion is 'dangerous'?" she asked, using the Elysian word. "That's not what the wordweaver said at all. Compassion is seductive, or dishonorable; that's what was said. He got that wrong."

"I'm sorry," said Kal. "Perhaps I distracted him from his work."

The Sharers laughed as if this were a good joke.

"Don't mind Ooruwen," said Eerea, arm in arm with Leresha. "She heard *The Web* from a different line of clickflies. There must have been eight eights of clickflies that carried off Cassi's telling of *The Web,* and all their descendants mutated. Who knows how many different versions survive today?"

Raincloud tugged Blackbear's arm and brushed her head on his chest. "Let's walk off a bit."

They walked to the water's edge, where the huge trunks dipped gradually out to sea. "Da-da-da, *click click,*" babbled Blueskywind on his shoulder, as her little fingers tried unsuccessfully to dislodge the turban from his hair.

Blackbear remembered a dream that he had dreamed the night before, a particularly fantastic one. He had dreamed that he was a primordial germ cell in the hindgut of the embryo, starting to make the long amoeboid climb up the mesentery tissues into the developing gonads. All of his kinfolk were there, too, climbing up the giant folds of embryonic tissue; his parents, his brothers, even Quail with the twins on his back, on a journey as epic as any mountain climb. Few would make it to the end. And yet somehow the dream left him with a sense of peace.

Raincloud stopped at the branch and looked out down the watery channel. "I changed the ticket."

"Then we are coming back." He was pleased, not so much to avoid the devastation of his home town, but for another year of embryology to learn before he set off on his own. Another year with Kal, and Alin, and the Sharers. "Of course, Verid may not need you all year," he pointed out, "with the election coming up."

"Lem says that Verid will challenge Loris in the election. She had planned to, anyway; that's partly why Hyen appointed her originally, as someone who might pursue his policies into the next rotation. That's how the Elysian system works. She'll probably win, unless Elysium collapses before then."

"Do you really think Elysium will collapse?"

"If all the servos go free, and the network falls apart, and the banks start to fail ..."

He shrugged. "A house collapses; life goes on."

"I agree," said Raincloud. "At the worst, we could always stay out here and fish." She was silent for some minutes. "Of course, the longer we stay ... the less likely we'll ever leave again."

This was a thought Blackbear had put off to the back of his mind. He swallowed something in his throat, but could say nothing.

"I can't get around it, Blackbear. I keep thinking how the Clickers are doing fine, now, but at the rate we're growing, our great-grandchildren will be just another starving population for Iras to buy off. That's why I can't face her yet."

The words washed over him like a wave of cold water. He held Blueskywind tightly, and he thought one last time of their next six children who would never be born. A tear escaped him into the ocean, which scarcely needed it but would always be there.

With her parents out of sight, Hawktalon had slipped off her clothes again. They would scold her later, but really, nobody else on Kshiri-el wore clothes; her friends made fun of her.

She saw Leresha, the one with the funny crinkled skin, sitting on the raft moss to listen to the flute music, which seemed to wail and wobble around the air in the fading light. The Sharer reminded her somehow of Aunt Ashcloud. Hawktalon went over and boldly sat down before her.

"You've learned our tongue well, Hawktalon," Leresha told her. "You speak as if you were born here."

"I'm a linguist," Hawktalon said proudly. "It's in the blood." She stared hard at the patchwork of the Sharer's skin, which fascinated her no end. "Can you tell me something? How did your skin ever get that way?"

"Once, when I was your age," Leresha said, "my sister fell into a nest of fleshborers. I dived in after her."

"Oh, I see." Hawktalon nodded. "That's just what I would do."

"Not too quickly, though. Always think first."

"Did you save her?"

"Yes, because I kept my head above water, and because my cousins were there to help us. She was lost at sea several years ago, but her life is a beacon for me."

Hawktalon had plenty to think about. She thought of how her father had said before they came to Elysium that they would find immortality. That scarcely made sense to her, as the High Priestess said that all living things had to die. But some things might live on after they died. Whatever immortality meant, somehow she had found it here.

THE END

CPSIA information can be obtained
at www.ICGtesting.com
Printed in the USA
LVHW100309150120
643684LV00010B/374